MADELINE WAITED FOR A GLIMPSE OF LORD ESHER

He came through the trees, leaping the ditch with uncanny grace. His hair had come loose and flew in the wind so that he looked not at all like an English gentleman, but rather a barbarian who'd ridden through some portal of time to invade the serene countryside.

Madeline almost could not bear to look at him. In his dishevelment he was as unrepentantly virile as a stallion in a field of mares. "You look like a savage," she said disdainfully, but there was an unaccustomed roughness to her voice.

His eyes, almost turquoise in the bright light, blazed. "And how would you know? How many savages have you seen?"

"None." She lifted her chin. "Nor have I seen elephants from India, but I assure you I'd recognize one if I did."

He laughed, tossing his head with impudence. A small, hot ripple touched her.

Books by Barbara Samuel

A Winter Ballad
A Bed of Spices
Lucien's Fall

Available from HarperPaperbacks

Lucien's Fall

⤜BARBARA SAMUEL⤛

HarperPaperbacks
A Division of HarperCollinsPublishers

This is a work of fiction. The characters, incidents, and dialogues are products of the author's imagination and are not to be construed as real. Any resemblance to actual events or persons, living or dead, is entirely coincidental.

HarperPaperbacks   *A Division of* HarperCollins*Publishers*
10 East 53rd Street, New York, N.Y. 10022

Cover illustration by Jeff Monti

First printing: September 1995

Printed in the United States of America

HarperPaperbacks, HarperMonogram, and colophon are trademarks of HarperCollins*Publishers*

❖ 10 9 8 7 6 5 4 3 2 1

For Tony and Lisa Putman,
who gave me a larger world

ACKNOWLEDGMENTS

Many thanks to my critique group, Linda Stachler, Janet Greer, and Sharon Stealy; to Kathy Fischer-Brown, who always comes up with the right music or the perfect book; and to the able and talented women of GEnie Romance Exchange. And as always, thanks to the Sisters—you know who you are.

Prologue

To souls oppress'd and dumb with grief
The Gods ordain this kind releif;
That Musick shou'd in sounds convey,
What dying Lovers dare not say.
                            —John Dryden

Lucien Harrow was drunk. It was not uncommon. In his set, to be sober at three of a muggy early summer morning would have been a far more unusual occurrence.

What was uncommon was the fact that he sat in his shirtsleeves in his study, his brocaded waistcoat flung over the back of a chair, dipping his quill again and again in a pot of ink.

A powerful sense of desperation—unblunted by the spirits he'd consumed—drove him to scrawl notations over the paper. In his head pounded a wild, ringing gypsy music, a swirl and a dance, a little turn. . . .

He squeezed his eyes closed and pushed away from the writing table, dropping the quill and picking up his glass. His head bobbed in time to the sound in his mind, the notes undrowned. Unsteadily, he aimed himself for the sideboard and the decanter of claret.

Crystal bottle in hand, he hummed the music aloud, over and over, swinging the bottle as if he were conducting. And as he hummed, he saw the notes as a river of colors. They rose and swirled, like an elaborate braid, each strand woven around the others, none muddied or muted. Unless he wished it.

The claret shone in his glass, ruby colored, like the sound of viola. Lucien pushed his hair from his face and drank deeply, then stumbled back to his desk, carrying the glass. Some splashed onto his hand. A burn in his belly warned him to cease, but he drank it all in a single swallow.

He then gathered the sheaf of papers over which he'd been laboring, and calmly, deliberately held them over the flame of the candle until they caught fire. When they were black and curled, he tossed them on the grate and stumbled toward bed, having silenced the sounds one more time.

One more time.

1

Black or fair, or tall or low,
I alike with all can sport.

—Thomas Stanley

A rose thorn bit Madeline's finger, another tiny, stinging scratch to add to the many marks covering her hands. Absently, she straightened. Sucking welling drips of blood from her finger, she eyed a cloud of dust that marked the arrival of yet another pair of visitors. Their figures were haloed against the lowering gold light of a late May afternoon.

Guests had been trailing in most of the day in a slow, sporadic trail, Londonites fleeing the strange early heat of the city. Among them would be the marquess Beauchamp.

Madeline wondered if one of these might be he, the man who would, with any luck, be her husband before the year was through. As this pair, one on a horse, the other a phaeton, raced through dusty bars of sunlight on the drive, Madeline doubted seriously either of them was the marquess. She'd heard he was a conservative man.

Since it was the marquess she awaited, Madeline turned away. Overly warm and feeling dusty, she knew she ought to go inside and bathe before supper, but a curious stubbornness kept her wandering through the ragged hedges and neglected flower beds, pausing to peer at one bush or another with a frown.

Once the gardens at Whitethorn had been famous throughout England, the legacy of the first earl of Whitethorn. Madeline had often thought the man was her spiritual grandfather, for she alone among his descendants had been born with his passion for the place. Juliette, her stepmother, was in favor of allowing it to go wild in the fashion of the day, but Madeline couldn't bear the thought.

Unfortunately, there was simply not enough money left in the estate to pay the gardeners required to maintain formal gardens of this size. And not even Madeline, with her love and the knowledge she'd laboriously uncovered for herself, could hope to do it alone.

With a sigh, she shook her skirts and wound her way toward the house over a path covered with lemon thyme. The sound of the two riders pounding up the graveled drive reached her. She brushed away a stray lock of hair as she looked through the *claire-voie,* a window cut in the eight-foot-high topiary hedge.

The riders raced up the road madly. The gleaming, sporty phaeton rocked dangerously in the rain-rutted course. The other man rode on a beautiful, lean black horse; beast and man were illuminated with the bars of hazy light falling through thick tree branches. They were young men, London rakes, a breed of man beneath Madeline's contempt. She found their arrogance and idleness a bore.

And yet, as they laughed and shouted, each goading the other to a faster pace, Madeline felt her blood rise in a strange excitement. It was in particular the man on the horse who caught her eye. He wore no powder or wig, and his thick dark hair was drawn back into a queue with a black ribbon. His body was long and sinuously made, and he rode as if he and the horse were one being. From where she stood, his face gave the impression of exotic tilts and powerful bones.

But it was the hedonism Madeline ordinarily found so distasteful in such men that drew her now, made her take up her skirts and run toward the opening of the maze so she would not lose sight of him behind the hedge.

She broke through to the open stretch of lawn between the maze and the Elizabethan house of Whitethorn just as the man urged his horse into a full run. Light dappled faster and faster over his dark hair, his dark horse, his long legs. Next to him, only a little behind, the phaeton rocked noisily.

As they neared the end of the drive, Madeline burst into a run. The man on the horse left the road and bolted across the same lawn. His speed was almost dizzying, and he headed with purpose for a shoulder-high hedge that edged the house garden.

Madeline froze. They would both be killed.

But even as she clamped a hand over her mouth, watching in horror, the black beast leaped with stunning grace over the squared hedge. Horse and man hung—haloed and gilded by the afternoon light—for an endless time against the sky.

As he hung there, suspended in midair, looking like Pan, like some untamed beast come in from the wild, the man laughed. The sound rang with robust defiance into the day, and Madeline felt her heart catch with a sharp pang.

To be so free!

Horse and rider landed nimbly on the other side of the hedge. For one long moment, Madeline stared after him, her heart pounding. Then, setting her mouth, she gathered her skirts and turned away to slip into the house by a side door. She didn't wish to greet anyone in such spirits, and particularly not the man who'd risked life and limb for a foolish jump.

The sound of the free male laughter, the easy camaraderie of bets won and lost, followed her as she ducked into the house.

Lucien Harrow dismounted with a victorious cry. "Foolish bet, Jonathan!"

Jonathan leaped from the carriage nimbly and set his wig aright. "I would have won it had you not taken that suicidal leap!"

From the top of the wide stone steps came a female voice, at once mocking and congratulatory. "Well done, Harrow! We saw it from the windows."

Lucien leaped up the steps and took her hand, his breath still coming fast. The widowed countess, though well past the first blush of beauty, was still generally counted to be the most glorious creature London had ever seen—and word was her sexual appetites were as prodigious as her beauty.

Lucien had never been her lover, but he never ruled out the possibility. With a mocking smile of his own, he lifted her hand to his lips and pressed a bold, moist kiss to it.

A flicker of approval danced in the violet eyes. "Dear boy, I'm so glad you could come!"

Jonathan elbowed Lucien aside, not at all covertly, and swept the countess into a lewd embrace. Over his head, Juliette met Lucien's eyes with a tiny smile, lifting one eyebrow lightly.

"Jealousy doesn't become you, Jonathan," she said in reproof, tapping him with her fan as she moved away, trailing lace and brocade and the scent of her omnipresent cosmetics. "Come have refreshment, gentlemen."

Jonathan shoved Lucien, only half in play. "This is one you'll not spoil, man."

A slow smile spread over Lucien's face. "You know I cannot resist a challenge, Jonathan. Do you so doubt your prowess?"

Jonathan, recovering, laughed. "Hardly." As if all was forgotten, he gestured for both to go inside.

But both of them knew Jonathan had revealed too much. Lucien smiled to himself, plucking a rose from the bush alongside the door. Jonathan in love—fancy that. And with the most notoriously unfaithful woman in all of England.

Interesting indeed. Lucien doubted he'd try to seduce her himself; for all her beauty she was a female of surprisingly sharp edges. He fancied women a little softer.

Nonetheless, there was nothing like a good tangle of amour and vice to brighten the dull countryside. Perhaps his exile would not be so deadly boring as he'd feared.

Juliette sailed into Madeline's chambers just before eight, dressed in a gown of apricot silk that displayed her awe-inspiring bosom and flawless skin to perfection.

Pearls gleamed around her long neck, and coquettish curls framed a perfectly shaped ear.

"Ah!" she said in her resonant voice. "You're nearly done. Wonderful!" She rounded Madeline, examining her. "And you are beautiful tonight, sweet."

Madeline held her head very still, allowing the maids to finish dressing her hair, which was piled high on her head and laced with emeralds. Wryly, she gazed at Juliette. "Thank you."

It was impossible to feel any sense of beauty in the presence of the countess, and Madeline had long ago ceased to try. Even her youth was no benefit where Juliette was concerned—every single detail of the woman was exactly what it should be to draw the attention of men. Her teeth, her eyes, her hair; her magnificent figure and modulated voice.

The maids finished with her, and Madeline waved them away to don her long gloves, which would effectively hide the scratches on her hands. "Is he here?" she asked, not looking at Juliette.

"Yes." Juliette smiled and stepped forward to take the patch box from Madeline's hands. "He's rather impatient to meet you."

"I've heard he looks like a pig—all pink and beady-eyed. If he's that awful, I'll not marry him, no matter how much money he has or how close to the throne."

Juliette's lips tightened infinitesimally. "You'll marry as I wish, or lose this estate. Your father gambled far too much and we are paying the price."

"Oh, it was his gambling," Madeline said with a lift of a brow. "Fourteen years ago?"

There was a flicker of steel in the violet eyes. "Do try, Madeline, this once?"

Madeline took her fan from the dressing table and

flicked it open in an expert, mocking imitation of Juliette. "I'll try," she said.

When Madeline would have walked out with Juliette, the countess stopped her. "No, my dear," she said, smiling. "You'll enter alone tonight."

Madeline inclined her head and let her stepmother go down ahead of her. Before her trip to the Continent, Madeline had oft been used as a foil for Juliette's jeweled loveliness. Tonight, perhaps the aim was to display Madeline in a better light.

Certainly no expense had been spared on the dress, made of brocaded forest green velvet, cut in a wide square at the bodice—or what there was of a bodice. The color agreed with Madeline's pale skin and dark hair, and the necklace of emeralds, so cold at first, had warmed and now lay with a comforting, glowing weight against her chest. The fabric and jewels made her feel a little less the dull child. Cynically, she supposed if she were to wed a marquess, she'd get used to such things.

All the same, she paused for an instant outside the door to the salon. From within came the chuckling of bawdy jokes, a lascivious undertone to the notes of the string quartet playing in the corner. She clutched her hands together, wishing for the veiling of a gauze fichu to cover her bosom. She wanted nothing to do with this sort of a life, filled with parties and meaningless dinners and too much drink.

The trouble was, she seemed to have little calling for a religious life, either. She had only an eccentric need for solitude, a wish to spend her days with plants and in study of poetry and music. Had she been born male—

But she had not, and for all her resentment of

Juliette's pushing, Madeline knew the estate needed a new source of cash. For the gardens, for the house that was her legacy, Madeline could marry as Juliette wished. Touching the armoring weight of emeralds at her breast, she took a breath and pushed open the door.

A little ripple of halted, then hastily resumed, conversation flew around the room. For a moment, Madeline paused, allowing them to admire her as she'd been instructed, then cast her gaze around.

There were a number of dazzling, beautiful women in the room, women Madeline had met in London with her stepmother. They stood in little groups with men in embroidered and brocaded coats and satin breeches in colors of her spring garden—new leaf green and lilac and sky blue—and red-heeled shoes.

Madeline greeted them graciously. She answered their polite inquiries, smiled and allowed kisses to be brushed over her cheek. The men bent over her hand, letting their eyes linger over the body that had been so thin when she left two years before. They commented upon how well she'd grown up.

None were the marquess. Trying to contain a frown, Madeline looked for her stepmother. As if Juliette could read her mind, she heard her name called out, sweetly, "Madeline!"

She turned, bracing herself as well as she might for the sight of her husband-to-be. Instead, she saw Juliette standing with the two men from the race this afternoon. The one from the phaeton was pale and very thin, quite perfectly elegant in his presentation. The way he hung close to Juliette, Madeline thought he must be Juliette's current lover.

Thinking of the strange longing the other man had aroused in her, Madeline folded her hands before she allowed herself to look at him, and took a breath to steel herself against his heady aura of freedom. She looked up—and found his gaze boldly upon her. A jolt of—something—passed through her stomach, hard and bright, then gone.

He still scorned wig or powder, and his hair seemed as violently alive in the candlelight as it had in the gold dappling of sunshine this afternoon. It was caught back from his face again in a queue neatly tied with a black ribbon, and rippled halfway down his back, thick and wavy and glossy.

Now she could see the details of the handsome face: high cheekbones touched with a flush of color, an aggressive and hawkish nose, a mobile and sensual mouth. It was his eyes that gave him an exotic cast— very dark blue and slightly tilted. Like a large cat. And like a cat, the smile he gave her was both predatory and elegant.

Madeline had long been acquainted with the habits of rakes. At fourteen, this sort of insolent and knowing smile had turned her knees to mush. At twenty, she was beyond melting under the gaze of any man— even one who was, she had to admit, quite compelling.

Still, she did not blush or hastily look away, but affected boredom as she approached the knot of them.

"Madeline, my dear, these are friends of mine from London," Juliette said. "This is Jonathan Child, viscount of Lanham."

The pale man bent over Madeline's hand. "A pleasure."

"My lord."

"And this," Juliette continued, indicating the other man, "is Lucien Harrow, Lord Esher, heir to the earl of Monthart, and quite the worst rake in the history

of England." This last was said with a hint of sup-
pressed laughter. "Beware of him, sweet."

Madeline glanced at Juliette, surprised to hear such
bold warning. The countess had already fixed her
gaze rather brilliantly upon Lord Esher, who took
Madeline's hand with a startlingly strong grip. He
stepped close, so close that the crown of that thick,
living hair brushed the tops of her breasts when he
bent over her hand.

She stepped back. He lifted his head, affecting a
quizzical expression that could not entirely hide the
glitter of amusement in his eyes. "Do not be alarmed,
Lady Madeline. She jests."

His voice was as rich as the breath of a cello, and it
was oddly alluring to have him so close, to see from a
few inches the depth of those eyes, to smell the dusky
fragrance of his skin. He held her hand and her gaze
for a beat longer than was proper, a tiny smile playing
at the edges of his sensual mouth.

Madeline frowned, yanking her hand away. "Do
not attempt such flirtations with me, Lord Esher. I'm
afraid I find men of your ilk transparent and boring."

He tucked his hands behind his back, allowing her
to put distance between them. But his grin was
crooked and set alive a dimple in the cheek. "Are we?"

"Yes."

"Madeline, how rude of you!" Juliette said, amused.

Madeline, knowing her stepmother applauded her
silently, said, "No ruder than men who think of
women as little toys."

Lord Esher laughed. "What a wise daughter you've
raised, Countess," he said. His gaze never strayed
from Madeline's face, and she found the steadfast
perusal unsettling.

"Stepdaughter," Juliette said, and spatted him with her fan.

"Oh?"

Juliette lifted her chin. "I am not near of an age to have a grown daughter! Her mother died in childbed. 'Twas tragic."

"Ah. I remember the story now. You wed the earl soon after, though, did you not?"

The countess pouted, very prettily. "Yes. But I was a mere child."

Madeline looked toward the long windows showing the setting sun framed by damask drapes, amused in spite of herself. Juliette, who was the daughter of a dressmaker, did not like being teased about her humble beginnings. Lord Esher evidently knew it. Madeline glanced at him from the corner of her eye.

Boldly, he admired Madeline's figure, making no pretense of doing anything else. The nearly violent blue of his eyes touched her shoulders and breasts and waist with approval.

Juliette caught the examination. "I did train the girl, so you needn't work your charms—she's immune to the wiles of seduction."

"Is she now?"

"Quite," Madeline said.

Mockingly, he dipped his head. "Then all I may do is bow."

Madeline inclined her head in return, just as mockingly, a smile on her lips for the first time. If he did not exert himself too much—and why would he—she'd grow used to his extraordinary appeal very quickly. It was only the suddenness of his appearance that made her feel so unsettled. She'd had crushes on far more magnetic rakes than this.

A stirring at the front of the salon caught her attention. Madeline turned, hoping it would be the marquess. A man came through the door, nodding distractedly at the guests.

Madeline stared for a long moment. He was not the piggish creature she'd feared, nor was he at all handsome. Too plump, too soft. His clothes were a bit askew, as if he'd hurried or been careless, and his forehead already showed two half-moons of skin where his hair was falling out.

Behind her, Madeline felt the presence of Lord Esher. His voice fell in her ear. "I hope you won't mind one single compliment, earnestly extended." The warmth of his breath brushed her earlobe.

She looked over her shoulder.

The smile faded from his face, leaving a sober and intense expression. "You are the most exquisitely fey and beautiful creature I've ever seen."

The tiny hairs on her neck raised. Abruptly, she flicked her fan. "If that's sincere, I'm the queen of England."

His crooked smile returned, and he straightened as Juliette moved close to Madeline, nudging her. "Psst. There is your husband, child. At the door."

Madeline stared at the marquess, knowing her life hung in this moment. As she waited, the marquess caught sight of her, and the round, unremarkable face was transformed by a smile of deep and singular sweetness. He gave her a small, courtly bow.

Her heart pinched.

"Our troubles are over, my sweet," Juliette murmured, urging Madeline forward. "Go to him."

For an instant longer, Madeline hung back. All her dreams of romance, of love, were swept away. She might one day grow fond of this round little man, but she would never love him.

As if to point out the contrast, the heated, moist breath of Lord Esher brushed her shoulder, a whisper of a caress as dangerous as a serpent's tongue. "One would think the marquess a perfect man for a woman who so dislikes men of my ilk."

A tiny shudder rippled over her arms. "Yes," she said with more certainty than she felt, and moved forward. She smiled at the marquess as graciously as she was able, feeling a cool brush of air replace the breath of Lord Esher against her neck.

She did not allow herself to look back.

2

*Fain would I change that note
To which fond love hath charm'd me.*

—Anonymous

Lucien had a headache. Mild at the moment, but the smell of perfume in the salon aggravated it, and he found himself hoping supper would soon be called. Food might help.

The party was not particularly large, seven men and an equal number of women. In comparison to London affairs, it was minuscule indeed. But as Lucien watched the group assemble into knots according to friendship and alliance, he knew there were endless possibilities for amusement.

Next to him, Jonathan glowered and tried not to watch every move Juliette made. By the door, Juliette fawned over the young marquess, while her step-daughter less enthusiastically, but politely, allowed her hand to be kissed.

"Why's the countess angling for a marriage between those two?" Lucien asked Jonathan.

Jonathan, involved in a pinch of snuff, wiggled his nose in satisfaction. "Look around. Whitethorn is suffering. The countess has done well to hold it all together, but the old earl was a notorious gambler and pissed away most of the estate before he died."

Lucien narrowed his eyes to watch the trio by the door. Lady Madeline smiled politely at the young marquess, but in subtle signs Lucien saw her reluctance to be with him: in her hands, clutched tightly together in front of her, in the way she only halfway faced him, as if she might flee at any moment; in the rigidness of her jaw. "The girl doesn't look particularly thrilled at the notion."

"Can you blame her?"

Lucien gave his friend a wry smile. "No." The marquess was young, but that youth was the only thing he had on his side. Plump and dull and earnest, his already thinning hair covered with a hedgehog wig, he was hardly the stuff of a girl's dreams.

And yet, the young man was obviously and thoroughly smitten with Madeline. His eyes shone with a naive worship Lucien found almost painful to observe.

Jonathan lazily snapped his snuff box closed and tucked it back into the pocket of his waistcoat. "Why don't you offer for her, Lucien?"

"Marry?" Lucien echoed in genuine amusement. "Why don't you do it? Snuggle yourself close to the countess?"

His face darkened. "I haven't the fortune they need. You do."

Lucien looked intently at his friend and realized Jonathan had already offered and been turned down. Curious. He glanced back to the glorious Madeline—and for one instant, he gave the notion of marriage a fleeting consideration. One had to do it eventually. It might as well be to one as beautiful as this, whom a man might enjoy for the brief time before boredom set in.

"Wouldn't that please my father to no end?" he said dryly. He lifted his glass of port and sipped of it, thinking of Madeline's arch acknowledgment of his status as a rake, and her disdain. She'd not marry him even if he offered.

"It *would* please your father, actually," Jonathan said. "He's likely to cut you off if you continue to defy him the way you have."

"His only son? He's a cold bastard, but I doubt he'd go that far."

"You have cousins."

Lucien blinked at a trickle of sharp, light-edged pain that seeped through his skull. In truth he had several cousins and an uncle, all of whom would be delighted to get their hands on the Monthart fortune. "So let them take it."

A derisive noise escaped Jonathan's throat. "We'll see how your tune changes when one of them succeeds in stealing it away from you."

"They won't."

"Suit yourself."

"A man so intent on being a lapdog to a woman ought not be so free with advice," Lucien said.

Anger flashed in Jonathan's eye. "If you weren't my oldest friend, I'd call you out for that."

The light-studded knife twisted in Lucien's brain, blinding him momentarily. Harshly, he said, "So do it. I'd be inclined to let you kill me."

"God, you're in a temper. What ails you?" He frowned. "Surely you can't be worried over that boy!"

"What boy? God, no." Lucien frowned and waved the notion away. Helena, his most recently discarded mistress, had stirred the passions of a melodramatic young actor, who vowed to avenge Helena's "humiliation" at Lucien's hands. "No. He's misguided, as he'll learn soon enough."

Jonathan clipped his watch closed with a sharp snap. "Well, whatever it is spoiling your mood, overcome it, will you? Juliette is rather counting on a smooth evening here tonight."

Lucien made no reply. Smooth evenings bored him. Again his gaze strayed to the girl, speaking earnestly now to the marquess. Her skin carried a peculiar luminosity he found quite extraordinary. It almost blended with the shards of light in his headache, and he found himself a bit adrift in a rather fanciful vision of her, clad only in that thick dark hair. "Marriage, no," he said, half to himself.

"Not seduction, Lucien," Jonathan protested. "Juliette will quite have your head."

"Is that so?" he drawled, and paused just long enough to plant doubt in Jonathan's mind before he said, "No. Innocents are rather dull." He let his gaze linger instead on Juliette, who caught the bold examination and tilted her head proudly in acknowledgment. "I much prefer women of some experience."

Jonathan said nothing, but Lucien felt him grow rigid next to him. A mottled red stained his cheeks below the loose blond hair, giving brilliance to his green eyes. Lucien didn't miss the amused and challenging glance Juliette shot toward Jonathan.

"She's going to drive me mad," Jonathan said, his mouth twisting as if he tasted something vile.

"It's a fatal mistake to fall in love, Jonathan. She'll use it against you."

"She's doing it now," Jonathan said, "flirting with you."

"So flirt another way."

Jonathan smiled, very slowly. "Best not meddle in things you don't understand, my friend." He left the room.

His departure caught Juliette's attention. Her coquettish mask evaporated and Lucien thought he caught the tiniest of frowns on her smooth brow. With a murmured word, she left the marquess and Madeline alone and hurried from the room.

Curious, Lucien thought.

By the time the meal was announced, Lucien's headache had trebled. Each step from the salon to the dining room caused a new explosion behind his brow, and he had to struggle to keep his expression even.

As they settled around the table, he concentrated on the quartet providing music from one corner of the room. A mistake. While they were passably good musicians, they fell short of true inspiration, and their dropped notes, sliding sharps, and unpleasing flats grated on his ears, harshly exaggerating his headache.

In the dining room he saw that the countess pinned down the top of the table, with Jonathan and himself seated on either side of her. To Lucien's right, across the table, sat Lady Madeline and the marquess. At Lucien's side sat a matron of the small hamlet, her wrinkled bosom dressed in violets, her powder rather grimly patted into the crevices. Lucien thought she must be at least ninety, and he was surprised to find her a quite learned and agreeable companion, who distracted him from both his headache and his rather disturbing attraction to Lady Madeline.

Serious she was, and quite different from the rest of the women at the table. Her eyes, a cool gray in color, showed a sharp intelligence. He liked intelligent women. They bored him less quickly, and often had bold and pleasing sexual imaginations to go with their clever repartee.

He gestured toward a footman for his glass to be refilled. The smells of the meal sat ill upon his stomach, and he plucked disinterestedly at the roast pheasant, unable to summon any appetite. The wine sloshed in his empty belly, but enough of it might numb the growing pain in his head. After dinner he could slip away unnoticed, or perhaps walk outside for a time. Fresh air sometimes chased away the worst of his headaches.

Luckily he wasn't called upon to make much conversation. The woman next to him started a lively debate on the merits of early or late shearing with the squire to her right, and Juliette's attention was on Jonathan. By the flushed expression on both their faces, Lucien guessed there were things going on below the table he'd rather not examine.

A footman took his plate and replaced it with an aspic that quivered sloppily, its shiny edges gleaming against the candles. Looking at it, Lucien feel faintly nauseous.

To distract himself, he gazed again toward Madeline and her marquess. He seemed a plain enough fellow who ate rather a lot but didn't seem particularly lascivious about it. He chatted politely, but uncomfortably patted his wig more than once, as if afraid it might slip. Which it did each time the marquess patted it.

Whatever the girl thought of her courting lord and his struggles didn't show on her face. Except once. Lucien caught her taking a deep, heartfelt sigh. Her expression at that moment—oddly stricken, somehow sorrowful—was so fleeting Lucien wondered if he'd really seen it at all. The rest of the time, she was the very model of civility and good breeding. Juliette had trained her well.

She was an exquisite creature. Thick ebony hair, piled artlessly on her head, pointed out the clear, light gray of her eyes, eyes at once smoky and bold and naive; a mouth—oh, yes, quite a mouth—cut wide and full for passion, and as yet unawakened.

As if she could hear the lascivious turn of his thoughts, Madeline looked up, straight at him. Her expression was cool, disguising any thought. Lucien touched his chin, wondering what sort of seduction it would take to shake free that aloof and haughty expression, and if it would be worth it.

Her hands rested at the edges of her plate, and her body was still, as unmoving as statuary in the gardens. He pursed his lips, touching his mouth with his finger as he considered.

Under his gaze, her breath caught. Only a bit, but he saw the quick rise of her breast, the smallest flare of her nostrils. He smiled, letting her know he had seen her reaction.

She tilted her chin, and the disdainful brow rose eloquently before she turned away to listen to something the man to her left was saying. Lucien smiled, satisfied. That coolness, then, was shallow, hiding currents of feeling at which Lucien could only guess.

A smooth, lyrical voice spoke against his ear: Juliette's dulcet voice, a voice that had lifted the daughter of a dressmaker to the glittering heights of countess. "Not that chicken, Wolf."

Lucien allowed himself a lazy smile. "I wouldn't think of it."

"No?"

"Virgins bore me," he drawled. "I am curious, however. Why have we not seen her till now? Surely she's past the age of a debut."

A flicker of annoyance crossed the exquisite face. "She would not allow it."

"Would not allow it?" he echoed.

"She preferred to continue her education on the Continent. Had to go to Italy and explore the gardens."

"Odd choice for a young girl."

"She is not impressed with society, as you may have gathered."

"But what else is there for the daughter of an earl?"

"Just so."

Lucien glanced back over his shoulder. In the flickering blaze of candles, her thick lustrous hair gleamed like the pelt of some elegant animal, and emeralds winked through the dark strands. He was caught by the flawless curve of her cheek, faintly rosy, unpainted and unpowdered. There was an appealing arrogance in the tilt of her head, a disdain he found more alluring than all the perfumes of Arabia.

He shifted his gaze. "She's a beauty, Countess," he commented with just the right note of lust in his throat. "Wise of you to marry her to the marquess before she falls into the clutches of some fiend."

Juliette's color rose. "Beware, Lord Esher." He saw she struggled to maintain her composure, but a hint of shrillness betrayed her. "I am mindful that men of your ilk find challenges irresistible."

"True."

She leaned forward, and Lucien allowed himself to admire frankly the display of creamy shoulders and bosom which her golden gown exposed. "Listen closely, Lord Esher. If you cross me, I'll not bother with cutting you at parties or arranging a duel, as has contented so many of your lovers."

He chuckled, raising his hands in mock terror. "What, assassinate me?"

She smiled, her eyes glittering like cold jewels. Under the table her hand crawled up his leg. Her meaning was completely clear. "Not even so easy as that."

Lucien inclined his head in acquiescence. He had no doubt she meant exactly what she said. "Very well, madam. I shall look elsewhere for my prey." As if he meant *her,* he let his gaze drop to her lips, as if wondering what taste they would carry. Slowly, he raised his eyes to hers again and smiled.

The mark was true. A sultry look bloomed in her eye, and her vanity was appeased.

God, it was too perfect! As he met that avaricious gaze, Lucien made up his mind to seduce the girl. What rake worthy of the name could resist? Juliette, no small rake herself, fairly begged to be taken down a notch, and she seemed utterly sure he would listen to her bidding.

Deflowering a virgin from a family his father would approve deeply could only add sweetness to the pot. It wasn't as if he had any pressing business the next few months—in fact he would likely be forced to duel a foolish lad in London if he returned.

Yes, he would seduce Madeline, under the watchful

eye of her guardian, and meanwhile let Juliette think he was intent on seducing *her*.

It might be his most splendid adventure to date.

A pang of conscience touched him as he looked toward Madeline—for she'd have to be publicly ruined if Lucien's father were to learn of the debauchery. A pity he'd have to do that.

As he looked at her, his headache swelled suddenly, sending a swift, sharp pain through his brain. And behind it, like a wisp of wind, Lucien heard a faint, disturbing bar of music. He shut it away, fiercely, along with his conscience.

Lucien would be doing Madeline a favor by seducing her. She deserved a taste of the sweeter pleasures before shackling herself forever to the doughy marquess—if he'd even have her when the scandal got out. Lucien rather thought he would as long as his pride were not too injuriously marred; if marquesses only married virgins, there'd be no little marquesses about at all.

Under the table, Lucien felt a kick. He glanced up in surprise to find Jonathan glowering at him across the table. With a quizzical smile, he lifted a brow.

All was fair in love and war. And this, it seemed, was going to be both. For a moment, his headache eased a tiny bit.

Ah, yes. The weeks in the country this year would be splendid indeed.

Madeline tried to ignore Lord Esher, but he made it difficult. Throughout supper, he watched her with the relentlessness of a cat stalking a songbird. It was a little unnerving, but Madeline had the marquess to think of.

To her relief, Charles Devon was not an unpleasant

companion. He seemed to feel no need to grope at her, as was so often the case with such beefy, rich men; nor did he bore her with stories of the hunt. Instead he had a rather charming fondness for archeology, a subject in which Madeline had no particular interest, but no particular objection.

Nonetheless, she was glad to escape him after supper, ducking outside to one of the small terraces that edged most of the rooms on the lower floor of Whitethorn. A sliver of moon hung above the trees in a clear night sky. Scents of yew and moist ground reached her, and she breathed them deeply.

It was only then, under the narcotic spell of the night, a night that seemed especially designed for lovers, that she let despair invade her. How could she possibly marry the marquess? Listen politely to him forevermore, her heart permanently boxed and put away? It seemed a gross violation of what love should be.

Pulling her shawl around her shoulders more tightly, she walked toward the stone balustrade edging the terrace. She wasn't at all like the other girls she knew—dreaming of some great love affair. She'd seen all too many love affairs in the salon of Whitethorn. They seemed tawdry and untidy, and love rarely outlasted passion.

Or so she had believed. Tonight she realized she'd harbored those same silly dreams herself.

At the edge of the terrace, she paused, leaning her hip against the balustrade. From this vantage point, she could see the formal gardens, the maze and topiary, the beds planted in patterns of lace. All of it desperately needed her attention, her time, and money she simply did not have.

With a sigh, she knew she could marry to save it. She would.

Behind her came footsteps, the sure strong footsteps of a man of some height. Madeline smiled, unsurprised. "Join me, Lord Esher," she said without turning.

"How did you know it was I without looking around?"

Madeline looked up at him. "I think there must be a book of rake's etiquette," she said lightly. "First rule is one must always follow one's prey into a moonswept night."

To her surprise, he laughed. "Well done." Inclining his head, he asked, "What then would be my next step?"

Madeline straightened, knowing she must not show any hint of shyness or of blushing sensibility. If she were to put him off properly, he had to understand she knew well any technique he might attempt. "That would depend upon the woman, of course, and the rake." She frowned, inclining her head. "You don't have the same look as some of the men from London, so I'd guess you were educated elsewhere."

"Good—you're right. How will that influence my choices?"

"Well, since you haven't a clue of what sort of woman I am yet, I expect you'd choose flattery first."

A crooked smile caught half his mouth. His voice dropped a measure. "Oh, but I do know a little of you, my lady."

"Do you? Pray tell, then, what tack you've chosen for your foray into my seduction."

He chuckled, low and deep, the sound almost sinfully rich against the flitting notes of a minuet in the salon. "Are you absolutely certain I've chosen to seduce you?"

"Yes, though you didn't make up your mind until supper."

This time, he did not smile. The artfully wrought lines of his face grew still. Madeline knew she'd scored a point, and the slight, growing apprehension in her shoulders eased a little.

"I believe you'll be more of a challenge than I thought," he said quietly. "All the better, of course."

"Of course," Madeline replied. "Not that you'll succeed."

"Well, that's the test, isn't it?" He leaned on the balustrade, and his elegant, sinuous form took on a lazy grace. For a moment he looked at her musingly, and Madeline forced herself to look evenly at him in return, showing no quiver or disturbance.

At last he spoke in an intimate voice, low and rounded. "I think my first step will be simply to look at you."

A prickle touched her spine, and Madeline clutched her shawl more closely in her fingers. "Simple," she said, but the word was breathier than she would have liked.

"Yes." Infinitesimally, he leaned forward. "I think you haven't been gazed at enough."

Madeline didn't move, but the prickle under her skin spread. A breeze came from behind him, carrying notes of the garden, and stealing notes from his flesh to fling against her. It was a man-scent of perspiration and musk and horse, and something else, like hay in the sunshine. She dared not breathe it deep.

"When I'm gazing at you," he continued in his slow, quiet voice, "I'll be touching you in my mind.

Your nose and hair, your throat. And I'll be thinking you are ever so much more beautiful than Juliette, who has stolen your light for far, far too long."

She hid the trembling of her fingers inside her shawl and managed to say calmly, "A good choice, sir. You are very observant to have seen so much in so short a time." Her courage ran out, and she turned from the balustrade. "Amusing as it's been, I must return to my guests."

"By all means do not neglect your marquess." He gave her a short, stiff bow.

Madeline hurried away, relieved when she was again safely within the brightly lit salon, embraced by the frivolous notes of the quartet. Lord Esher frightened her.

And yet, she had no choice but to meet him toe to toe. Otherwise she'd disappear as certainly and quickly as claret on a gamblers' table, lost to the extraordinary appeal of him.

She had no choice but to fight him—on his ground.

Lucien went to sleep well enough but awakened sometime before dawn, in the blackest part of the night, haunted. Music rang in his head, shattering sleep and thought, riding on a sharp blaze of light-struck pain.

There—there were the oboes. He winced and blinked, trying to push them away. But in came the cellos, the drums, the clarinets. They crowded in, triumphant in spite of the port he'd drunk, the food he'd eaten. They came, his demon notes, to haunt him.

Over the years, he'd learned that there was only one cure for them, one way to drive them from his mind. In his nightshirt, he stumbled from the bed and lit a brace of candles. He flung his hair from his eyes and began to write.

When he was finished, he burned the pages completely, thoroughly, to curled black flutters.

The headache ceased.

Lucien slept.

3

I dare not ask a kisse,
I dare not beg a smile;
Lest having that, or this,
I might grow proud the while.
—Robert Herrick

Madeline, dressed in an old, worn gown, made her way to the gardens long before the rest of the house stirred. Dew clung to the grass, wetting her slippers and dampening her hem. A blackbird sang from some dark and hidden place, the sound wistful in the still morning. As she walked, she pulled on cotton gloves that cost the earth, and yet were necessary to help protect her hands.

Thin mist clung to the landscape, and Madeline felt a catch in her chest—she had missed this place! All through Europe she had hiked, visiting out of a sense of duty the main sights thought to be suitable for a young woman. In truth, she'd gone for the gardens—and everywhere had found people sympathetic to her passion, those willing to share it by showing off their own gardens. It had been singularly pleasing. Sharing those well-loved places, Madeline had finally come to a clear sense of herself as apart from any-thing anyone else expected of her. And in this garden, she would please her own expectations.

Basket and shears in hand, she knelt in one of the small wing gardens that offset the maze on all four sides. Each plot had once been designed to illustrate a different sort of lace, but at the moment, most of it was unrecognizable for the weeds and overgrowth.

As the sun rose and the mist burned away, she clipped lavender borders and dug out the tiny paths between clumps of flowers to illustrate the lace pattern. In two hours, she managed to remove enough debris and unruly growth from a three-foot section so that it at least began to resemble the pattern. Rocking back on her heels to admire it, she wiped the back of one hand over her forehead, and felt a gritty mark streak her skin.

Yes, it would take some time, but she would restore the gardens at Whitethorn. They were her legacy.

Perspiring and hungry, she picked up her basket of tools. Shaking her skirts to loosen the grass and leaves clinging to it, she looked up and was aston-ished to see Lord Esher approaching. It couldn't yet be eight, and yet he was immaculately dressed in a dark blue coat and breeches, his hair neatly queued and tied with a bright ribbon that fluttered on a cur-rent of wind. On his feet were tall black boots.

A quiet stir touched her blood at the way he moved, so loose and free, and as he came closer, she thought of his wild leap over the hedge yesterday, of his rich shout of laughter as he reached the very height of the jump. He could not have known, in that moment, whether the horse would find its feet—

whether he would live or die. It hadn't seemed to matter.

There was no hurry about him. When he was a few feet away, she slapped her gloves together to shake some of the damp earth from them. "Rare for a gentleman of leisure to rouse himself so early, sir."

"I like to ride before the day is too long." With the insouciant ease that marked his every movement, he glanced around him. "It is unfashionable, but I find I enjoy the morning, before the tedious noise and babble begins." He smiled to take the sting from his words.

Madeline smiled. In the kindly light, he looked far less dangerous than he had the night before, his eyes clear, his complexion hale and healthy. She shifted her basket on her hip and used her scissors to cut a late blooming rose for him to put in his lapel.

"Yes," she said, handing him the flower. "I can't stay in bed past dawn most days. I'd rather be out here."

He smiled, tucking the flower into his coat. "Beware," he said, "you'll give me tools to aid me in my seduction of you." But his smile was rueful, self-mocking, and she took the words as the light jest he intended.

"So be it." A tangle of weeds had grown around the rosebush. Fronds reached strangling arms clear to the top. Madeline frowned and set down her basket so she could wrestle the vine from the bush. "It would be impossible for you to stay long at Whitethorn," she said, "without learning my primary interest is in gardens."

"Ah." He looked around him. "It would seem you have quite a job ahead of you."

"You have no idea." Madeline dropped the

uprooted woodbine to the ground. "If I were to do nothing else, just the maze would take me a year."

"It alone looks well tended. Surely there isn't that much work to be done."

"Looks can be deceiving." She hadn't intended the double meaning but heard it as soon as the words left her lips. She cocked her head toward him, grinning.

"Truer words were never spoken." For a moment he gazed at the maze. "Will you show it to me?" A glittering challenge lit his eyes.

"Another time," she said, lightly. "I'm afraid I'm quite famished."

"Pity." He lifted one perfect brow. "I have weakness for these old gardens and would have enjoyed a tour."

"Leading a rake into the maze, Lord Esher? Alone? The rake's book of rules would surely insist that such a gesture is an invitation to certain ravishment."

"You speak boldly."

"It saves time."

"Yes." He lifted his hands as if in surrender, and backed away with a short, quick bow. "I'd hoped for a narration of its virtues, from someone who obviously loves it well, but perhaps you're right. I'll go alone."

"Impossible. You'll be hopelessly lost."

He gave her the faintest hint of a smile. "Then I suppose you'll be rescuing me before supper tonight."

Madeline hesitated. She genuinely loved the gardens, and as anyone did, loved to share her knowledge. Was his interest genuine, or a ruse to lure her into a secluded place? She didn't know. "Most find the old style of formal gardens a bore nowadays."

"Yes, I know." He clasped his hands behind his

back, that restless gaze traveling over the ragged topiary all around them. "My boyhood home had formal gardens of this sort. My father had them razed and replanted in the new style after my mother died." He looked at her. "It was a gruesomely destructive act."

"My stepmother would do the same here." Somehow, they were walking slowly toward the entrance to the maze. "It would be a tragedy. This hedge is nearly a hundred years old."

"Show it to me," he said again. "I vow the place will be your ground only. Within, I'll be only Lucien, your friend."

"My friend." She drawled the words with as much skepticism as she could muster, stripping her damp gloves from her hands. "All right," she said. "If you misbehave, I'll simply leave you in there to starve."

His crooked smile flashed. "Very well."

"Choose your path."

He considered and pointed. "The left."

Together they entered the hallways of green. Immediately all sounds were muffled. The sun had not yet warmed the paths here, and shreds of mist clung to the ground and hung in streamers around the small, secret beds planted here and there.

"Do not attempt it alone," she cautioned seriously. "Once, there were markers to help the alert, but most are overgrown now. The right side is better, more easily navigated."

"Why is that?" Lazily he plucked a bud from a clematis vine and lifted it to his nose.

"The first earl of Whitethorn had a passion for puzzles. The two sides meet at the center, but it's impossible to get from one side to the other except there. On the right side, you alternate turning first left, then right."

"But how does one remember?"

"Carefully."

"And on this side?"

Madeline gave him a smile and tapped her forehead. "The pattern must be memorized."

"And you have?"

"It's been my retreat since I was a child." Here, on her own ground, in the one place on earth that belonged to her, Madeline felt calm. Lifting her head, she inhaled the scent of the yews, and the damp, bruised grass under their feet. It was longer here, unkempt, and her feet were quite wet before long. As they rounded a corner, Madeline gave him a secretive smile. "The *claire-voies* in this maze are extraordinary," Madeline said. "There are more than twenty of them."

"Claire-voies?"

"Yes." Madeline lifted a hand to indicate he should precede her around a corner, and he did.

There, framing a view of great expanse of the wild gardens beyond, was a window cut into the hedge. Lord Harrow paused midstep. Madeline thought he looked almost stricken before he recovered and glanced down at Madeline. "Breathtaking, isn't it?"

She looked at the view, painted pale gold with the soft fingers of morning, the greens in hues from gray to yellow, the stillness unbroken but for a cluster of ravens, shiny black, picking in the grass for breakfast. "Yes," she replied. "The whole maze exists only for the sake of beauty. It's extraordinary."

He lifted a brow. "You strike me as a woman who'd find beauty for its own sake a wasteful thing."

"No. Oh, no," she said, and let her gaze touch the exquisite view framed by the *claire-voie*. "Is beauty not the easiest of all things to claim? It's there for anyone."

Madeline felt his restless body quiet. In a resonant voice like a cello, he quoted: "'Full many a glorious morning have I seen/Flatter the mountain-tops with sovereign eye, / Kissing with golden face the meadows green,/Gilding pale streams with heavenly alchemy.'"

Shakespeare. Madeline recognized it immediately, but in his mouth, the sonnet sounded unlike it had in her own mind when she read it. He somehow gave the words a life and music she'd never uncovered. The lyrical rhythm stung her.

With a sharp breathlessness, Madeline looked at him. His head turned and their gazes collided. In the good, gray light, she saw that his eyes were quite remarkably beautiful, dark blue studded with sparks of yellow and green that seemed to have their own source of light.

Jeweled.

Abruptly, she turned around and started walking the direction they had come. Foolish of her to think there was any hope of resisting a man as accomplished in the art of seduction as Lord Esher.

"Lady Madeline! Wait! Why do you run?"

She whirled. "It was unseemly to bring you in here. I was wrong to do it."

"I've frightened you," he said. "I vow that was not my intention."

"It *is* difficult to seduce a terrified woman," she said acerbically.

He touched his chest and held out his hand in a gesture of sincerity. "Nothing I did here was for intent." He glanced over his shoulder and back to her. "I swear by my mother's grave I'll not try to seduce you here."

Again he looked back, toward the path leading inward, to the heart of the maze, with a yearning Madeline recognized on some wordless plane.

He waited, without moving or cajoling, only watching her with that pained, jeweled gaze. The stillness was gone from his body, and she felt his need to go on as clearly as a shout.

She was mad to do it, mad to open even the slightest hint of trust, but she sensed they were alike somehow, in some way hidden deep within both of them, and she wanted to find out what it was they shared. "All right," she said. "The maze is neutral ground."

"Not even simply neutral," he said soberly. "It's yours."

The *claire-voie* pricked music to life in his nerves. New notes, notes that he'd not heard. The ravens, so black against the green, the sky pale above, the dazzling butter yellow sunshine—all framed with the stillness of the living window, green and silent, made music burst to life in him.

And from his heart, or his chest, or whatever place it was the music lived, he heard notes. Violin. He frowned. No, viola . . . yes, and now a horn, soft and faraway.

As he stared through the opening, with Madeline wary and yet curious beside him, a raven lifted and flew into the morning sky, and with the bird's flight came a swell of notes. Lucien hummed them softly, catching them.

How long since music had come like that, without the breach of liquor? So long. And yet, he could not seem to resist it.

With a rueful smile, he offered his arm to the decidedly grimy Madeline. From her dress and skin came the earthy scents of bruised grass and hard work. Long untidy tendrils of hair escaped her cap to hang on her shoulders, and he wondered again what that hair looked like free and brushed to shining.

She shied away from touching him. "I'm very dirty," she said with a shake of her head, folding her hands behind her back. A thread of a second viola, playing counterpoint to the first, swirled in, and a violin. Yes. Andantino.

It was too perplexing to alarm him. Such bright, strong sounds—from nowhere, all at once? It made him feel slightly dizzy, as if he were not himself.

"It's almost enchanted here, isn't it?" he said quietly.

"Yes." Madeline didn't smile, but her eyes were bright. "I was afraid to come here at night when I was a child. I thought the fairies might carry me away."

"And now?"

"I don't know." She paused to bend over a particularly shrouded rosebush and firmly, but gently, tugged away the vines over it. A stone bench, beaded with dew, sat nearby, and a tangle of violets bloomed below it. She pinched one purple flower and held it to her nose. He followed her lead, smiling at the fresh, deep scent.

It was companionable. Lucien found it charming that she was so wary of him, that she kept a foot or two between them at all times, that she didn't pause for more than a moment at any of the quaint unusual features that littered the way.

The place was quite clearly her passion. He understood it. At one corner, she stopped and pointed out another *claire-voie*, this one looking inward, across several pathways, through more windows, to the center of the maze itself. He could see a stone bench, worn gray with time, set in the middle of an overgrown bed of herbs.

"Dazzling," he said, and meant it. "Thank you for your generosity."

She raised skeptical eyes. He sensed about her the long wariness of a loner and was surprised at the recognition he felt. "You're quite welcome," she said simply.

"Juliette tells me you've just returned from a tour of the Continent," Lucien said, politely. A little sunshine now began to penetrate the maze, awakening sleepy corners and drying the dew on the petals of tender flowers. Over the hedge walls, a tree with a dark trunk and pale green leaves was suddenly illuminated. In his inner ear, Lucien heard the waterfall tumble of harp.

Beautiful.

"I went to explore the gardens," Madeline said, bringing him back to the moment. "The Italians are particularly adept at the art, as I'm sure you know."

"The Italians seem adept at a great many things. I did not know gardening was another of their accomplishments." Idly, he plucked a trumpet-shaped flower from a vine and held it to his nose. No scent to speak of. "What makes them superior?"

"The climate is kinder than our own, of course, but I think it's more than that. Enthusiasm and an eye for detail, perhaps."

"Ah. Did you find ideas you hope to employ here?"

"A number of them, actually."

"For example?"

Madeline gave him a quick smile. "It's impossible at the moment, but I'd very much like to experiment with fountains and pools."

"Have you seen the fountains at the Villa d'Este?" he asked.

"Oh, yes! They're magnificent." She clasped her hands over her breast, and a bright passion filled her voice. "Water has a peculiar magic. The sound, the scent, the spirit of cool refreshment—it's quite extraordinary."

They passed a wide space, centered with a hedge in the shape of a triangle. Curious, Lucien slowed. Madeline, a smile curling the edges of her mouth, gestured for him to go in.

He peeked into the opening and saw another of the stone benches within, but this one sat amid a tangle of bushes. Small pink and red flowers with ragged edges and a spicy scent filled the narrow bed. On the gray stone bench, its tail swishing, was an enormous black cat. Lucien grinned at the billowing spill of his belly. "Hullo."

"Meet Boss," Madeline said, bending to scratch the creature's battered ears. "This is his domain—I've rarely known cats able to catch squirrels, but this one thrives upon them."

She knelt, almost by rote, and yanked a stand of grass from between the flowers. Lucien admired the smooth straight line of her spine.

Suddenly in the quiet, her stomach growled. She colored faintly. "I'm afraid I'm growing famished," she said. "And Juliette will never allow me to come to the table this disheveled. I must return."

"By all means, lead us out," he said. "Not that such a lady as Juliette will have stirred at so ungodly an hour."

"You've a wicked tongue, Lord Esher."

"I am a wicked man."

"Yes." Madeline nodded. "That I can believe."

No one—under pain of dismissal—disturbed the countess before noon unless she rang for them. So at this still tender hour of nine, Juliette was indeed only just stirring awake. The room was agreeably dim, the heavy draperies drawn against the invasion of morning.

Juliette moved carefully, one limb and one joint at a time. She moved her fingers, then her wrists, keeping her eyes closed. Only minor stiffness. Her mouth was deadly dry and a dullness fogged her mind, but all in all, considering the copious amounts of wine she'd consumed the night before, it wasn't as horrid as it might have been.

She chanced opening one eyelid. A scene of some debauchery greeted her—her torn gown, a twist of stockings, a discarded pair of silk breeches lay in piles on the floor. Apricot silk and brocaded blue satin, tangled as their owners were.

A musky male scent touched her nostrils, and Juliette shifted, turning over to look at Jonathan, asleep next to her. His skin was hot, smooth, taut under her hand.

So young.

The night flooded into her mind—all that zest and energy were astonishing. He was an inventive, passionate lover. More than that, he shared her secret need of a certain brutality in the act. Sometimes both of them ended up bruised, scratched, bitten.

He moved under her hand, slow and sleepy and aroused. Juliette braced herself against the morning onslaught—always so much more difficult than the night, when wine blunted her emotions. Mornings, she was ill prepared for the clever plying of his hands that knew all the ways she liked to be touched, ill prepared for the heat of his mouth on her throat, or the warm sound of his need rumbling into her ear.

So gently he moved! A gliding hand, a sweet kiss, a reverent sigh. He used his youth to move in her slow and easy no matter how she tried to urge him into the torrent of wild, brutal love they knew at night. And young he might be, but masterful, and Juliette swallowed tears of despair and yearning as she succumbed once again. Anything else she might have resisted. Not the gentleness.

So young.

Damn him!

4

Present mirth hath present laughter;
What's to come is still unsure:
In delay there lies no plenty;
Then come kiss me, sweet and twenty,
Youth's a stuff will not endure.

—Shakespeare

Madeline spent the day in her greenhouse, making notes, sketching out beds and plans and schedules, calculating what she might be able to do on her own, what would have to wait.

As much as she enjoyed it, the sheer enormity of the tasks that awaited her made her feel weary. When the marquess sought her out to ask if she might like to ride in the cooling afternoon, she agreed heartily.

She met him in the stables. His round kind face, below the pate of thinning hair, was dewy, and a line of sweatbeads decorated his upper lip. Madeline tried not to notice, and he greeted her so cheerily it would have been churlish not to respond in kind. "It is a fine, fine day for riding, wouldn't you say?"

Madeline smiled. "Indeed." She took the reins of her gray mare from the groom and accepted the help of the marquess to mount. "Rare to enjoy such fine weather in an English spring."

"Yes."

As they rode out, making small talk, Madeline breathed deeply. Clouds danced across a vivid, blue sky, hinting that there might later be a very welcome rain. The air was light and dry, but the grass drooped on its stalks and a dullness in the colors of the leaves betrayed the lack of moisture these past weeks. A trio of birds played tag across the meadow, and the freshly mown grass gave the day an earthy scent.

In the rose garden, nearly every bush was in bud or blooming. The colors were astonishing. Planted in concentric circles, the flowers were arranged by color, going from palest, clearest white at the center to an almost burgundy red at the outside row. A tall, graceful willow tree grew in the center.

Madeline sighed. Like every other corner of the garden, the roses needed immediate attention.

"That sounds weary," the marquess commented.

"Perhaps a little," she admitted and lifted a hand to point. "In a few weeks, those gardens will be quite beautiful. I hope I'll have a chance to show them to you when they're in full bloom."

"I expect you shall," he said calmly. "Would it help for me to send for my head gardener? He can't be spared at the moment, of course, but I reckon it won't be much longer."

"Oh, that's very kind of you," Madeline returned, "but no, thank you." The exchange made her feel as if she'd been dropping some untoward hint. And yet, who could fail to notice the neglect so evident here? The willow tree, nearly eighty feet tall, provided lovely pale green contrast to the darker green leaves of the roses. The sturdy mums grew with abandon in their sunny beds.

But it was impossible to avoid noticing last year's rose hips uncut on the bushes, the dried brown stalks that needed pruning out, the clumps of grass ruining the lines of the carefully planned beds. With a determined tilt of her head, she commented, "Juliette hires three gardeners. Unfortunately, she is appallingly ignorant in how to direct them." She smiled to lighten her words. "By next spring, I'll have everything in order once more."

The marquess gave her a smile. "No doubt you will."

They rode down the road, past the maze—where Madeline found her thoughts turning to Lord Harrow, and she determinedly turned them away—along the clipped meadows, into the wilder forested land on the outskirts of the estate. "Do tell me of your travels, my lord."

"Oh, do call me Charles," he said with a pained smile. "'My lord' makes me think of my gouty father."

Who would no doubt have a gouty son, she thought unkindly, eyeing his plump fingers. Then, ashamed of herself, she nodded. "Charles."

He smiled.

"The countess tells me you've made several fascinating trips to the Continent for your excavations," she said.

"Oh, I wouldn't think of boring you with all that." He waved his hand. "All those dusty sites are hardly to the taste of a young woman."

"What dusty sites?" Madeline persisted. "Have you visited Pompeii?"

"Oh, yes." His mild voice took on a resonant timbre. "I spent nearly a year with Sir William Hamilton, the English ambassador to the court of Naples, helping to uncover some of the walls."

"It's a fascinating place."

"Do you think so?"

His earnest expression gave her a pang and caused her to tell a polite lie. "Yes."

But the small lie reminded her suddenly of the conversation in the maze. They were just alike, she and Lord Esher, only now it was Madeline prompting the marquess to talk about himself, so he'd feel flattered and happy to be in her company, so he'd think she'd be a good bride for him.

How did that differ from a rake flattering a woman in order to bed her?

It did not. And it was curiously humiliating to realize just how easy it was to appear interested when in fact one was not. Had Lord Harrow been bored this morning as she ran on and on about her gardens?

With a sense of chagrin, she sat up straighter, vowing to be as sincere as she was able with the marquess. As husbands went, she could do much worse.

From below his coat, he took a square of pottery and handed it to her. "I carry it with me all the time."

It was a small rectangle of painted stone, showing a single blue flower, probably flax. The color was vivid and the detail accurate. It moved her oddly.

"Isn't it marvelous?" the marquess said. "To think it was painted by a hand now dead for hundreds and hundreds of years!"

Madeline looked at him. The round face was lit with quiet wonder, his cheeks ruddy. For the first time, she noticed the still, calm quality of his sherry-colored eyes and she liked it.

And yet, the relic gave her the same unsettled feeling as the ruins had done. Without knowing she would, Madeline blurted out her feelings. "Do you ever wonder if all those poor people, dying in such suddenness, without recourse or escape, left some deep emotional scar on the place?"

He did not answer for a moment, only looked at her with peculiar intensity. "There are those who are very affected by the ruins. I've seen women carted away on litters." His eyes sharpened with interest. "Were you carried out like that?"

"Oh, no." She rubbed a thumb over the relic, absently. "I confess they made me feel terribly sad. I could barely catch my breath."

"I am a scientist and trained to cultivate objectivity," he said, tucking the artifact back into his pocket. "Perhaps that cancels out the deeper emotions." He smiled comfortably.

Madeline smiled in return. It struck her that the marquess was that singular creature: a man at home in his own life.

They'd been riding alone and undisturbed on the country lane, alongside the edge of thickly forested and hilly land. Now from within the trees came shouts and the sound of something—some large creature—crashing through the underbrush.

"What the devil?" the marquess said, stopping to peer toward the noise.

But even before they emerged from the trees, Madeline knew who it would be—the two London rakes, risking life and limb and horseflesh in their pursuit of adventure. She disapproved of such heedlessness, such irresponsibility, and yet she found herself holding her breath and harboring a curious stirring in her chest as she waited for a glimpse of Lord Esher.

He came through the trees first, leaping the ditch

with uncanny grace. His coat and waistcoat were shed, and his cambric shirt clung damply to his chest. His hair had come loose and flew in the wind so that he looked not at all like an English gentleman but rather a barbarian who'd ridden through some portal of time to invade the serene countryside. The bloodcurdling yell he let free did nothing to dispell the notion.

Jonathan emerged from behind, cursing loudly in the bright afternoon. He reigned his horse before it could take the ditch. "Blood hell, Lucien!"

"Mind yourself, sir!" the marquess cried. "There is a lady present."

"Oh, dear." Jonathan bowed toward her. "A thousand pardons, my lady."

Lucien laughed.

Madeline almost could not bear to look at him. In his dishevelment he was as unrepentantly virile as a stallion in a field of mares; he even seemed to smell of an extraordinary heat and pleasure. She found her gaze on the muscled length of his forearm, brown and strong below his rolled sleeve, covered with crisp hair that gave off gold sparks in the sun, and on his hands, long-fingered and strong, the sinews and bones covered elegantly with smooth, sun-warmed skin.

But it was his hair, loose and long and black on his cambric-clad shoulders, that alarmed her. "You look like a savage," she said disdainfully, but there was an unaccustomed roughness to her voice.

His eyes, almost turquoise in the bright light, blazed. "And how would you know? How many savages have you seen?"

"None." She lifted her chin. "Nor have I seen elephants from India, but I assure you I'd recognize one if I did."

He laughed, tossing his head with impudence. A small, hot ripple touched her.

Jonathan rode smoothly between them, effectively dousing the rising tide of heat in Madeline's chest. "Might we join you?" he asked.

Madeline wanted to refuse, and she could see by the amusement in Lord Esher's devilish expression that he not only knew it but knew the reason why: that she was moved by him, and that he provided an altogether unpleasing contrast with the marquess.

"I'm afraid you'll find us dull," she said levelly. "We're only chatting and riding calmly. No wild races—of which you seem overfond, Lord Esher."

"I? No, 'tis Jonathan who goads me."

His horse moved restlessly and Lord Esher moved easily with the beast, bringing him back under control. "Jonathan could not bear that I bested him yesterday, and begged a rematch."

The marquess spoke. "We'd be delighted, of course, to have you ride with us. I'm afraid I'd rather lost myself in regaling Lady Madeline with tales of my travels."

"Oh? What travels, sir?" Jonathan rode ahead, alongside the marquess.

With some annoyance, Madeline realized she'd lost the battle to rid herself of the rakes. Not only that, but the road was narrow, leaving room for only two horses to ride abreast. With Jonathan taking up the attention of the marquess, Madeline was forced to ride alongside Lucien Harrow.

"Do you mind so much?" he asked quietly enough for her ears only. "Jonathan desperately wants to ingratiate himself with Beauchamp for a business proposition."

"You mistake me, Lord Esher," Madeline replied,

her chin high. "It is always a pleasure to share the day with guests who might not be accustomed to our country lanes."

His grin was crooked and knowing. "Perhaps I was mistaken, but didn't you call me a savage only a moment ago?"

Steadfastly, Madeline avoided the lure of looking at him. "You're improperly dressed for a gentleman."

"Ah, but I am no gentleman. And even when I pretend to be so, I am not very proper about it."

Madeline lifted an ironic brow. "At least you're honest."

"Only when it suits me."

For a moment, Madeline regarded him. If he used honesty like any other tool in his quest for seduction, then he must believe somehow she needed to know he planned to seduce her, that a direct approach would be more effective than another method. What benefit could there be to it?

She frowned a little. It seemed important to stay abreast of his motives as well as she was able; he was too clever by half and she was rather too sharply attracted to him. A slight carelessness and Madeline could easily be lost.

As if he'd been waiting for her conclusion, he looked at her with no expression at all, and said not a word. She flushed and faced forward.

The road, following the river, broadened. With relief, Madeline rode up beside the marquess and Jonathan, who were discussing again the Italian countryside. Madeline seized upon a bit of overheard conversation from the other two men. "Have you been to Pompeii, Lord Esher?" she tossed over her shoulder.

"Yes."

She glanced at him, but he seemed disinclined to say more. "You did not care for it?"

"On the contrary, I cared very much for it." He turned his head. "It moved me as much as anything I've seen in my life."

A bitter applause was on Madeline's lips—wasn't that just the sort of calculating thing a rake would say to engage the emotions of his quarry?—when Jonathan let go of a derisive laugh.

"It put him on the melancholy, he means. I vow he was drunk for days and never did gather his courage to go back."

"Madeline said it affected her the same way," the marquess said. Madeline heard in his offering the soothing oil of justice of one who dislikes conversation to belittle anyone else. She admired his fairmindedness. "Only a moment ago," he went on, "she was suggesting that perhaps there's some lingering impression there, left by those so suddenly killed."

Lord Esher looked at her, his eyes very still. "So you are not the pragmatist you'd have us believe."

"Oh, but I am. Why cannot there be some scientific explantation for the strong emotions some people feel there?" she said. "You felt them, as did I—at different places and at different times."

"Please!" protested Jonathan, blustering. "Surely you can't mean there is some magic force at work, holding the emotions of fifteen hundred years past in thrall. If that were true, why wouldn't all who enter the ruins feel the same things?"

Madeline frowned, looking toward the treetops of waving green fronds and into the pale blue English sky. In her imagination, she saw ash-whitened columns, the forgotten gardens, all buried alive one violent day and thus frozen for all time.

"I think," she said slowly, "one must be tuned to it, or not. Yes," she said, "perhaps that's just what I do believe. There was such trauma that day that it has left behind a lingering cry to echo through the ages, but only if you have a certain sort of—" she struggled with a word that would sum up her feelings, "openness will you notice it."

"I believe Lady Madeline has the soul of a poetess," Lord Esher said. The words did not seem to be ironic.

"No poetess," she said. "Only a simple woman who mourned those poor people, torn from the middle of their lives so violently."

"Would you not agree, my lord?" persisted Lord Esher, his eyes upon Madeline.

"Perhaps she does." With a kindly smile, he winked at Madeline, a jest for the pair of them. As she returned the smile, she wondered if it were luck or accident that he had thus thwarted Lord Esher's attempt to flirt with her.

"Does that make you a poet, too?" she asked Lord Esher, and immediately wished she could call the words back.

It was not he that replied, but Jonathan. "Don't you know his painful history?" There was again tension in his words, a sharp glitter in his eye that said he knew his words would hurt or embarrass his friend. Madeline looked from one to the other, wondering what caused the enmity. "The great Lucien's prodigal talents?"

"Jonathan," Lord Esher said. The word carried deep warning.

Heedless, Jonathan rushed on. "He was nearly as famous a prodigy as Mozart when he was ten. Played Vauxhall and Bath."

"Really? What did you play?" Madeline asked.

"That's enough, Jonathan," Lord Esher said. His posture was deceptively relaxed.

"Played everything!"

Madeline sent a questioning glance toward the marquess, who shrugged in bewilderment.

"The antics of a trained monkey," Lord Esher said dryly. "No more."

A dark burn of annoyance or anger colored his cheeks. Madeline watched him in some wonder, surprised to see such deep emotion in him.

"It's that passionate Russian blood, y'know," Jonathan said.

Real fury flashed in the jeweled eyes. To forestall the fisticuffs she could see brewing, Madeline rode between them. "Are you Russian, Lord Esher?" she asked lightly.

"Half. My mother was Russian, from Saint Petersburg. My father met her on a diplomatic trip." Along his jaw, the muscle pulled tight, but he took a long breath as if to calm himself. "I spent much of my childhood there."

"How romantic," she said, again playing the flirtatious hostess attempting to hold her raucous guests at bay. The marquess gave her an approving nod. "Do tell us a little of it."

"It's been too long," he said dismissively.

"Oh, surely you remember something."

He turned to her, and even as Madeline watched, he seemed to take on some wild power from beyond himself, gathering a wide appeal from the very air.

The power centered in his face, on his mouth and in his eyes, and he focused it with particular intensity upon Madeline. "I remember," he said, and there was the faintest rolling to his *r*'s, "the white nights and the ladies in their dazzling gowns dancing in the soft bright midnight."

Madeline swallowed. "It sounds lovely."

"There was music," he said, his voice rougher, lower. "Everywhere. Everywhere," he repeated. "I remember the snow, too, falling from a dark cold sky, dancing like diamond feathers on unseen winds."

His gaze moved from her eyes to her lips as he spoke, and he lifted a finger to touch his own mouth. Transfixed, Madeline watched his long, lean finger move on his firm lips, and found herself leaning ever so slightly forward . . .

"Why that's rather poetical, too, isn't it?" the marquess said. "Bravo, Lord Esher."

"Indeed," said Jonathan.

Startled by their voices, Madeline realized her posture, realized her lips were slightly parted and her breath came between them in hurried fashion, and that Lord Esher smiled, an ironic and triumphant gleam in his eye.

Abruptly, she straightened, feeling a warm flush crawl in her cheeks. A distinct tingle remained in her lips as she tried to recompose herself, and she bit down on them hard, trying to drive away the oddly aroused sensation.

He was very, very dangerous. It would take every shred of skill she'd accumulated to resist him.

As they neared the house, he rode close enough to brush her calf with a hand, discreetly so neither of the others would notice. "I won that round," he said, his voice inaudible more than a foot away. His fingers caressed her leg as if in promise, then he let her go.

With a wicked, free laugh, he rode away from them, coaxing his horse into a hard run. They moved together as one creature, Lord Esher low over the horse's neck, his hair and the horse's mane flying out on the wind, his shirt a billowing flag of white.

"By God, he'll kill himself," the marquess said, aghast as Lucien rode for the hedges at a dead run.

"No," Madeline said.

The trio paused to watch. The wind picked up, blowing a scurry of leaves into the path, but there was no other sound until Lord Esher cried out into the darkening day, "Go!"

Horse and man leaped and flew and hung against the sky. Madeline's heart swelled. Barbarian beast he might be, but she doubted she'd ever met anyone so free as Lucien Harrow.

How in the world could she ever resist his ploys to bed her?

There was only one way. She'd stay away from him as much as she possibly could until he tired of chasing her. And tire he would. Another woman would catch his fancy, a chambermaid or a matron at a party or some heiress from town.

She simply had to wait him out.

But that might make her seem as if she were more of a challenge. She frowned. That wouldn't do—he'd only pursue her all the more, and she couldn't bear a full assault. Even she, with her impatience for matters of the heart, would fall to the concentrated sensual powers of an accomplished rake like Lord Esher.

What, then, would she do?

The real trick would be to seem not much of a

challenge, or to make it seem as if she were chasing him. A shudder touched her. Too dangerous.

No, she'd simply have to spend as much time as possible with the marquess and hope that when she had to greet Lord Esher, she'd be filthy from the garden.

Soon or late, he'd tire of the chase.

5

Lucien believed there was no woman who was completely immune to seduction. Some could be wooed with flowers or sweet words or food. Some only needed a slight encouraging push; some a good deal of cajoling flattery; still others needed to be plainly ignored.

From the beginning, that first night on the balustrade when she surprised him with her bold talk, Lucien had known Madeline would prove to be more difficult than most to woo. Not only had she been raised by the countess of Whitethorn, who was nearly as notorious as Lucien himself, but Lucien also sensed an innate goodness about her, and a sensibility not easily ruffled by the usual sleight of hand of good looks, flattery, and charm.

He watched her. Experimented a little with a bit of flirting, a little flattery, a little of the promised watching—which served to unnerve her, make her blush, but little else.

Until now, Lucien believed all woman had a need to save the unsalvageable rake—to be the one woman who could redeem the most hardened heart. But not even that singular motivation seemed to hold much sway over Madeline. She was not vulnerable to the call of a rake's lost soul, sensibly concluding it was a loss of his own making.

And after all, saving souls was for the vicar and the church and God. She made no pretension to being any of those.

He'd met difficult cases before. There was always a weak point, and a clever man could use such a point to gain a woman's trust.

Lucien observed her.

She was not invulnerable to him. A pulse in her throat beat faster when he smiled at her, and her pupils grew larger, her lips softer—women gave themselves away with a hundred tiny details.

Mornings were invariably spent in her gardens—as long as she dared, for he also learned it was not a pursuit Juliette particularly approved. If Madeline had been ladylike, taking a bonnet and gloves and prissily clipping a flower here, a flower there, it might have been all right, but as with everything else she did, Madeline took to the gardens with a wholehearted gusto Lucien found surprisingly erotic. Such passionate attention in the bedroom might be interesting indeed.

From the garden, Madeline changed and ate with whatever guests happened to be present in the dining room, sampling tidbits from the constant feast laid out at the sideboard—kidneys and eggs and rashers and bread. Afterward, she escaped to her greenhouse if she possibly could, otherwise she allowed herself to be drawn into promenades about the grounds or she read in the study or she played the spinet in the music room.

The greenhouse was her first choice, however, and he watched her through the windows as she made notes like a scientist on various plants she grew. At such times, she donned a pair of spectacles from her pocket.

She posted a great many letters, and Lucien bribed a servant to learn where they were going. She carried on a lively correspondence with several renowned naturalists, and exchanged chatty letters with two friends, one in London, another in a hamlet to the north; girls she'd evidently met on her travels. Another correspondent was less clear: a Sir Julian in London. He waited to see what that might mean, but Lucien thought it must be another of her botanical friends.

At night, she played the piano and sang a little with the others, politely laughing and conversing; at such times she seemed the very epitome of the graceful lady—her unruly hair neatly tamed and dressed with ribbons or jewels, her creamy bosom proudly displayed in one dazzling gown after another, her cheeks dusted with a discreet brush of rice powder. The powder amused him. For all the care she took with her hats and long sleeves, her skin had taken on a ruddy warm glow from the sun, and bright streaks ran through her hair like veining in black marble.

In those lazy evening hours, he admired her, and amused himself with pleasant images of disrobing her. Over the festive suppers—at which Lucien found himself always seated very far from Madeline and very close to Juliette—he toyed with images of kissing a particular freckle high on her left shoulder.

But for all that she was enchanting in the evenings, it was the mornings he awaited with eagerness, when she came from the gardens after her early work. Her hair was mussed, falling loose from her cap, her clothes askew, her hands dirty. Often she smelled of light sweat and the earth and a peculiarly arousing perfume of sunlight that seemed to come off her in waves. He wanted her deeply at such moments, and did not want to take her comfortably in a bed or after she'd washed—he wanted her just like that: musky and overheated and tasting of her work.

The power and violence of his wish surprised him. It should have warned him.

It did not.

Madeline told herself she should be wary of the cheerful Lord Esher when he joined her at five of a drizzly Friday morning. He was dressed for working in a pair of scuffed boots and sensible woolen trousers. His head, predictably, was bare, showing the wealth of thick, dark hair that adorned his well-made head. She thought he might be vain about his hair, the way he never covered it.

"Good morning!" he said in greeting.

Madeline glanced up, as if she'd just seen him. "Good morning." She was working in the rose gardens this week, going from the middle outward, clipping rose hips and dead blooms and pruning out deadwood. It was her third day at the chore, and she'd only managed to make it to the middle pink tones. "What brings you out here so early?"

"I'm here to help you," he said, spreading his hands.

"What do you know of gardening?"

"Nothing at all." His grin was crooked and unrepentant. "But I'm easily bid. Tell me what you need done, and I'll do it."

"Why would you drag yourself out of bed so early to do such a thing?" She brushed a lock of dampening hair from her face so she could see to cut a withered stalk from the middle of an ancient bush. "It's tedious work and not to most people's liking."

"True," he replied, "but I'm here to win your good favor."

Madeline paused. For a moment, she took his measure, from the top of his head to his boots. "I suppose it doesn't matter what your motives are. I am not foolish enough to dismiss help when I can get it." She pointed out a pair of pruning shears. "Take those. But watch me first. I don't want you butchering the good wood."

Agreeably, he picked up the shears and watched carefully as Madeline illustrated the process of pruning. "If you'll cut off the dead branches, I can trim away the rose hips and old blooms."

With a neat precision she would not have expected, Lord Esher did as she'd shown him. "Like so?"

She smiled her approval. "Yes."

They quickly developed a pattern: Lord Esher trimming the bush of its worst deadwood and old branches, Madeline following behind to neaten the overall appearance. She was glad of his help; the work was less tedious when there was someone to talk with, and whatever else his failings, he was an intelligent man.

They chatted lightly about books and horses and dinner parties. Madeline learned he like poetry, and that his taste ran to the lusty works of a hundred years before, but he didn't like the current crop of romances.

"Why not?" Madeline asked in challenge. "One is just a longer version of the other—love and drama."

His crooked grin flashed. "And carefully described moments of passion."

"Sex you mean."

"Yes." His dark blue eyes glowed with approval.

"Still, I think those poems appealed more to men, less to women, as novels appeal more often to women than men."

"Perhaps."

It surprised her that he didn't seem to need to be proven right on every statement. In that way, he was unlike most of the men of her acquaintance.

"I like this one," he said, touching the velvety blossoms of a dark rose bud, still curled tight and beaded with silvery rain. "The color is extraordinary."

"Yes. I like it, too. It's particularly compelling in this light. I'm not sure why, but there are some of them that seem to have greater intensity in lower light. This cloud cover brings out the vividness."

He wrestled a thick, dead branch from its stranglehold. His mobile mouth turned down at the corners. "Hmmm. Perhaps it's like your theory of Pompeii."

"I don't understand what you mean."

"A field of some sort, that has a vibration influenced by outside factors. One must be of a certain nature or frame of mind to perceive the vibrations at Pompeii, and with the flowers, the light must be at a certain hue."

Madeline considered that, pursing her lips as she glanced over her shoulder toward the willow tree at the center of the concentric circles that made the garden. The soft green leaves veritably glowed against the pearl-gray sky. White roses, beautifully displayed now that Madeline had pruned the bushes, made blurry marks against the light, with the yellow climbers against the wall almost dazzling. "The colors are all more vivid in this light," she said.

"Yes, to some degree." He turned, barely touching her shoulder to point toward the farther reaches of the garden, to the still-wild beds that had not been cleared. "Look at that red one."

Amid the dark green foliage, the flower blazed, almost impossibly bright against the dim morning, its color so vivid it was almost painful to look upon. Before she could speak, Lord Esher strode to the bush and clipped it, bringing it back to her.

He held it loosely in his long-fingered hand. "It's so beautiful, I want to eat it."

Madeline laughed. "It sounds odd, but I know what you mean. It's not enough to simply look at it— it's so impossibly fleeting and vivid you want to absorb it on as many levels as possible."

"Yes." As with the flowers, his eyes were doubly blue in the strange gray light. He put the flower against his nose and inhaled, closing his eyes as he did so.

A strange, sharp pang rushed through Madeline's chest. His black lashes, long as a child's, lay in a wide sweep against his high, elegantly hewn cheekbones. The bright soft petals of the flower touched a jaw not yet shaved this morning, and the contrast of rough and hard against delicate and sweet made her ache.

He opened his eyes, then deliberately put the flower against his mouth and tasted it. He grinned. "Not much flavor or scent, really. We're meant, I think, only to look at it."

One delicate petal snagged against his mouth, and tore. Madeline backed away, unaccountably upset, and bent her head to her work. "You may have all the time in the world, my lord. But I have work that must be done."

"And I promised to help you, not distract you."

"Your presence is a distraction," she said. "I think perhaps I'd rather not share this quiet morning time. If you want to help me, please come back later."

He said nothing for a moment. Madeline dared not look at him but kept her eyes on her task. He stood still, but some emotion emanated from him, turbulent and unidentifiable. "I meant nothing untoward, Madeline."

"I did not give you leave to call me by my Christian name."

"Forgive me." The turbulence increased, and he took a step forward. "I was only—"

She looked up, her heart rushing. "Trying to seduce me."

"No!" The word was vehement, and Madeline stepped back once again. "I vow it—for once, I was not—it was only conversation."

She did not know whether to believe him. And he seemed more dangerous for her own indecision. It was not Lord Esher who was to blame for his extraordinary appeal, she noted with some embarrassment. It was she who responded to it so vehemently.

"Very well, you may stay," she said abruptly.

"No." The word was heavy. "No, you're right. I lied." Madeline lifted her head.

He put the flower in her hand. "It was all designed for seduction. The flower, the conversation." He gestured toward his clothes. "Even my being here this morning."

Madeline turned the flower in her fingers slowly. "Do you have any idea who you are under all those disguises?"

"None at all."

"It doesn't matter, you know," she said, gathering her shears, "whether you came out here to seduce me, or win my favor as you put it, or to discover something lost, which I think is more likely."

He lifted an ironic brow.

Madeline ignored it. "The fact remains you've halved my work this morning, and I'm grateful."

His eyes narrowed. Instead of taking the shears, however, he shook his head. Without a word, he left her, striding into the morning mist with a rigidness on his spine. Madeline watched after him for a moment, admiring with some small part of her woman's heart the taut, muscled length of his legs.

A puzzle.

At the end of the garden, he turned around. For a long, long moment, he simply looked at her with no expression at all on his handsome face. Madeline bore it for a time, then she put him out of her mind and trimmed her roses.

When she looked up again, he was gone.

Juliette, restless and weary, climbed from her bed, disturbed by something she couldn't name—only knew it had taken her from sleep. Jonathan had not slept with her last night. He started his foolishness about marriage again, and she'd been forced to send him away when he appeared at her door. There were rules.

She missed him with a vague, aching hollowness in her belly. Trailing her amber silk dressing gown behind her, she rubbed the hollowness with her palm and drew open the drapes over the long French windows. A dreary, misty morning greeted her and she leaned against the wall, gazing out on the grounds.

From here, she had an eagle's-eye view of the maze and rose gardens, and also of the open meadow, lined by elms, that lay beyond. Madeline's gardens. How fiercely she protected them!

And there the girl was, amid the roses with her basket of tools at her feet. Even from this distance, Juliette could see the muddy hem of her old gown. She smiled fondly. In truth, the girl had a rather dazzling talent for flowers, inherited from both sides of the family. The earl's ancestors had built the gardens, of course, but Juliette's mother, too, had had a passion for flowers. Although she died when Juliette was twelve, and the flowers she coaxed out of the mean back garden in the rough London slum where Juliette had grown up had hardly compared with this grandeur, Juliette remembered that small plot with great joy. It had been the only spot of joy in her mother's short, hard, brutal life.

Too bad she did not live to see Juliette's stunning success and the granddaughter that so resembled her. Where Juliette was blond, Madeline was dark, with the same creamy English skin as the grandmother she'd never seen, didn't even know existed.

Only Juliette and a handful of trusted servants knew all the secrets of Juliette and Madeline's lives.

And this gray, gloomy morning, Juliette wished she could tell Madeline of her true parentage, that she looked like a grandmother long dead; that her love of flowers had come from that long-dead woman.

As she stared at the girl in the dim light, a figure emerged, dashed toward one end of the garden and came back to give Madeline a flower. Juliette grasped the edge of the drapes.

Lucien Harrow. There was no mistaking that elegant, graceful figure. Unlike most of the dandies in his crowd, Lucien was a restless, physical man, and it showed in his trim body. He was rather roughly dressed and appeared to be working with Madeline on the roses.

Juliette narrowed her eyes. Not bloody likely he was doing it without good reason. And Juliette knew just what that reason was.

She frowned.

For months, even before Madeline's return, Juliette had researched the possibilities of a husband for the girl. It was important to Juliette that the man not only be rich enough to save Whitethorn, but that he have a reputation for kindness—and that he not have a wandering eye. Madeline was a biddable girl to some extent, but she'd not tolerate unfaithfulness, however fashionable it was at the moment. Her husband would be husband to her in more than name, or a wife he would not have.

Her quest brought her directly to the doorstep of Charles Devon, the marquess of Beauchamp. She had contrived to meet him and had rattled at length about her beautiful, intelligent stepdaughter, showing him the miniature Madeline had sent from Milan. By the time Madeline had actually returned from her extended tour of the Continent, the marquess was like a ripe peach, ready to be plucked.

Her joy had known no bounds when the marquess took one look at Madeline—the girl was quite astonishingly beautiful—and fell irretrievably in love.

Perfect.

Except for the presence of Lord Harrow. Briefly, she considered sending him away. But that wouldn't do—it might even rouse his anger and cause him to seduce Madeline for sheer spite.

In the garden, the pair stood a few feet apart, a wide tension radiating from them. Neither saw what to Juliette was plain; an arc of sexual tension sizzled between them at every meeting. Madeline was skeptical; Lucien amusedly and lazily in pursuit. But there was potential for great disaster there. Juliette could feel it in her bones.

There was, really, only one possible option: she would seduce him herself. It might mean losing Jonathan. The thought was almost insanely painful—but he'd soon tire of her anyway. It was better this way. She'd chase away a lover who'd grown too tiresomely passionate with his avowals of love, and reel in a new one who knew the rules and would not break them.

And Madeline would be appalled, forever protected from the advances of Lord Esher.

Perfect.

6

Among thy fancies, tell me this,
What is the thing we call a kisse?
—Robert Herrick

    Madeline dithered over her gowns before supper. It was the time of her monthly, and she felt thick and moody. Her hair on her neck was hot and heavy. Her bodice was constricting. Beyond the window, as if to reflect her mood, the sky was thick and dark and gray. From far off came the sound of thunder.

"Must you pull it so tight!" she snapped to the maid tugging her corsets closed. "I can scarce breathe."

"Aye," the maid returned calmly. "Yer mum sent up this new brocade and bid me tell you wear it."

Madeline eyed the gown, a watered silk the same passionate dark pink as the rose Lucien had plucked in the garden yesterday morning. It would suit her coloring, setting off her dark hair and the olive notes of her skin—her papa had often teased her about being a changeling child, switched by fairies for a Spanish baby.

But the bodice of the gown was so low it barely covered her nipples. The fashion was low cut, but this was ridiculous. When Madeline put it on, she felt miserably self-conscious and found her hand straying to be certain she had not inadvertently exposed more of her breast than she wished.

"I hate this dress."

"It'll suit ye well, my lady. You'll see." The girl smoothed a hand over Madeline's cheek. "I'll bring ye a bit of my special medicine in a little, all right?"

Madeline nodded gratefully.

Juliette sailed in, smelling of the cloves and pine nuts in her Imperial Water. She wore a Caraco gown in shades of plum. "How do you like the dress, my sweet? I think it will drive the marquess to distraction."

"I don't think he's the sort of man who allows himself to be inflamed by improper displays of women's bodies." The corset pinched as the maid laced the dress. Madeline yelped. "Leave me be. I'll have my mother's help now."

The girl looked a little wounded, but Juliette shook her head as if to say, "Pay her no heed," and mollified, the girl left.

Juliette picked up the laces. "All men are inspired and motivated by lust, my dear," she said. "Never forget it."

"Not Charles," Madeline returned stubbornly. She tugged the bodice fretfully. "And I'm not wearing this. It's cut too deep."

"Charles, too. Turn around." She frowned when Madeline did as she asked. "I see what you mean. Where is that gold lace fichu?"

"I gave it away. It itched." She took another from her drawer, letting loose a scent of lavender as it unfurled. It was gauzy and light. Madeline crossed it over her chest demurely and began to tuck the ends into her bodice.

"Oh, not like that! It will ruin the effect completely!" Summarily, she took it from Madeline's hands and rolled it into an elegant twist that she tucked into the edges of the bodice. Madeline's nerves screamed, but she forced herself to be still until Juliette was done.

When her stepmother was finished, Madeline moved before she snapped at Juliette. Taking up an exquisitely simple diamond pin, she tucked it into her dark hair and admired the subtle wink of it. "Yes."

Juliette kissed her. "Wonderful, *ma cherie.*"

They walked down to the salon together. A quartet of musicians played in the corner, viols and clavichord, a sweet background note. Lightning flashed against the long French windows, illuminating the gray-green fronds of the trees tossing in a powerful wind. "It's going to be quite a storm," Madeline commented.

The marquess joined them, bowing deeply over Madeline's hand. His wig was rather more solid tonight and didn't slip forward the way it often did. He'd left it unpowdered. The sable color gave life to his complexion, a brightness to his eyes. "You look especially well this evening, Charles," Madeline said.

"Thank you." His mouth was dry on her hand. "I might say the same for you, but it would be blasphemous to compare my humble health to your blazing beauty."

Madeline chuckled. "Quite poetic, my lord."

"Ah, there's Lord Esher," Juliette exclaimed. "I have an important matter to discuss with him. Excuse me."

With a pang, Madeline glanced up. Lucien—for she'd come to think of him as Lucien, not Lord Esher, which sounded stuffy and elderly—paused at the door, as if deciding whether the company were to his taste. He cast his gaze toward the quartet, and Madeline saw him wince before he turned toward the rest of the room. His expression darkened when his gaze fell upon a new member of their party, Anna Stiles, the countess of Heath, an old friend of Juliette's who liked to escape her elderly husband whenever possible. Lucien, staring at her, looked quite as thundering as the sky, but the countess only smiled.

"Looks like we'll have a quite a storm," Charles said conversationally.

Madeline returned her attention to the man alongside her. "Yes," she said. "You're almost certainly correct this time." From the corner of her eye, she watched Juliette in her plum gown sail through the room.

From a corner, Jonathan suddenly appeared and waylaid her with a hand to her arm. He bent close to whisper something in her ear. Juliette tried to pull away, but Jonathan held her steadily, and in moments, Juliette appeared to sway toward him.

Then, abruptly, Juliette yanked away. With a sharp, quiet word that Madeline could only guess at, Juliette stormed through the little knots of people toward Lucien. Madeline looked back at Jonathan, and quickly away, for there was on the young man's face an expression of naked yearning of such vastness it pierced her clear through.

"Poor chap," Charles said. "He's quite besotted, isn't he?"

"I'm afraid so." Madeline watched Juliette approach Lucien, who stood lazily at one end of the room, gazing at the party with an air of aloof amusement. Juliette, tiny and perfect, her bosom as creamy and white as rose petals, smiled up at him. Whatever she said caused Lucien to laugh.

A tiny wave of something unpleasant washed through Madeline. With effort she said dryly, "It looks as if my stepmother has marked other prey."

"Indeed." He offered his arm. "Shall we walk?"

Tucking her hand into the crook of his elbow, she said, "Perhaps we ought to wander over there and chat with Jonathan. He looks quite devasated."

"Yes, let's do."

But before they could move, Jonathan spun on his heel and left the room. Into the air rang Juliette's high, clear laughter. Madeline narrowed her eyes. "I've despised her cruelty since I was a young girl."

"She was not cruel as long as your father lived. Perhaps it broke her heart when he died."

"Grief does not excuse cruelty." She saw Lucien lean foward as Juliette chattered, her color high, as if she were aroused. As Lucien bent over, his thick dark hair captured the light of the candles nearby him, and produced a deep mahogany gleam. As if in admiration, he touched Juliette's shoulder, and his elegant, long fingers stayed there on her bare skin.

A single, sharp pain shot through Madeline's heart, and she turned away. "They deserve each other."

Charles gave her a measuring gaze, and for an instant, Madeline wondered what he made of her behavior. But he said mildly, "Of course."

*   *   *

The dining room faced the gardens and the maze, giving a view of splashes of color and the tall trees. As the small party trailed into the room for supper, a violent flash of lightning blazed over the sky, almost immediately followed by a hard crack of thunder. A collective cry rustled through the guests, and there was even one short, tiny scream from Lady Heath.

Madeline frowned. "I don't think this is an ordinary storm," she said to the marquess, who lightly held her hand over his elbow. It was a familiar gesture, and a greater liberty than he'd hitherto taken, but Madeline allowed it. It was a comfort. *He* was a comfort—so solid and steady and calm. "Look how heavy those clouds are! Practically black!"

"It's the wind that concerns me. The farmers at Kirkton will be fretting it, I reckon. The new wheat won't take kindly to it."

As if to underscore his words, a full-throated gust roared over the balustrade and slammed into the windows with such force one of the doors blew open and crashed into the wall. Another cry went up.

It was the quick-footed Lucien who caught the door before a second gust could catch it and break the small panes. "It's all right," he said, lifting a hand to the guests. "Just wasn't fastened properly."

Madeline wondered fleetingly if she ought to check the greenhouse, but servants were already carrying in the first course. She decided to wait until after dinner.

As she was about to sit down, Jonathan appeared. He looked smoothed, as if nothing had bothered him earlier at all. To the marquess he said, "Will you do me a great favor, my lord? Go take my place nearby the countess and allow me to sit with Lady Madeline."

Madeline gave Charles a slight nod. Already Lucien and Juliette were laughing and teasing at the head of the table. How artful she is! Madeline thought, watching her stepmother bend close to Lord Esher—just close enough to be seductive.

"Of course," Charles said. "Take good care of her." He walked to the head of the table.

Jonathan helped Madeline settle. He sat to her left, so he could watch Juliette while he spoke to Madeline. The ploy was so transparent Madeline smiled. She glanced toward her stepmother.

Juliette's eyes blazed. Madeline was taken aback. It was quite unlike her stepmother to care about any particular lover too much.

"She looks ready to tear you to pieces," Madeline commented lightly, setting her napkin in her lap.

He shrugged.

Madeline noticed that his high cheekbones were flushed with emotion. His unpowdered blond hair was caught back from his face, and for the first time, she really looked at him. His was a very sensual face, and younger than she'd realized. He glanced down the table again, and his green eyes showed a sullen blaze much like Juliette's. Madeline shook her head. If both of them wished to be together, then why all the bother? Both were well past the age of consent.

"It isn't terribly flattering to be an object of service," she said, dipping her spoon into clear soup.

"I'm sorry." He looked up, rather startled.

"I lost a dinner partner who admires me so you might make my stepmother jealous. Where is the reward in that for me?" She smiled to show it was not meant too deeply.

His expression eased. "I can say without vanity

that most girls your age would choose my company over your marquess."

"I'm not most girls."

"No. You aren't, are you?" Casually, he looked past her, then back. "It's Lucien who tantalizes you, isn't it?"

That strange, sharp feeling went through her again. "Don't be ridiculous. What earthly good is a rake of his sort?"

"Look at him."

Madeline turned her head. Lucien ignored his food and leaned back in his chair, his elbows braced against the arm rests, his fingers steepled in front of him. Dark amusement glittered in his eyes, curled his full lips. He looked like nothing so much as a cat in certain pursuit. When he caught Madeline's eye, he winked.

Next to her, Jonathan chuckled. "He has no interest in Juliette, you know."

"No?"

"He wants you only."

Madeline bent over her plate. "I'd rather talk of something else," she said.

"Very well. Name your topic."

Just then, a broad slash of lightning burst with a blinding sizzle across the sky, followed instantly by a crack of thunder that sent dishes clattering and the overhead chandelier swaying on its chain.

"Strike me blind!" Madeline swore, jumping to her feet. A torrential rain began to pour from the sky.

Dinner forgotten, the guests left the table to crowd around the windows, exclaiming to each other over the power of nature. Madeline went with them, pressing her face as close as she could into the pane.

Within moments, huge raindrops filled the small terrace beyond with water. Rain slammed against the doors. Wind tore leaves and small branches from the trees, and Madeline glimpsed small shreds of red and pink and orange borne away—flower petals torn from tender plants.

In the press of people, Madeline did not at first notice the heat along her arm and spine. Not until she scented a particular and distinctive smell did she realize she was hip to hip with Lucien. She shifted to break contact, and he did not follow but stood so close behind her she could feel the brush of his breath over her bare shoulder blade.

"Magnificent, isn't it?" he said.

Annoyed, she tilted her head to look at him. "Must you stand so close?"

He lifted a finger to his lips. His eyes held a bright, glittering look. "Listen," he said, with an odd note in his cello-rich voice. A kind of reverence. "Do you hear the music?"

She frowned, all too aware of his hand on her shoulder, just as it had been on Juliette's, his bare fingers on her skin. Hot and uncomfortable. She squirmed a little, but his light grip tightened.

"Listen," he said again.

The word was so insistent that Madeline inclined her head and opened her ears to the sounds all around them. "Rain, wind, the rising and falling of voices," she said aloud.

"Closer," he said, almost whispering. "How many notes there are in the rain!"

Madeline looked at him. He closed his eyes, and there was on his face an almost transcendant look of joy. She wanted to hear what he heard and she closed her eyes, too. Many notes in the rain? She listened. Yes. The heavy splat of fat drops hitting the stone balustrade, the higher, sweeter tinkle of it striking the glass, and the hollow splash of it on the empty brass planters on the steps. "I hear it!" she exclaimed.

Lucien opened his eyes, and his fingers moved very slightly against her neck. "What else do you hear, Madeline?" He touched her earlobe with his index finger. "Listen."

There were dozens of sounds, some faint, like the clatter of a serving spoon against china as a footman stirred a dish. Some boomed, like the hard stomp of thunder. Skirts rustled, voices swirled, rain pattered and slapped and tinkled. "Wonderful," she said.

So intently was she listening that she heard the hail a split second before it hit the walkway beyond the windows. It came roaring in, tearing at the trees and gardens, coming toward the house—

"Move away from the windows!" she cried.

Two- and three-inch ice stones crashed through the windows, pelting guests with glass and freezing rain. Someone screamed. People scattered, knocking chairs over, screaming, heading for the opposite wall.

A pane of glass exploded in front of Madeline's face, and the hailstone smacked her lip.

"Get out of the way!" Lucien cried. "Everyone away from the windows!" He grabbed Madeline none too gently and shoved her into a chair. The noise was outrageous, as if there were a thousand men atop the roof, running and shouting.

She tasted blood and touched her lip.

All at once, she remembered the greenhouse. With a little cry, she jumped up and ran out of the room. Someone called her name, but she paid no attention.

The guests and servants were huddled in a knot against the far wall of the dining room, so the halls were eerily silent but for the pelting, thundering rain and hail. Madeline ran, skidding madly in her satin slippers, and kicked them off to gain purchase on the marble floors of the passageways. She thought she heard someone call her again, but it was impossible to know through the roaring noise of the storm.

The greenhouse was at the far southwestern end of the house, through a series of connected rooms. She passed no one.

As she entered the main foyer, the hail seemed to slow a small bit, and she heard an odd, strangled noise. Thinking there was an animal caught somewhere, she glanced over her shoulder—

—and slammed into the wall in her surprise. Through the library doors, in the dark, dank room, were two people silhouetted against the stained glass. The noise came from one of them, the woman, who made it again as Madeline stared, literally transfixed by the sight. A wash of pale brown light from the Madonna's gown in the stained glass spilled over the woman's white, naked hip, in high contrast to the gold and plum skirts bunched around her waist. Her head was flung back, her bare legs gripping the man who moved between them in almost violent passion.

Juliette and Jonathan.

Choking in embarrassment, appalled and aroused, Madeline averted her eyes, trying to find breath enough to move. Feeling oddly dizzy, she put a hand against the wall, and finding it cool, pressed her cheek to it as well.

A cry rang out, helpless and ecstatic, and Madeline

closed her eyes tighter yet. Still too dizzy to move, too affected, she most desperately wished to escape.

Then Lucien was beside her. She smelled him, and opened her eyes. In his eyes there glowed a sultry look she hadn't seen before, and his nostrils flared. He took her hand and led her away from the library, pulling her by the wrist. Still a little stunned, Madeline allowed herself to be led. The hail slowed, and although it was replaced with more of the torrential rain, at least she could hear.

"Where were you going?" Lucien asked.

Madeline cursed and lifted her skirts. "The greenhouse." She started to run once again. This time Lucien ran with her.

At the door, she paused and peeked through the window. "Oh, blast!" she cried, and yanked open the door. A burst of cool wet air hit her. It poured in from the broken panes. Hailstones littered the tables and gravel floor, melting into puddles where they rested after their destruction had been wrought. It was worse than she'd expected.

The most urgent problem was the ice on some of the plants—the delicate orchids and exotic ferns she grew for pleasure; the exotic vegetables she grew for experimentation. The cold air would send them into a traumatic shock. Unmindful of her attire, she stuck her feet into a pair of boots and hurried forward to scoop ice from the pots and brush the worst of the shattered glass from tender leaves.

Lucien watched her for a moment. "May I help you? Tell me what to do."

"It'll ruin your clothes."

"I have more clothes than the king." He shucked his coat and waistcoat, and hung them with the aprons by the doorway. He took one of the long aprons and brought it to her. "You don't want to soil that beautiful gown."

He tied it around her before she could move, and his touch on her sides, impersonal as it was, sent a rippling over her skin. Rain poured in through broken panes, splashing into the pools already forming under the tables and along the walkways.

"It'll do no good now," Madeline said, brushing ineffectually at the water spots marking the sleeves and skirt. Her words were breathy.

"A pity," he said. Then he shrugged and took a handkerchief from his pocket. He held it by her face. "May I? You were cut by the glass. There's blood on your face."

"Is there?" She brought her hands up. For the first time, she became aware of the stinging scratches and the annoying thickness of a swollen lip. She touched the latter with her tongue, probing the soreness experimentally.

"Now there's a little mud, too," he said with a crooked smile.

"Oh. Please, then, wipe it away."

Wetting the cloth under a stream of rain pouring through a hole overhead, Lucien gently wiped at her cheeks, then her forehead. He stood close, but not obnoxiously so, and his body seemed peculiarly warm. A fine trembling stirred in her limbs. She reached behind her to brace herself on the table.

"Close your eyes," he said.

Madeline complied. He wiped gently at her eyelids, and again over her cheeks, then down to her chin. The curve of his knuckle, warm and dry, brushed her lower lip, back and forth as he lightly rubbed her jaw.

A flash of the scene in the library jolted through her mind—violence and sweat and desire—and the annoying heat pressed into her abdomen, aggravated by the light brush of Lucien's crooked fingers on her lower lip.

Madeline opened her eyes.

He stared down intently into her face, his cat eyes gleaming a wild combination of colors—gray and blue and green mixed in the most alluring gradations. "Your face is extraordinary," he said quietly, and stroked her jaw. "The lines make me think of the flight of birds, sailing along in perfect grace." His fingers swept along a cheekbone, over her mouth, swooped down the line of her nose and again along her lip.

A shiver rocked her, and she could see Lucien felt it. For a moment, the long muscle in his jaw tightened, and his lids grew heavy over the gloriously jeweled eyes. "It aroused you, seeing your stepmother and Jonathan like that."

"No," she whispered. "It embarrassed me."

His thumb settled on her lower lip, precisely in the center, and Madeline ached to open her mouth and suck it in, to taste it. As if he sensed that urge, he took a step closer, putting their bodies in contact. His thumb didn't move, just rested on her lip as if it belonged there. "I don't think so."

Madeline's breath caught and she made an urgent move to back away, but a table stopped her. Now he caught her face in both hands. His long fingers caressed the edges of her ears, and his palms were hard against her jaw, and there was a light in his eyes she couldn't read. "There's such passion in you, Madeline. Hidden, far away, deep so it can't hurt you. I wish I could set it free."

She thought he was going to kiss her, and the thought made her tremble even more. She didn't move away, only closed her eyes against the temptation of his beautiful face. There was a soft, moist sensation against her eyelids, first one and then the other, and she was abruptly free.

"You've got a couple of nasty cuts there. Don't leave them too long."

Rattled, Madeline said only, "No, I won't. Thank you." She looked around her, overwhelmed by the mess and the man, and breathless with both. A tiny pulsing quivered in her throat, and she felt dazed as she looked around her, trying desperately to give the room the attention it deserved. Almost half of the glass panes in the long room had been shattered, though most were contained at the north end.

"What shall I do to help?" he asked.

His words served to bring her practical nature to the fore. She smoothed the apron over her skirts. "Take the hailstones from the pots, first of all," she said as matter-of-factly as she was able. She illustrated by scooping out a now-soggy ball of ice that filled the cradle of her palm. "Most of these plants are delicate and won't take to this cold, so they need to be moved to a more protected spot."

He went to work, easily and efficiently doing whatever she asked. From the corner of her eye, Madeline watched him, aware of a dangerous and disturbing truth: she would have let him kiss her. She had, in fact, been aching for his mouth, and for his hands on her body. If she were honest, she still wanted it. The thought terrified her.

And yet, as she worked, her innate sensibility righted itself.

Today, the storm had stirred her up, then the carnal coupling of her stepmother and her lover, and the destruction of the greenhouse. She was bound to be more than usually emotional.

Yes, that was it. She'd simply avoid Lord Esher—better to think of him as Lord Esher than Lucien after all, until she was herself again.

Yes.

7

Kiss me a thousand times and
Give me a hundred kisses more

. . . .

We'll have no time to vex or grieve
But kiss and unkiss till we die.
— Alexander Brome

With Lord Esher's help, Madeline managed to move most of the delicate plants to a more protected location. She picked out shards of glass from many pots, swept messes from the tables and onto the floor. She might have gone on all evening, except it began to get exceedingly hard to see in the dark. At Lord Esher's insistence she left and went to her room to change.

Her dress had been ruined, of course. A pity, especially since Juliette had just bought it for her, but there was no help for it. She changed into a serviceable wool and went back down to see how the rest of the guests had fared.

Dinner had been forgotten in all the excitement. The remains of the soup course littered the table. Madeline ordered it cleaned up, and asked for trays of bread, fruit, and cheese, wine and tea, to be taken to the salon. The cook pointed to the cold pheasant waiting to be served, and Madeline nodded. "Might as well get some use from it."

Servants were already working to sop up the rain on the dining room floor. A few panes of glass had been broken in the French doors along the long front wall, but compared to the greenhouse, the damage was minor. She checked the salon, but it was sheltered somewhat by the branches of an old, sturdy oak and had been spared. The musicians sat idly in one corner. She set them to playing.

In short, she performed all the tasks Juliette should have been addressing, had she not indulged in her passion in the library where anyone might have seen her. Neither Juliette nor Jonathan were anywhere to be seen. Nor Lucien, though he had been as soiled as Madeline, and she imagined he'd gone to change as she had.

Most of the guests were badly shaken by the violent storm, and the mood in the salon was subdued. Even so, a game of cards started in one corner, and though the musicians played desultorily, they did provide some background music. Madeline found it all oppressive. When Charles did not reappear, she escaped to the music room.

She'd been working a long time to learn Handel's passacaglia for violin. The wistful notes suited her mood this evening, and in the dim, moist gloaming, she began to play. She had no true skill, no great gift for music, but it gave her heart and hope. Like most girls she'd been trained to play the clavichord and to sing. On her own she had insisted upon violin, and though it challenged her almost beyond any ability she possessed, she loved it.

Tonight in the somber mood, the music seemed only to add some new weight to the restless emotion in her breast, making her feel thick and annoyed and—

With an irritable sigh, she put it aside.

"Oh, please don't stop."

Madeline turned, startled by the voice that came from the gloom. The marquess sat on one of the striped silk sofas that lined the edges of the room. "I didn't hear you come in," she said. "How long have you been there?"

"A little while," he said, standing. He crossed the room into the small pale light of the candles. "I came looking for you, and when I heard the music, I stopped in. You play very well."

She smiled. "I do not, but I thank you for your gallantry nonetheless." A pin loosened in her hair and she lifted a hand to pat it back in place. "Why were you looking for me?"

Charles caught his hands behind his back and looked away for a moment. She felt his sudden discomfort and it puzzled her. "Is something wrong?"

"No." His smile was apologetic. Taking her elbow, he gestured toward the gardens beyond the windows. "Will you walk with me a little while?"

"Of course. It would be a pleasure."

"Good."

The air outside was cool and sweetly scented. "I love this smell," Madeline commented, lifting her skirts with one hand, holding his crooked elbow with the other. Again she noticed the calm he exuded like the bouquet in a fine wine. It soothed some of the irritation she'd felt all night. As if ridding herself of pent-up emotions, she breathed deeply and exhaled on a sigh. "Much better," she said with a smile toward Charles. "I do enjoy your company."

The tenderness on his face pleased her. "I'm very glad. The feeling is quite mutual."

With a gentle squeeze to his arm, she looked away again. "Shall we take the path down the avenue? Everything else will be too wet."

"Fine." He pointed out a large broken tree limb. "You've a good deal of work ahead of you."

Madeline nodded, wondering how the gardens had fared.

"Where did your stepmother go? Rare of her to disappear like that."

"Rude is what it was." A vision of the coupling in the library flashed in her mind, and she pushed it away.

"I expect she had her reasons."

"Yes, I'm sure she did," Madeline commented dryly.

For a time, they walked on in silence. Darkness grew thick in the shadows and spread from the corners across the vast grounds, until everything was the same color—sky and ground and trees and shrubs a colorless gray. Crickets sang in the underbrush, and the lawns were littered with birds dining on the worms soaked out of the ground. Their whistles and coos added sweet music to the evening. With a strange twinge in her chest, Madeline thought of Lord Esher, closing his eyes by the windows, telling her to listen.

"Madeline," Charles said, "I must return tomorrow to Kirkton. This hail will have devastated many of the crops, and I'll have to see what I can do about all that."

Surprisingly, Madeline felt a small pang of regret.

She looked up at him. "Will you come back when you've finished your business?"

"Would you like me to?"

"Yes."

He paused. In the creeping darkness, with shadows obscuring his plump face, highlighting only the strength of his nose and brow, and the surprisingly firm lines of his strong chin, he looked almost handsome. The sherry-colored irises darkened. "Madeline, I think it's no secret I'd like to marry you." He held up a hand. "Don't speak yet. I want you to think what it would be like, truly, to be married to a man as dull as I am."

"You aren't dull!" She touched his arm. "You're exactly the opposite—concerned and caring and passionate. I love that you're willing to return to your estate to look after the farmers who'll be fretting. Many lords would not bother with such squirish chores."

"Still," he said with gravity, "I mean what I say, Madeline. Think on it. Think if you may be fond enough to make a solid marriage between us. I only wish it if it makes you happy."

He bent quickly and pressed a kiss to her mouth. It was not without expertise. Madeline waited for the congestion she'd felt when Lucien put his hand on her shoulder. It didn't come. Charles's kiss was pleasant and tender, but not at all arousing.

She missed most of all the scent of Lord Esher. Somehow, she'd thought it was a smell men all carried when a woman got close enough to them. Foolish of her.

Disappointed and trying not to show it, she lowered her head. "Perhaps we'd best get back," she whispered.

"Yes, perhaps we should."

At the top of the stairs that led inside, Madeline paused. "I'll think on it," she said, and lifted on her toes to kiss him again, allowing her body to come into contact with his. Again the sensation was pleasant, nothing more.

At least it wasn't repugnant.

From the shadows of a turn in the wall, Lucien watched the marquess and Madeline.

Sweet the way they made protestations to each other. The marquess was so earnest a man could almost feel sorry for him, and would, if the woman he courted were anyone else. Not Madeline. At any other time, she'd be the perfect wife for the marquess—honorable and kind and good. Responsible, intelligent, pretty. Together they would tend the vast estates of Kirkton and Whitethorn with democratic grace and care.

Cynically, Lucien leaned on the balustrade above them, confident he would not be seen, as they paused on the steps to the hall. Yes, he could see them in their old age, clucking over the antics of the children, a pack of hounds sprawled at their feet, relics from the ancient world littering the mantelpieces.

Madeline bent her head, and the last dying gleam of day caught on the column of her neck, white and curved, unbearably tender at the nape. He thought of her standing in the muddy, sopping-wet greenhouse in her fine brocaded gown, her breasts near to falling out of the bodice in spite of the careful placement of the fichu. In memory, the scene was rendered in green and gray, rose, and cream and sable.

Desire moved in him. What could she hope to gain

with such a bland alliance with the marquess? How could she hope to ignore the passion that seeped from her very pores like the fragrance of a moonlit night?

He narrowed his eyes. She did not know it lived in her. Nor would she ever unless Lucien led her to it.

How would the marquess have handled that little scene in the greenhouse, with Madeline looking so delectably wanton in her ruined gown, a muddy smear across her chin and another adorning the swell of one nearly wholly exposed breast? Or worse, the one in the hallway, when Madeline had witnessed the sybaritic scene in the library?

When Lucien had come around the corner, she was staring like an owl, two bright slashes of color on her face, her bosom rising and falling in quick pace. The tiny scratches on her cheeks and the bloody lip, together with the pounding of the hail overhead and the love cries from the library, had aroused him as nothing had in more years than he could remember.

And in the greenhouse, he'd fully intended to begin his earnest seduction. He prided himself on exquisite seductions of great care and great rewards—when she fell to him, it would be a moment she remembered for the rest of her life, a moment of such passion she would not truly be able ever to regret it. Ever.

There in the moist, gray-colored greenhouse, with her hair coming loose, her mind filled with sexual images of an extremely passionate nature, Madeline had been ripe for the plucking. He'd planned to rouse her so thoroughly she couldn't breathe—the first step in any true seduction.

And yet, he had not done it.

The reason terrified him, sent him pacing here tonight. When he'd touched her plump lower lip and watched her eyes drift closed, a bolt of music so pure and clear he almost wept for the beauty of it had sounded in his mind. It was made of the sound of the gray-green rain, and the sharp red of Juliette's cry, and the umber warmth of the smell of damp earth and humid growth in the greenhouse. The violins and cellos hummed low.

It was exquisite and whole, and meshed in some way with the ravens on the grass the morning Madeline took him into the maze. And while it was on him, he could not bear to be cruel.

The trouble was, he had not written the other bit down and burned it, as was his habit. He let it play when it would, let it ring as he lay awake at night. He was afraid if he wrote it down, he would not then burn the music. And he didn't know what that meant.

Now, with both pieces humming, twirling, dancing in his brain, he was getting drunk. Only drinking could let him sleep on such a night. Only drunkenness could completely drown the sounds. Gratefully, there was already a blunting to the shimmer of colors; already they were fading.

Oddly, watching Madeline and Charles, he considered allowing them to go on, unmarred by his intention. He thought it would be a kindness to allow them their simple happiness, the steadiness that was apparent in every move both of them made.

But then he thought again of the undiscovered passion in her, the blaze in her eyes he caught sight of now and again, and he thought it would be a great tragedy to let her go peacefully into her life without ever tasting that fully. A tragedy. And perhaps it might even serve the marquess, for he might, too, be ready for an awakening.

Well pleased at this tangle of justifications, Lucien
went to bed and passed out.

The music awakened him before dawn. His head
ached massively, with the edging of color and light
that warned he would be ill with the headache, and
all through it was the sound of the gray-green music.
Queasy, blinded by the edging of light in his eyes, he
dragged himself to the small desk in his room and
dipped his quill.

The devastation in the garden the next morning was
overwhelming. Madeline could not even do any work
at first—she just wandered, first through the rose gardens. The roses she had managed to get pruned were
fine. Many of the others had been violently torn by
the wind and hail. The wounds showed like split skin.
From the roses, she walked the length of the meadow.
Everywhere were tree branches and broken shrubs
and the assorted tangles of debris left by nature's
frenzy.

Into the protected maze Madeline retreated. Aside
from an occasional branch in the path, most everything here had been little marred by the storm. It gave
her a sense of calm to find it untouched, and she
found herself letting go of a breath too long held.

The strange wild swollenness of the day before had
broken, leaving behind a clarity of thought as crisp as
the new-washed air. The scene she'd inadvertently
witnessed in the library, the oddly passionate and not
passionate moments in the greenhouse, now seemed
fogged, as if they were the product of a summer afternoon's slumber.

A perfect Michaelmas daisy bloomed against a gray

stone bench. Madeline bent to pluck it and held it to her nose idly, wandering through the maze until she came to a *claire-voie* that faced the meadow. At this early hour, there was naught but stillness over the landscape, stillness and the impossible green of copious rain. The shining air was washed clean of impurities.

As her mind had been.

She felt an almost fatalistic sense of destiny. Fate had sent the storm to force her hand. The mullioned windows of Whitethorn had been as devastated as her gardens. She'd sent the butler around this morning to count and didn't look forward to the tally. There was no money to pay for such extensive repairs. Already, Juliette had sold off a magnificent diamond necklace given her by the earl in order to pay for this summer fête and the clothes in which to dress the prize— Madeline.

Thinking of that sacrifice, Madeline knew a painful slash of guilt over the rose silk she'd ruined yesterday. Perhaps it could be salvaged. Often Jenny, the cook's helper, could perform miracles with her brushes and potions. Still, it had been uncommonly thoughtless of her.

With a sigh, she meandered farther into the maze. Boss, the cat, sat in the middle of a path, cleaning a paw. He stopped to yowl at her, plaintively, and she chuckled. "Didn't much like the storm, did you?"

He yowled again and bumped into her skirts. Madeline bent to lift him into her arms, the big lug of a tomcat, battered and arrogant and yet still in need of attention. As she rubbed his massive head, a ragged purr rattled from his throat and he tucked his nose into the hollow of her shoulder.

She laughed. "Silly cat."

Some disturbance in the ordinariness of the maze caught her eye. Madeline looked back, letting her eye rove slowly over the details she knew so intimately but didn't immediately see anything amiss. A sprinkle of blackish feathers, rather mangled, lay on the grass, evidence of Boss's breakfast. "I thought I smelled bird breath," Madeline said.

Boss meowed in reply but didn't lift his head. Luxuriously, he settled more closely into the crook of her arm.

Madeline started to walk on, thinking she must have imagined the disturbance, when a slight, uncommon sound came to her. It sounded like a moan.

With a frown, she headed for the center of the maze, wondering if some new servant had become lost and had had to spend the night in the place, in that cold and horrible storm. "Hello?" she called.

There was no answer.

Boss stirred at her hurrying steps but made no move to get down. She was glad of his heavy warmth and didn't even mind the small pinpricks of his claws as he held on. "Hello?" she called. "Is anyone here?"

Sounds traveled oddly in the maze because of the *claire-voies* and the muting of the bushes. It was impossible to pinpoint where a sound originated. But Madeline had not imagined it. That moan had been as human and real as her own breath.

She checked every hidden spot along the route, some behind a simple wall, others in hidden circles accessed from secret places—tiny mazes within the maze. She found no one. At each window cut into those hedges, she paused to look through, calling out.

Nothing. Until she turned the last corner into the

very heart of the maze. There, looking for all the world as if he were dead, lay Lucien Harrow.

Madeline froze, clutching the cat to her chest as if he were some living shield. He protested mildly, touching his cold wet nose to her neck in reminder of her human duty to felines. Absently, Madeline rubbed his body.

Lord Esher lay flat on his back on an old gray stone bench, one leg bent at the knee to brace him from toppling onto the ground, the other flung along the length of the bench itself. One hand touched the earth, the bright white of his lace cuff making his brown, graceful fingers look even darker. He wore only a cambric shirt, unlaced at the neck, tight dark breeches, and a pair of muddy boots. His hair had come loose and spilled over the gray stone in glossy abundance, and his jaw was covered with a dark shadow of bristly beard. In the center of that roughness, his beautifully cut mouth was vulnerable.

The sheer length and breadth and stillness of him took away her breath. She thought he must have stumbled here drunk and passed out, and the moaning she had heard was only the well-deserved misery of too much drink. Still she couldn't seem to move. That hard pulse pounded, that painful aching that seemed to shimmer to life every time she saw the big, lazy, drunken oaf. It made her chest hurt.

Abruptly, she put the cat down and launched herself forward, moving over the grass in a blur, halting only as she came up even with him. Clutching her skirts, she said, "Lord Esher! Wake up!"

He did not move. Not a muscle or a twitch of a finger. But his eyes opened. The color was almost green, the color of the sea, and the whites were bloodshot in the extreme. She noticed his flesh looked quite pale and was drawn tight over his cheekbones. Well she recognized the signs of debauchery on a man's face—heaven knew, she'd seen it often enough as a girl.

"Get up," she said harshly. "I dislike drunks littering my garden with their foulness."

He still said nothing. Only gazed at her. It was disconcerting.

"Are you deaf? Get up."

Very slowly, he dampened his lips with his tongue. And in a voice rasping almost unrecognizably, he said, "I would love to oblige you, dear lady, but I do not believe it will be possible for me to move."

With a disgusted sigh, Madeline held out her hand. "I'll help you."

"Oh, not even a hand will do." He had obviously aimed for an amused, sardonic tone, but the last words were a deep ragged whisper. He closed his eyes.

Madeline made a move toward him. He opened his eyes suddenly. "Please, unless it is your pleasure to torture a man—do not put your hands on me."

She frowned. "Am I to leave you here to starve, then?"

"Your cook gave me a potion the last time. Ask her for me what it is."

"A cure for your excesses? You might simply try drinking less." Her gaze fell on his lashes, lying thick and black on his face. A hard line of tense muscle corded from temple to jaw, and there was a faint, unhealthy flush on his skin. He looked feverish and in pain.

Holding up her hand, she said, "I only want to touch your head. I'll not jolt you, I swear." Without waiting for a reply, she gently opened her hand against his forehead. His skin felt taut and overly stretched, and she thought him a little feverish.

He tensed at first, but eased. She felt the tension flow from him. "The music," he said. "This is the price I paid for it."

"The music?" Madeline said, touching his temple, his cheekbone.

"Yosef told me it would ask a price." He lifted one hand and put it over hers, pressing her palm closer against his head. "Your fingers are so cool."

"It is a fever, Lord Esher."

"No." He opened his eyes, and for a moment, Madeline had the impression that light sharded there as if on Juliette's prized crystal goblets. "No," he repeated. "It is my punishment."

"For overindulgence?"

He gazed at her steadily. She saw him swallow. Under her hand, the bones of his face seemed fragile. "Yes. The music."

Almost absently, he pulled her hand down and pressed a kiss to her palm, then tucked her hand under his chin. She felt the prickles of dark, unshaved beard against the back of her wrist, and the sensation was oddly, sharply erotic.

Violently, she yanked away. "I'll go for the cook."

He moaned, and as if the motion had sent him completely off balance, he rolled to one side. His hair tumbled black and thick and glossy around his face, over his shoulders. Madeline clasped her hands together.

As he slowly braced himself on the bench and struggled to his feet, she found herself staring at his legs, lean and long and muscled beneath the tight, dark breeches, and his buttocks, so firm and round, and his long, elegant back. With a sense of horror, she realized she wanted him with a surprising force. He seemed to know it. He found his footing and turned to face her. The cambric shirt gaped, open to the waist, and Madeline felt a blaze of shock jolt her at the intimate view of his chest and stomach. Her entire body reacted with a ripple of heat and longing.

His chin tilted sardonically, and even though his mouth was drawn in some pain, he was unbearably desirable, standing there like that. "It's in your eyes, Madeline," he said, still with that ragged edge in his voice. "All that passion you want to deny. Do you think it would be the same for me to kiss you as it is with your marquess?"

She took a step backward and found the hedge at her back. Branches stuck her. "I should not forget, Lord Esher, that you still need my assistance to leave this maze."

"Do I?" The careless, aloof expression flickered, and Madeline watched as he lifted an almost involuntary hand to his head. His shoulders seemed bowed with the weight of his head. Still, his lips twisted. "I've practiced. I know how to get out."

Torn between wanting to help him and needing urgently to escape him, Madeline found her feet frozen in place. "Are you so sure?"

He moved with excruciating slowness to point vaguely at one of the openings cut in the hedges. "The *claire-voies* must stay to one's left. The small rooms are always to the right."

The fact that he really was quite ill finally penetrated her selfish, inward conflicts. "Oh, by Jupiter," she muttered, moving toward him. "Put your arm around my shoulders and we'll get out of here."

"No." His voice was harsh. "I'll walk."

"Very well." He was the most exasperating man. "Do as you wish. Charles is leaving this morning and I must return to bid him farewell."

He said nothing. Madeline headed for the outlet. As she turned the corner to leave him, he said, "You'll be thinking of my mouth when you kiss him good-bye."

She didn't pause, only clutched her skirts and kept going. Let the blackhearted wretch starve to death out here. How dare he?

How dare he?

8

> . . . *dying is a pleasure*
> *When living is a pain.*
> —John Dryden

Juliette and the countess of Heath had been friends since both were in their early twenties. Both prided themselves on their independence in a man's world, the independence to choose their lovers and lives the same way a man would do. Both had used beauty and a talent for the bawdy to work themselves up in the world.

Both were now facing the slow, steady downward spiral toward middle age. As they sat on the terrace underneath a carefully draped fabric designed to shade them from the harsh sunlight, eating sliced strawberries and fresh bread, Juliette thought she was aging rather better than her friend. Likely, Juliette thought, because her own husband had obligingly passed on, while Anna was forced to manage her dull, dowdy country earl with cunning and deftness.

Still Anna was beautiful, as dark as Juliette was

fair. Juliette enjoyed, as always, the contrast between them. It had served to set each apart all the days of their friendship.

"How is the campaign going?" Anna asked lightly, buttering a roll. "Will we be hearing wedding bells this fall?"

Juliette licked a sprinkle of sugar from her index finger. "I think so. Charles is quite besotted, and Madeline is a sensible girl. She'll do what's best."

As if on cue, Madeline wandered out to the table, her hair brushed and neatly arranged, her skin glowing with the health and clarity only youth could boast. A deep, sharp pride ached in Juliette's chest—her daughter was by far the most beautiful of all the girls this season. And she was brilliant, as well. In a rush of fond feeling, she touched her hand. "Good morning, dear heart! Will you have some strawberries?"

"Please." She looked around. "Where is Lord Lanham?"

"I'm sure I don't know. Why ever do you ask?"

"I thought I saw him come this way," Madeline said with a shrug. "Must have been mistaken. Perhaps he's gone riding or something."

"Speaking of Jonathan," Anna said, leaning forward, "it was wicked of you to invite me here while Lord Esher stays under your roof."

"What? Why?" Juliette frowned. "Have I made some dreadful social error?"

"My dear!" Anna laughed. "You mean you don't know?"

"Evidently I do not."

Madeline spoke, reaching for cream to pour on the strawberries. "Do tell, Countess."

Juliette looked up at the odd tone in her daughter's

voice. A drollness was not uncommon on Madeline's sharp tongue, but there was something else here now. Juliette frowned.

"Well," Anna said, blotting her lips, "there was a terrible scandal. I can't think how you missed it, unless you were on the Continent at the time." She inclined her head. "Yes, perhaps you were. The summer of '73. Or perhaps '74."

Juliette knew it would only lengthen the story if she attempted to rush it from Anna's mouth. With a soft, slight sigh, she folded her hands. Madeline caught her eye and gave her a slight, wicked wink.

"Lord Esher was only a youth, perhaps not quite twenty. I met him at a ball, and he pursued me relentlessly. At first, I resisted—I'd had other lovers by then of course, but none so young as he, or quite as forceful. I think," she said with a conspiratorial laugh, "he frightened me a little."

A footman in livery put a fresh basket of bread on the table and whisked away the old. Madeline motioned for more tea.

Anna continued, "Well, one thing led to another, and we became"—she smiled coyly—"intimate. He was quite passionate, even composed music for me."

"Music!" Juliette interjected. "How quaint."

"What sort of music?" Madeline asked, and Juliette saw a strange, intent expression on the girl's face.

"What difference does that make?" Juliette said. "Go on, Anna."

"Oh, I think the music mattered rather much to Lucien," Anna said. "He studied in Vienna with the masters until his mother died—she was Russian, and you know how the Russians are!" She tittered. "I gather his father was not quite as supportive of his composing."

"I should think not," Juliette said. "An earl who composes!" She laughed. "The singing earl! Can you imagine?"

"Quite," Anna said, and they laughed together.

"But what *happened*?" Madeline asked.

Anna lifted her shoulders in a single shrug, the motion brimming with ennui. "I tired of him and broke it off." She leaned forward, pausing dramatically. "Do you know, he challenged my husband to a duel!"

"No!"

"He did! Called him out, and poor Harry was really bothered by it, poor thing. He didn't want to hurt the young man, but after all he'd had a commission in the Navy and was quite deft with his weapons."

"I should think so."

"But Lucien was insistent, and Harry dutifully met him at dawn one morning. Harry only nicked him, and Lucien was humiliated, but everyone thought it just the bravest, most romantic gesture, and they all invited him to their parties after that."

"Though all have been careful to do so when you are not there," Juliette said, and gave Anna an apologetic smile. "I'm so sorry, my dear. I'd quite understand if you returned to London just now."

"And what of his music?" Madeline asked.

"Oh, I wouldn't think of leaving!" Anna said. "It might prove most interesting, after all these years. He's grown into a rather fine man, hasn't he?"

Madeline leaned over and put a hand on the countess's arm. "What of his music?" she asked again.

"Madeline!" Juliette admonished.

Anna smiled. "He said he'd never compose again. I laughed at him, you see." She sighed. "I didn't really intend to wound him, but I was young then, too. Other men were bringing me jewels and furs and exotic fabrics. Lucien brought a sheet of music and a violin."

"How quaint," Juliette said. "It's hard to imagine the present Lucien as such a callow boy."

Madeline stood. "It's a terrible story," she said. "I hate the way you use people so freely, as if they were handkerchiefs to be tossed aside when soiled."

A gleam of amusement shone in Anna's eye. "Ah, to be so young and passionate again," she said dryly. "Do you remember, Juliette, when you vowed never to use a man for your own ends, but only to be with one for love?"

"I was never that young," Juliette said, and was embarrassed at the edge in her words. She gestured. "Oh, Madeline, do sit down. It isn't as if Lord Esher never recovered. He's this very moment fleeing a difficult mistress, hiding here until her new lover calms down."

Madeline shook her head slowly. "That isn't the point, Juliette. It is dishonest, the way you live—taking lovers as you will, discarding them as you wish, taking them back up when it suits you."

The girl was staring rather pointedly at Juliette, and she frowned. "What is this about?"

"Why do you think I'm speaking to you?"

Just enough anger edged the words to let Juliette know Madeline was indeed speaking directly to her. "We'll discuss this later, shall we?"

"That won't be necessary." She flicked her skirts from the table. "It won't make any difference what I say anyway."

Anna laughed. Juliette frowned, watching Madeline walk away, her head high. There was something

Juliette ought to be noticing, something just out of reach.

"Oh, don't look so worried," Anna teased. "She's only earnest with youth."

"Yes," Juliette said slowly. But she wasn't entirely sure. She must be very alert over the next few weeks. Madeline was not a malleable, biddable creature—never had been—but Juliette would hate to see her make some terrible mistake out of a misguided and naive sense of righteousness.

Shaking off the mood, she looked at Anna. "Did Lord Esher really compose for you?"

Madeline left the countesses, feeling a strange disquiet. Part of it lingered from the upset in the maze a few hours before, when Lucien had put his mouth on her palm. She'd heard women say they could still feel the imprint of a man's lips hours or days later. Madeline only wished that were true. Instead, what she felt was that bright, hot shock of arousal all through her every time she thought of it.

She'd been very angry with him when she left him in the maze, and now she wondered if he'd got back all right. He'd been ill, after all. Perhaps she ought to check.

It was crushing to hear that story of his youth—it had almost made her cry to listen to the peacock countesses laughing at the earnest youth he'd been—in love enough to compose something, and then to have it flung back in his face. In love enough to call out her husband, knowing the scandal it would cause, and then be humiliated by an experienced soldier who "pitied the boy." She could just hear the earl saying it in his bluff, hearty drawl. Oh, it was excruciating to imagine it. How much worse it must have been to be a prideful, emotional young man and live through it.

Little wonder he was cynical.

But on top of all those mixed and disturbing emotions was another: shame. Was she not indulging in the very same behavior for which she condemned the countesses? Was she not trading her feminine gifts to gain something material? Yes, it was marriage, and it was logical, and it was done all the time. But was it really any different?

The trouble was, Madeline knew Charles harbored genuine emotion for her. It couldn't have been easy for him to come here, plain and round and unfashionable, to court Madeline. To his eyes, she was beautiful and bright and desirable.

And what had Madeline done through his whole visit here? Flirted with Lucien Harrow. She pretended to avoid him, but in truth wasn't she always hoping he'd find her? In spite of all he was, a rogue and a rake with a dead heart and no direction, she found him deeply compelling. In a way, she'd even used Charles to shield her from her feelings in that way.

Hurrying now, she felt her cheeks flame. How could she have considered marrying such a good and honorable man as Charles Devon? He deserved far better than she—someone who would at least be honest in her emotions, someone who would not be calculating the cost of window glass while he kissed her.

She hoped she could catch him before his party left. Lifting her skirts, she ran for the stables.

The group of them were about to depart—Charles on a fine black gelding he managed with that surprising adeptness, his wig askew as usual. A button had popped open on his waistcoat from the strain of the past days' eating.

"I'm so glad I caught you," she said breathlessly. "Must you leave right now, or may I have a moment to speak with you?"

A small frown creased the openness of his face, a flicker of something Madeline could not quite read. "A few moments, but I'd rather not let the horses get too restless." He waved to his man. "Go on. I'll catch up in a bit."

"Very well, sir." The small cluster of men and horses walked from the stables into the sunlight, leaving Madeline standing alongside the horse, looking up at the marquess. Now that she was here, she didn't quite know how to say what was in her heart.

"I've come to tell you, Charles," she blurted out, "I cannot marry you."

For the space of a heartbeat, he was silent. "I see. May I ask what brought you to this decision?"

"I don't love you," she said, halting on each word. "I like you," she hurried to add. "I enjoy your company. But I'm only thinking of marrying you so that I might save Whitethorn, and you deserve better than that."

To her surprise, he smiled gently. Dismounting, he gave the reins to a stableboy and gestured for Madeline to walk outside. A gilded morning danced around them, yellow and green treetops against a full clear sky. The marquess took her arm and walked with her away from the outbuildings, to stand against a great old rowan tree, bending thick gnarled branches in canopy. He stopped and looked at it, smiling. Then he looked at Madeline.

"It would have surprised me very much to learn you had any other reason to marry me—or anyone else—than to save your ancestral home." He looked over his shoulder and lifted a hand toward the house, neat enough but obviously in need of care. "It is a beautiful home, and deserves the devotion you give."

"But I—"

He lifted a hand. "I'll not lie to you, Madeline. I am in love with you, and you're more wife than I had a right to expect, given my appearance and my ungallant ways. I'd like to marry you, and I will take my chances that you might come to love me one day."

His small, dignified speech gave her a pang. "Oh, you are too good!" she said, and flung her arms around his neck impulsively. "I am not a good enough wife for you," she said against his shoulder.

In a low voice he said, "Think on it, Madeline. I'll not die of heartbreak if you decide against my suit, but it would bring me great joy if you accepted it."

Very, very gently, he pulled back and tipped up her chin and pressed a kiss on her mouth. Just as his head closed out her vision, a sharp, clear picture of Lucien bolted through her imagination.

"You'll think of my mouth when you kiss him good-bye."

Madeline felt a sharp, deep pain—regret or despair, she didn't know.

"All right, then?" Charles asked, holding her arms.

Looking into his kind, sherry-colored eyes, Madeline thought what a good father he would be to her children, and what a steady husband he would make. She would stake her life on his faithfulness. "Yes. Hurry back," she said, and meant it on more levels than she could express.

She thought he knew that, too. "Yes," he said. "That I will do."

*   *   *

The potion the cook gave Lucien, together with a few hours' sleep in his darkened bedchamber, helped to ease the light-sharded pain in his head. It lingered, dangerously, at the base of his skull and the edges of his eyes, but for the most part, it was better.

On his table were the notations he'd written last night. When he saw them, his headache leaped a notch. He grabbed the sheaves of paper in a great handful and dumped them in the fire. He watched the embers catch and curl the paper, erasing the clefs and quarter notes decorating the pages in black slashes and delicate dots.

As the paper dissolved into cinders, great open wounds devouring the night's demonic work, he could not breathe. Sorrow mixed with savage pleasure—he'd never have that work again. It was gone. Forever.

When it was finished, he washed his face carefully and allowed his man to pull his hair into a queue and help him into fresh clothes. Even such small movements were difficult; he held his head carefully, as if it were a cracked egg.

As he was finishing these small tasks, Jonathan appeared. "There you are," he said, coming into the room. "I was beginning to think you'd fallen into the sea or some such thing."

"I'm here."

"Let's ride into the village for the afternoon. I'm bored beyond expression."

"Bored?" Lucien turned his head carefully. "Or outcast?"

A bitter twist touched Jonathan's mouth, and

Lucien saw the lines of strain around his eyes. "I've never known such a bewildering or annoying woman." He flopped in a brocade chair. "She's driving me mad."

With a wave, Lucien indicated he could finish on his own. Deftly, he tied a snowy cravat at his neck. "So leave her and find another."

"I do not want another woman."

Lucien smiled. He'd known that would be the answer. "She's been making advances at me, man. Let her go."

"I saw her. Don't fancy she wants you, Lucien. She simply means to be sure you do not seduce her daughter, and if she sleeps with you, the virtuous Madeline will have nothing to do with you, no matter how hard you try to seduce her."

"Is that what it is?" Lucien drawled.

A brittle expression touched Jonathan's mouth. "Yes." Restlessly, he jumped up and paced the room, round and round, touching a curio and the window casings and the edge of the door. "How goes your pursuit of the little dove, anyway? I saw the marquess leave this morning. That should make your way clearer."

"Perhaps." A tiny white shard stabbed his temple. "She's not all that simple to seduce, actually. She's far too aware of the tricks. I spout poetry, she spouts it back at me. I offer food—she offers more." He frowned, untying the knot of his neckcloth. "Yesterday, I thought to steal a kiss and I still have not decided how she averted it." He tossed the cloth aside. "Let's ride, then."

It was never easy to force himself into physical activity after one of his bouts with the debilitating headaches. Sometimes riding would send him howling back to a dark room, but more often than not, it chased away the lingering traces of illness. Lucien believed in trying, anyway. There was nothing but infirmity to be gained from hiding away in the dark.

Today it was no different. His neck and head screamed at first, but slowly the joltings of his horse ceased to be so vicious, and the fresh air worked its magic. By the time they reached the village, he felt much clearer. A good meal and a cool glass of ale might be just the thing.

The village, named for the estate nearby, boasted quaint medieval cottages and a dark, satisfyingly ancient pub with shutters and rough tables. Lucien asked the goodwife to bring him a plate of her best, and she, blushing and curtsying, hurried off to comply.

Over tankards of surprisingly good ale, Jonathan leaned forward. "Lucien, all jesting aside, I need this woman." The admission cost him. "Without her, I cannot sleep. I'm miserable."

"God, you've done it, haven't you?" He measured Jonathan over the rim of his cup. "And Juliette, of all women. How did you let such a thing happen?"

"I don't know." He flushed, and stared mulishly toward the back of the room. "Does one choose when to fall in love?"

Lucien shrugged.

"I did not know I'd even done it until you and I came here. Or at least I didn't know how deeply I'd fallen." He gripped his tankard and leaned forward. "I've had my share of women, Lucien, but you've a special knack with them. They all fall in love with you. How do I make Juliette fall in love? How do I snare her?"

"Snare her for what?"

"To marry her, of course."

Lucien threw back his head and laughed. "You can't be serious!"

Grimly, Jonathan waited. "I assure you I'm quite serious." His voice grew rough. "I must have her."

The goodwife brought Lucien's food—a thick mutton stew with chunks of onion and carrot, and a hunk of bread alongside. Lucien nodded, giving her a wink. "Thank you."

He gave his attention to the food for a few bites and let Jonathan drink another cup of ale. Then he said, "If I wanted Juliette, I would ignore her. She's the sort of woman who cannot abide being ignored."

Jonathan perked up. "I can see that might be true. Go on."

"There isn't much else. I'd flirt madly with the other women." A wickedness bloomed in his mind. Jonathan did not know of Lucien's affair with the countess of Heath. Or if he did, he'd never said so. "Use her friend the countess, and make sure Juliette knows you've slept with her."

Jonathan looked doubtful. "I might lose her completely if I sleep with her friend."

"You might," Lucien agreed. "But you'll certainly lose her now."

"Perhaps I ought to seduce her daughter," Jonathan said, and gave Lucien a lift of one brow.

"And perhaps I'd be forced to call you out."

"Ah!" Jonathan smiled. "Careful, Lucien, that you do not fall yourself."

"No," he said comfortably. "I fell early and raw, and learned my lesson well. My heart was mortally wounded. What no longer exists cannot be engaged."

He paused, thinking of Anna in those days—nearly ten years ago. He'd been sure he would die of the pain and turmoil and embarrassment. "Hard to imagine being so young again." Then with a sort of honor he wasn't aware he possessed, he said, "It was, in fact, Lady Heath, who so wounded me. Perhaps you'd be well advised to beware."

"What does not exist cannot be engaged," Jonathan echoed. He lifted his cup. "And what is engaged cannot be misplaced. Countess Heath is an attractive woman, but she is not Juliette."

"No." He suddenly remembered the passionate embrace he'd glimpsed in the library. "Forgive me for saying so, Jonathan, but I happened to pass by the library yesterday eve. It did not seem you were, er, having trouble with Juliette at that moment. In fact, neither of you reappeared all evening, as I recall. That would suggest some harmony."

Jonathan lowered his head, staring into the bottom of his tankard with a grim expression. "It is complicated." He had the grace to look abashed. "God, I wonder if anyone else saw us."

"As it happens, Madeline did." He remembered her expression, the flush on her forehead and chin as well as her cheeks, the limpid look of her eyes. It had undone him a little. "We did not linger."

Jonathan said nothing.

They let the subject go and turned to a friendly game of dice. By the time they were ready to return, it was late afternoon. Lucien's headache was gone for another day, and the rigidness of Jonathan's mouth had eased. Lucien thought his friend might be a little drunk.

When they rode back to Whitethorn, long gold sunlight slanted through the trees, highlighting the destruction the storm had wrought—the boarded windows and broken plants and mangled greenhouse. Lucien had a sudden thought. "You say they haven't the funds to maintain Whitethorn?"

"No, they don't."

Lucien smiled. "I've a wicked thought, then. Let me find my man and send him to the village for some men to work for me, for her." He clapped his friend on the back. "If I fix her greenhouse, leaving her funds to fix the rest, she'll be happily in my debt."

"Yes."

"I amaze even myself at times," Lucien said unabashedly. He leaped up the front steps cheerily, and at the top, caught a wisp of sound. He paused.

From the open French doors to the music room came the sound of a violin. A Marais composition Lucien had never much liked. It was insincere, lacking real emotion. And yet, whoever it was on the violin certainly played with vigor—if not expertise. He winced as she missed a finger placement, making a flat where none was intended. "It's not flat," he muttered under his breath. And yet, the violinist went on happily, oblivious to the missed note.

"Oh, there you are!" The pair of countesses—the Peacock Countesses, Madeline called them, much to his amusement—appeared at the doors. It was Juliette greeting them, a swallowed-canary look about her. "We were just wondering where you'd got to."

"Why, Lucien," Anna said, holding out her hand, "what a magnificent man you've become." A hard glitter lit her dark eyes.

"And how old you've grown," he said, ignoring her to bend over Juliette's hand. At the last moment, he turned it over and pressed his mouth to her palm instead, and lingered. If she was not to interfere with his seduction of Madeline, she had to believe her seduction of him was working. When he straightened, he let his eyes wash over her bosom appreciatively, lingeringly, then he gave her his practiced and most devilish smile.

Jonathan, into the breach, grabbed Anna's forgotten hand. "Forgive his manners, my lady," he said, bending with a courtly gesture as elegant as Lucien's was practiced.

Lucien didn't miss the way Juliette's eyes darted toward her lover. A flash of anxiousness whisked over her face and was gone. "Come, let's all have tea, shall we?"

She led them into the vast, marbled foyer. Through a gilded door to the music room, Lucien saw a figure silhouetted against the light, slim and simple— Madeline. As he watched, she bent into the instrument, still earnestly playing with an inexactitude that made him wince and plucked his heart all at once. It took all he had to resist the lure of going into that room, taking that instrument from her—

A dulcet voice spoke into his ear. "A pity it isn't a composition of yours, my dear," Anna said. "But you don't do that anymore, do you?"

Before he could turn, violence in his chest, she laughed lightly. She wandered toward the veranda, waving her fan lazily, casting him an amused glance over her shoulder.

He held her gaze steadily, furiously. No verbal answer was required.

In the music room, Madeline missed her note again. Lucien turned on his heel and bolted up the stairs. Anna's derisive laughter floated after him.

9

*She like Fate can wound a Lover
Goddess like, too, can Recover;
She can Kill, or save from dying,
The Transported Soul is flying."*
—Thomas D'Urfey

The workmen started arriving midmorning the next day. Madeline was gathering shredded tree limbs and rose branches when the first group arrived, three men she recognized from the village, with a wagon piled high with supplies.

The front man gave her a note. "Milord bade me gi' it to ye," he said, and shifted on his feet restlessly. Small pox scars ravaged his face, but his eyes were clear and there was no smell of gin on him.

Madeline broke the seal on the note.

*My dear Madeline,
    I knew you would not accept such an offering from me directly, so I made arrangements from afar. These men are here to do your bidding, and I've arranged to be billed for any costs they incur. I've ordered them to begin with the house windows and move to the rest as they are able.*

*You are under no circumstances to misread my
gesture as a measure of coercion. You must know
the money is of no consequence to me—and I so
dislike seeing you suffer and worry; consider this
a gift from a friend only and freely accept it in the
spirit it was given.*

*I expect I will return to Whitethorn within a
fortnight and we might then discuss our other
plans. Until then, I remain,*

   Your ever faithful
   and affectionate,
   Charles Devon, Marquess of Beauchamp

Madeline looked at the workmen. "I'm very sorry,
but I cannot pay you. You'll have to go back—and
take the supplies with you."

The headman looked over his shoulder. "Milord
already paid us for a fortnight. All three of us, and
enough for lunch, too, so ye needn't worry about new
mouths to feed."

"Is that so." The expression was less a question
than an admission of surprise. She took a breath.
"Well, then, I expect I shall have to show you what
needs doing."

She'd no sooner got them going on removing the
shattered glass in the dining room than a second
group of workmen wandered up the lane, four this
time. Sturdy, strong men. Madeline met them at the
steps. "May I help you? If you've come about the windows and storm damage, I'm afraid the positions
have already been filled."

The lead man, a burly man with forearms like
hams, pulled his forelock a little uncertainly. "We
were already paid to help w'yer gardens, milady. And

the greenhouse?" He stepped forward. "I did some repair work last year in London, to one of the great houses there. I have me references."

"Who paid you?"

"Weren't no one I recognized—a London-lookin' lord."

"No powder or wig?" she guessed.

"That's him."

"He sent no note with you?"

"No, milady."

Madeline eyed the group of them for a moment. In sudden decision, she said, "Wait here."

Catching her skirts in one hand, she stormed up the stairs. It was one thing for Charles to expend such lavish amounts on her since she intended to marry him. It was quite another for Lucien Harrow to do so. At his door, she scratched perfunctorily, then barged in.

The dark silence surprised her. The drapes had not yet been opened, and she stormed across the room to yank the cord, letting gold morning light in to spill over the fading Arabian carpet and the bed with its curtains drawn. She reached for them, then hesitated, awash suddenly with what she was doing. What if there were some woman with him—a village girl or a servant or even one of the guests? Most everyone had drifted back to London, but the countess of Heath was not without her charms, and they had once been lovers.

No. He had gone too far. She flung open the bed curtains.

The bed was empty. It didn't even look touched.

With a frown, Madeline glanced around. A pair of boots littered the floor, carelessly flung where he'd taken them off, and a yellow silk brocade waistcoat hung over the back of a chair.

And there, slumped against the back of a chaise longe, was Lucien Harrow, dressed in his clothes from the day before, a scattering of papers all over the floor around him. A pot of ink and a newly cut pen rested on the small desk beside him. He snored softly.

Tiptoeing, Madeline bent to pick up one of the sheets of paper. Music. Scrawled, hard to read, for it had obviously been written in some haste and in poor light. She peered at it, trying to pick out something she knew. There, a glissando, sweet and light, moving in to a more somber series in a minor key. Haltingly, she tried to hum a little of it.

"What the bloody hell do you think you're doing?" Lucien roared. He snatched the paper from her hand and threw it in the fire.

Before she could answer, or even react a little, he turned with a sound like a wounded and dangerous animal, feverishly scooping the rest of the paper into a pile he then threw into the coals. There wasn't enough fire to burn them quickly. He grabbed a poker and jabbed at them violently.

It was only then Madeline thought to move. "Don't!" she cried, and dived for the sheaf of papers. His poker narrowly missed her hand, but she managed to snatch them off the coals before more than just the edges had sparked.

Lucien caught her by the arms and yanked her backward, reaching for the papers. Madeline yelped but held them out of his reach, turning and freeing herself to scramble away. He came after her. "You have no right!" he cried, grabbing her again.

He was right, of course—Madeline had stormed into his room and invaded his privacy—but there had been something in that small glimpse of the music that she longed to know better. It seemed horridly important that she not let him burn the work. He held her hard against him, her back to his chest, his left arm a vise around her ribs, his right reaching for the sheaf of papers in her hand. They struggled silently, Madeline holding it just out of his reach, grunting as she struggled against him.

"Let me go," she cried.

"Give me the papers."

She suddenly became aware of the intimacy of the embrace. He held her so tightly his breath was moist with heat on her neck, and his arm was close beneath her breasts, lifting them even higher into the low square of her bodice. Against the length of her, his body was hard, muscular, uncompromising. Her breath caught.

He heard it and stilled. "Why did you come here this morning, Madeline?" He yanked her closer, and with a savageness that frightened her, bit her neck lightly. "Did you decide after all to come to me?" His hand lifted dangerously close to her breast, and with a single, violent move, he turned her, slamming her against the wall behind them. It jarred her teeth.

Lucien leaned over her, intentionally close, his breath coming faster than normal. So close she could smell him—port and spice and fire. "Did you come for a taste of me?"

She stared up at him, at the burning of his eyes, darkened now with violence. His mouth did not have any softness about it, and there was only heat and darkness and anger in him. She lowered her eyes. "No." She shoved the papers into his chest, afraid of him. "Take your notes and burn them. I don't care."

He snagged her when she would have ducked under his arm. "No, you don't," he said silkily. "You came to my web, little fly, and now I'm going to eat you." He half dragged her to the fire. "First, we'll let these burn."

She yanked, but he held her easily with one arm. It was the first time she realized how much larger he was than she. The lingering sensation of his teeth scraping over the flesh of her neck still burned, and it burned lower, too, with a wildness she did not like. Her heart was pounding with both fear and hunger.

Desperately, she knew she had to flee. When he let down his guard a little, she let her weight drop all at once. The sudden dead weight pulled him off balance. He dropped the poker with a clang against the flagstone hearth. At the same moment, a flash of light burst as the paper caught fire. Madeline and Lucien tumbled to the floor. He fell on top of her, pinning her. The naked flesh of his chest, exposed by the unbuttoned shirt, touched lightly the swell of her breasts over her bodice, and Madeline let go of an involuntary gasp at the sensation.

He held her hands above her head. "Are you one of those women who need to think the decision is beyond them? Do you need to feel forced to avoid responsibility?" Thick disdain dripped from his mouth. "Are you Clarissa, needing to be ravished?"

"No!" she spat out.

Her head spun dizzily, and her body was alive with sensations she didn't dream existed—a pounding in her chest and in the tips of her breasts. Her mouth felt empty, as if it needed filling.

"I don't like it this way," he said. "I don't like playing

the forceful game at all. But a kiss I can steal without guilt."

Madeline tried to turn her head, but he caught her chin in his hand and put his mouth over hers. At the first heated touch of his lips, she knew she was lost.

It was a long, slow, deep kiss that was nothing like the dry whisper of Charles's mouth. Lucien's kiss was wet, and not neat, and sinuous. It filled the empty places of her mouth, made the pounding in her breasts and belly ache more fiercely. It stole her breath.

Wild panic grew in her, and he yet held her tightly; she couldn't move. She wanted to arch against him, wanted that hot, too wet, mouth against other parts of her, and the knowledge was damning. With a cry, she turned her head away.

Undaunted, Lucien availed himself of her neck, supping at the mark he'd made with his teeth—and Madeline shuddered. He touched his tongue to the lobe of her ear, and licked her jaw with slow, excruciating intent. Madeline trembled violently but managed to hold herself rigid.

"Let me go," she said, balling her hands into fists. Her voice was raw and deep, unlike her ordinary daily voice, and it shamed her. "Please," she whispered. "Please, let me go."

Abruptly, he did just that. One moment, he was hot and hard against her, the next he was just not there, and Madeline lay on the floor, her clothes akimbo, her cap gone. With embarrassment on her face, she rolled to her side and got to her feet, smoothing her clothes.

Lucien stalked over to the window, putting his back to her. "Leave me, please," he said roughly. His hair, too, had come undone in their struggle. Wisps clung to his face, which was damp with sweat. He wiped a forearm over it. "Leave me, Madeline, I'm warning you," he said again, still without looking at her.

With as much dignity as she could muster, Madeline picked up her cap from the floor. "I invaded your privacy," she said unsteadily, "and for that, I apologize." She lifted her chin. "However, I came to ask you if you'll come down and send away the men who came to the door this morning to fix the greenhouse."

"No."

"Pardon me?"

He turned, his face unreadable. "I said, no. I'll not send them away. You need the help, do you not? Isn't it for Whitethorn you marry?"

"Well, yes, but—"

"I only free you, my lady, to do as you wish, not as you must. Is that too much a quandary for you?"

"Such a noble speech," she said sharply. "It is not for Whitethorn you do it, but to have your way, so I am in your debt. I dislike that feeling."

"Is it so much simpler to be indebted for life, than for a single night?"

Madeline frowned, feeling swayed by his reasoning. "Better honor than disgrace."

"Is it?" he said, and his voice was thick with cynicism. "I do wonder about that."

"Having tasted honor, I know which I prefer."

"Ah, but there is much freedom in disgrace."

"I fervently hope I never taste such freedom." The primness in her voice annoyed her. "Come—send your men away."

"They've already been paid," he said. "Consider it a gift. I'll count the kiss I stole just now as payment enough, unless you choose to pay more." He looked at her, full on, deeply and intensely.

It took extreme effort to say calmly, "There will be no further payments, Lord Esher. I am going to marry Charles, and that is that. You waste your time."

He did not argue. "Very well, then. Consider it my pleasure, a tribute to the gardens that were destroyed in my youth."

Madeline nodded. "Thank you."

He did not reply, only stared out the window with a rigidness on his spine, the paper on the hearth smoking in black curls.

She fled, running down the hall as if a devil nipped at her heels. There was no clear thought in her mind at first, only a sense that she desired sanctuary. The maze—no, it was marred with Lord Esher's laconic teasing yesterday. And in the greenhouse, she'd think of his thumb on her lips, and in the rose garden, the tearing petals of the flowers against his mouth.

Even the library—that dim and musty retreat—was marred with his presence and the stain of sex.

Oh, how had he so thoroughly invaded all her private places so quickly? There were none left where she might sit in silence and peace and consider what was to be done.

Business first. She stopped outside and told the men to go ahead with their work. She gave explicit directions to the headman and let him know she would check on him in an hour—men were notorious for ignoring the orders of women.

As she came back toward the house, she saw Juliette and Anna on the veranda, having breakfast below their parasols. They were dressed for riding.

Juliette called out to her, "Madeline, join us, darling!"

Reluctantly, Madeline wandered toward them. Jonathan, coming out from a side door, joined her. He, too, was dressed for riding.

What a handsome man he was, she thought, vaguely; though that blond noble look was not at all to her tastes, his strong nose and sensual mouth were quite appealing. "Good morning, Lady Madeline," he said cheerfully, offering his arm. "Are you not going to join our ride?"

"I'd not heard anything of it."

"Oh, yes," Juliette cried. "We're going to escape all the workmen's hammering. I've had a picnic prepared. You must come, my dear."

Madeline shrugged. Lord Esher was nowhere in sight and had showed no signs of going anywhere when she was in his room a few minutes ago. She'd rather ride with this trio than be here in the house with him lurking about. "I'll go change."

"My dear," Juliette said, standing to come around the table. "What have you done to your neck?"

A bolt of guilt slammed through Madeline, but she managed to frown—convincingly, she hoped—and touched the front of her throat. "My neck?"

Unerringly, Juliette brushed her closed fan over the exact place where Lucien's mouth had fallen only a little while ago. "Here."

Madeline affected guilelessness, brushing the back of her fingers over the place. "I've no idea. It doesn't hurt."

"Perhaps your marquess was more than a little enthusiastic in saying good-bye yesterday, hmm?" Jonathan suggested lazily.

Now Madeline blushed, for it was plain by the bright, knowing look in his eye that he knew exactly where she'd received the mark on her neck—and she remembered his room was next to Lord Esher's. She had presumed he was with Juliette, but perhaps she was wrong. "Charles is a gentleman," she said softly.

"But even gentlemen can be passionate." Juliette beamed. "Is it he who sent all these workmen, my sweet?"

Madeline shot a quick look at Jonathan, who spread jam on a thick slice of bread. His eyes glittered. "Yes," Madeline said. "He sent quite a kind note, as well, and said he will return to Whitethorn in a fortnight."

"Wonderful!" Juliette kissed her head. "Go and change and we'll go riding."

To her dismay, Lord Esher joined them after all. When Madeline had changed and met the little party at the stables, he was already mounted and ready, looking off into the distance with an expression of boredom as Juliette and the servant woman dithered over how much wine to take. He spared a single glance for Madeline when she came up, but she ignored him, self-consciously adjusting the gauzy fichu she wore to cover the pinkish bruise he'd left on her neck.

Lady Heath was the one who commented on Lucien's appearance. "My goodness, Lord Esher," she said lightly, "did you spend the night brawling?"

Lucien lifted his eyes blandly. "After a fashion."

Madeline saw that he'd changed his clothes, but they were carelessly donned—his waistcoat loose, the neck of his shirt open, the lace jabot hanging carelessly to either side. His jaw was unshaved.

"Leave him alone, Anna," Jonathan said lightly, riding flirtatiously nearby her. "He fancies himself a doomed sort. The ladies in London find it ever so appealing to try to save him."

"I can well imagine," Juliette said in warm approval, staring boldly at Lucien.

He ignored her.

Brightly, Juliette said, "Shall we?"

They rode toward a hilly ground covered with thick woods, where small meadows opened here and there. The ruins of a castle crowned a hill a few miles ride from the house, and Madeline knew they would picnic there. It was one of Juliette's favorite places.

Juliette rode in the lead. She was an accomplished rider, and her mount displayed her treasures to perfection, her good posture, her abundant bosom, her glorious skin. Just behind her rode Jonathan and Lady Heath, riding two by two. There was, Madeline thought, a considerable flirtation going on there, though she couldn't decide which of them had instigated it.

Lord Esher rode beside Madeline without speaking. In spite of what Jonathan had said about his donning a doomed attitude for effect, she thought he looked rather grim. "Are you feeling better today?" she asked politely.

"Better?" He lifted a shoulder. "Oh, yes. Yes, whatever it is that's in that potion of your cook's is quite effective."

"Probably opium!" Madeline laughed. "She's a great believer in numbing all pain."

Juliette looked over her shoulder at the sound of Madeline's laughter. "Oh, Lucien," she called, "do ride up here and keep me company."

As if bored beyond expression, he nodded at her. "Excuse me." He rode up next to Juliette and murmured something that made Juliette laugh throatily. A sharp, hot pluck of jealously ripped through Madeline's stomach.

And that in itself was alarming. Jealous? What did she think to gain from Lucien Harrow besides sorrow and disgrace?

There is great freedom in disgrace, he'd said this morning. And as he rode in the bright morning, his hair gleaming down his back, his jaw unshaven because it suited him, his disdain for all of them thick as honey, she thought she caught a glimmer of what that meant.

It frightened her that she could even begin to understand it.

Lucien stuck close to Juliette all afternoon, laughing at her jokes, teasing her with bawdy double entendres. She laughed a bit too brightly, her eyes, though she tried not to show it, stayed on Jonathan and Anna, drinking a wine from the bottle as they viewed the world from a high perch on the tower wall.

Madeline viewed them all with a cynicism Lucien would not have expected from her, but then, he supposed she'd grown up with such love affairs brewing around her all the time. After they ate, she ambled off by herself, and he glimpsed her through the openings in the broken castle walls, picking wildflowers. She shed her cap, and her hair streamed over her shoulders in disarray, down her back and to her hips. She thought herself unobserved, he knew. Once he saw her absently touch the side of her neck, the place where he'd bruised her.

She didn't know that she looked as if she'd been well and thoroughly loved, her lips bruised and swollen, her jaw scraped by his beard, that mark, red and raw, on her neck. He couldn't look at her without getting hard, and avoided her altogether in Juliette's presence. She'd see what he tried to hide, and the game would be finished.

Anna and Jonathan disappeared, and Juliette grew fretful, though she tried not to show it. Brightly, she suggested to Lucien that they walk along one of the paths that led into the forest from the castle. Under other circumstances, Lucien might have been somewhat leery of the invitation, for he had no wish to bed her, and he might have suspected some sort of ploy in that direction. Today, however, he knew she sought Jonathan and Anna, to thwart whatever dalliance they planned.

"What about Madeline?" he asked.

"Oh, she's out there dreaming of her marquess. They're going to be married, you know."

"Ah!" he replied dryly. "No, I hadn't heard. How wonderful for them."

"It's plain you share my love of marriage," she countered, ducking under the low arm of a tree. "But your father must be nearing his seventieth birthday. He must be concerned that you'll need to produce an heir?"

Lucien smiled bitterly. "Oh, yes, it worries him greatly. And thus I avoid the very thing he wishes."

"You sound as if you hate him."

"Hate is too strong—it implies some level of concern. I take joy in shaming my father, but I do not hate him. He's below my notice."

"But why?"

Lucien lifted his chin, thinking of the beatings his father had administered when Lucien returned from Vienna. "It's completely mutual, I assure you. I am a great and terrible disappointment to him, as he is to me. If I were not his only son, he'd take pleasure in disinheriting me." He smiled. "Unfortunately for my father, the estate would pass to my cousin, and my father hates him more than me."

There came through the trees a sound of high feminine laughter. Juliette went rigid beside him, and he saw by the movement of her bosom that she was extremely agitated. He took her arm. "Perhaps we should return."

She hesitated. The voices came closer. With a quick movement, Juliette shoved Lucien against a tree and kissed him.

It infuriated Lucien, and he shoved her away before Lady Heath and Jonathan broke through on the path. He narrowed his eyes at her, seeing her misery as Jonathan entered the tiny clearing. Her eyes leaped upon him as if he were some magnificent feast and she only an orphan, peering in the windows. For one brief instant, Lucien felt sorry for her.

The moment passed, for on Jonathan's face was a rare expression of rage. He attempted to hide it, but a thin white line edged his nostrils and his pale eyes went nearly black with enlarged pupils. A hard red flush burned on his cheeks. Lucien regarded him steadily, hoping he'd see what was plain—it was only a ploy to make him jealous, and meant nothing.

Instead, Jonathan turned to Juliette and took her hand summarily. "You'll excuse us," he said, and stormed into the underbrush, dragging Juliette behind him.

In the stunned silence they left behind, Anna lifted an eyebrow in Lucien's direction. "Where have I seen that mad jealousy before?"

Lucien didn't even spare her a glance. Without a word, he turned and went back the way he'd come.

Juliette stumbled behind Jonathan, a little frightened but much more aroused by his anger. He nearly yanked her arm from her socket, and she stumbled twice when her skirts tangled in the branches. By the time he stopped, she was aflush and ready for him. She smiled up at him, lifting her arms to put them around his neck. "Did you like that?" she said.

"Yes," he said on a growl, and kissed her, hard, his lips punishing. But instead of taking her against the tree as she had anticipated, he only lifted his head. "Juliette, why do you toy with me this way? Why must you torture me to find any pleasure in the act?"

"That is not so!" she protested.

"No?" He lifted his head, and light cascaded like a gilded waterfall over the beautiful planes of his face. "Then come to me tonight as an ordinary woman. Or let me come to you as a husband might come to a wife. No ropes or drunkenness or torn clothing—just the pair of us, naked and alone with each other."

Her knees softened at the notion, at the visual picture that assailed her just then, of Jonathan naked against the moonlight in her room. She shoved him away. "I don't wish to make love like a wife."

He moved away from her, his face aloof. "Then fuck someone else."

He turned to go.

"Wait!" she said. "All right! I'll come to you like a wife then, if you take me now."

Slowly, he shook his head. A tiny, knowing smile touched his mouth. "Not now," he said. "Later. Come to me as a wife."

And Juliette, who'd never done a man's bidding in her life, nodded slowly, helplessly.

She hoped she was not falling in love. That could be rather messy.

10

Now cold as ice am I, now hot as fire,
I dare not tell myself my own desire.
—John Dryden

Madeline returned to the castle ruins to find everyone else gone. Not that she minded. The cross-currents between them were like thick, slow-moving tides, pulling this way and pushing that. Jonathan and Juliette seemed to delight in strange tortures of the other, but now was added the knife-edged sharpness of Lady Heath's tongue, which was, as often as not, directed at Lucien.

The tumbles of stone on the hilltop were the ruins of a twelfth-century Norman castle. All that remained were two walls and a tower. Within the tower was a circling staircase that was yet strong and sturdy, and rose to its original height, perfectly intact. A single wall, crumbling and dotted with former embrasures at various floor levels, led up to it on one side. On the other side, the wall had long since fallen. Madeline ducked into the cool shade of the tower and climbed the stairs to the top. The wood floor had rotted, but there was a thick rim of stone on the topmost floor, wide enough for a body to stand and admire the surrounding landscape. As a girl, she'd often ridden here to play princess and knight. The memory made her smile.

Gingerly, she walked the stone rim toward her destination, a stone seat carved from the wall, made smooth by centuries of rear ends. It looked over the surrounding meadows and forests, to the thin bluish ribbon of the river. Softly rolling ground undulated back toward Whitethorn. Madeline breathed deeply, admiring the view, thinking of all the animals housed in those trees. The sun was warm on her face, the world silent, though she could hear the distant echo of laughter. Far below, the horses were hobbled in the dappled shade beneath a copse of trees. Their tails switched lazily at stray flies.

A whistle broke the stillness and Madeline glanced over her shoulder, disappointed that her private moment should come so quickly to an end. Her heart gave a quick, hard beat, for it was Lord Esher coming out of the trees, looking more rakish than ever.

As he neared the ruins, he lifted a hand at her. Madeline waved back. He stopped at the foot of the long wall that sloped upward to the tower, its topmost edge a capricious straight line high in the air. Lucien eyed it, then shed his coat and leaped nimbly atop the lower edge of the slope.

Madeline leaned over the embrasure. "Lord Esher, take the stairs in the tower. That wall is rotten."

A crooked half-smile lit his face. He found his balance on the wall. Slowly he walked toward her. Most of it was a gentle slope upward, but the few yards were a hard climb—Madeline knew, for she'd done it as a girl and been petrified—over jutting stone held in place only by crumbling mortar.

Lucien tackled it boldly, seeking purchase with his hands and feet. Once he stepped hard on a stone and it crumbled, nearly taking him with it. It skittered out from under him and his body swung out with it. Only sheer luck gave him help. At the last possible instant, he caught hold of stone yet firmly mortared in the wall.

Madeline slapped her hands over her mouth to catch her scream. His feet dangled in the open air, his body tilting at a mad angle as he looked for a better grip with his hands. The stone that had come loose hit the piles of crumbled rock below with a thudding crash, and Madeline gave a sharp cry. Briefly and cowardly, she closed her eyes.

When she opened them again, he had somehow managed to regain his balance, but rather than retreat, Lucien simply steadied himself and moved forward once more. With her breath held back in her throat, Madeline watched as he topped the highest portion of the wall, standing alone sixty feet in the air. He rested there a moment, gazing around him in obvious enjoyment. "It's rather magnificent," he said to Madeline.

"Yes." She gripped the edge of the wall. Small dusty rocks bit her fingers. "Do take care! I wish you'd climbed the stairs."

He seemed not at all bothered by the great height, but sat comfortably on the broad wall, feet dangling down on either side. He looked at her, his eyes a hard bright blue in the sunny afternoon. "Have you never climbed the wall?"

"Only as a child, but I didn't truly understand the danger then."

"But 'tis the danger that makes it so thrilling." With a sudden, graceful move, he shifted his feet and cautiously, confidently stood.

A hard pain stabbed her. She covered her mouth with both her hands to keep from gasping or screaming.

"Shall I run to you?" he said, that crooked smile devilish.

She shook her head, unable to speak.

"Perhaps walking is enough," he said agreeably. There were perhaps three yards of high wall between him and Madeline. He stood a moment with his arms outstretched, his chin up as if scenting the air. A slight breeze ruffled his full white shirtsleeves and lifted a lock of dark hair on his shoulder. His feet were one in front of the other in the scuffed boots.

And he began to walk, swinging one foot out and around and putting it down, and then the next, and the next, just so. Madeline's chest hurt with watching, but she could not stop. She feared with some illogical part of herself that she must keep her eyes on him or he'd fall to his death.

One booted toe kicked a loose stone, and it dislodged without a sound, breaking free to tumble down, down, down. The sudden movement threw Lord Esher off balance and he suddenly squatted, grabbing the wall for a moment. There still was no fear on his face, only a wild light of joy. He stood up again and lightly dance-walked the rest of the way to the tower. He leaped nimbly to the stone ledge and walked toward her.

"I am the prince of Gobbledegook," he said with a bow, "come to save you from the evil king, my dear princess." His eyes glittered.

Madeline stared at him. How had he known the game she played so often here as a girl? "You might have been killed," she said.

"Yes, I might have been." Slowly, he walked around the stone circle. "But one must do what one must to save endangered princesses."

Reluctantly, Madeline smiled.

"Ah, there it is!"

"What?"

He stopped a foot from her, too close, really, but Madeline didn't move away. Her heart beat hard. "Your smile, Madeline. You have such mischief in your smile."

"Must you ever be on the prowl?" she asked in exasperation. "I'd not mind your company nearly so much if it weren't plain you only speak to a woman in order to bed her."

Lucien laughed. "Is that so? Do I thus speak to your stepmother? Or Lady Heath?"

"I assume you never count any woman outside your realm." Madeline turned away from him to lean her elbows on the wall. "It is rather tiresome. However, I somehow have a tendency to like you in spite of it."

"Do you now?" He, too, leaned on the wall, and Madeline didn't dare look at him. He kept his distance, but she felt his heat and presence brushing her, bumping her as distinctly as if he were pressed against her. "Then if I am your friend, I have a better chance of bedding you, am I correct?"

She gave an exaggerated sigh and shook her head. "You'll not bed me at all, no matter what technique you pull from your arsenal, Lord Esher. My heart belongs to the marquess."

"Oh, good." He settled on the wall. "I admit that gives some relief. It's a burden to bed every woman one meets, but what is a rake to do?"

Madeline laughed at the twinkle in his eye and shook her head. "I hereby grant you leave to consider me a lost cause, and therefore a friend only."

"Graciously granted." The aerial view seemed to strike him again. "This is magnificent. Who lived in the castle?"

"I'm sure there are records, but I don't know. The first earl of Whitethorn was given the land by Queen Elizabeth, in return for some service he performed, and the castle was already in ruins by then."

Meditatively, he gazed at it. "Odd that entire generations lived and ate here, danced and dreamed and"—he shot a glance at her—"made love here. And now they're lost to all of time."

"Like Pompeii," she said quietly. "You never did say what bothered you about it."

"The same things you mentioned. The suddenness, the completeness. It seems unfair that all at once, all their lives were gone. So fast, so utterly without hope of escape." His voice deepened. "Why does God, if he is truly in his heaven, allow such things to befall people?"

Pierced, she looked at him, and saw anew the haggardness at his jaw, the carelessness of his dress. In her mind's eye she saw his wild walk along the wall, as if he dared death to snatch him. "Perhaps it is too large an answer for our small minds to grasp," she suggested.

Shaking his head, his eyes trained on the treetops, he said, "It never bothered you, this castle?"

"Oh, yes, it did." She rubbed a hand along the wall, moving dust and grit. "It brought on the melancholia deeply when I was about twelve or fourteen. I'd come here and think of my mother and weep." She smiled, quickly, remembering. "Young girls are often melodramatic. If there had been no castle, I'd have wept over something else."

"Do you remember your mother?"

"Not at all. There is a painting of her on the wall in the library. She's beautiful and delicate, and it's plain she would not have lasted long whether I was born or not."

"She died in childbirth?"

"Yes. And they thought I would die, too, but I did not. I believe that is why my father married Juliette so quickly after—it was quite the scandal, but he had need of a woman to raise his daughter."

"Scandal," he said mildly. "My father scandalized his set with a marriage, as well. Married a Russian noblewoman twenty years his junior."

"Juliette was not even a foreign noblewoman, but a dressmaker's daughter."

"So I have heard." He turned toward her. "She has been good to you, though."

Madeline nodded. "Yes."

A bank of clouds suddenly obscured the sun, and Madeline looked up in surprise to see a storm was moving in. "Heavens!" she said. "We'd best get back."

"Yes." He straightened and turned away from her.

"Where are you going?" Madeline asked. "The stairs are this way."

His devilish smile flashed. "Back the way I came."

Impulsively, she caught his arm. "Please do not. I do not think I can bear to watch again."

"So do not watch."

"Please," she repeated.

His smile deepened. "It seems we must bargain again."

"No," she said, taking her hand from his arm and stepping backward. She rubbed her fingers against her side, trying to remove the impression of his flesh below the fabric of his shirt. "I am finished with bargains."

"All right, then. Back down the wall I go."

Madeline let him walk away, and gripped her hands together. He paused at the edge of the wall, as if to give her one more chance, and she simply stared at him.

But then he leaped to the top of the tower wall and her heart stuck hard in her throat and she was moving before she knew she would, rushing toward him. "Lucien, no! Please don't do it again, I can't bear it!"

He turned, so quickly he nearly overbalanced. For a long, agonizing second, he hung between earth and sky, wavering over a vast drop to a painful and horrible death. Then, like a cat, he found his balance and jumped nimbly to the stone ledge within the tower. A blazingly satisfied smile touched his mouth, and even reached his eyes. "You'll bargain with a rake, then?"

"Depending upon what he asks."

"Oh, it is a small, small price I ask, Madeline—I may call you Madeline, may I not, since you have used my Christian name?"

She blushed but held her ground.

He stepped close, so close his body nearly touched hers. Only a small outstretched hand could have fit between them. Madeline had to tip her head backward to look at his face. "What I wish, Madeline," he said slowly, touching her neck where the mark was, letting her know he'd seen it, "is one kiss, of my choosing, redeemable whenever I wish it."

"I—"

"One kiss, Madeline, that's all, I swear it."

She stared at him, sensing some trick. But the narcotic spell of his nearness enveloped her suddenly and she could not quite catch her breath. Her eyes seemed to focus, all without her help, upon his mouth—firm for so dissolute a man, perfectly cut, and as she knew, capable of giving great pleasure. "Just one kiss?" she asked.

"Yes." He moved his finger down her throat in a slow line. "One kiss. And you needn't give it to me now."

"You mustn't redeem it in front of other people."

He smiled, and his hand slipped from her neck, over her shoulder, along her arm, perilously close to her breast. "Is that your only requirement, that no one must see me take it?"

Madeline roused herself to think for a moment—should she require anything else? "Yes, that's all. It must be done privately."

"Very well," he said, "I will not walk the wall in return for a kiss from you at a time of my choosing, and in private."

"Yes."

"Shall we go down the stairs, then?"

A whistle again broke the quiet day. Madeline looked down and saw Anna, Juliette, and Jonathan grouped at the foot of the wall, staring up at them. Juliette did not look pleased.

"Let's get down the stairs," Madeline said abruptly. "It's going to storm."

"Yes," he said lazily, "I believe it will."

*   *   *

Late that night, after all had retired, Juliette dismissed the maid who had helped her undress and tended her clothes. Alone, she stripped away her undergarments until she stood nude in the cool room. Rain fell outside the windows, pattering and clean. Juliette washed carefully and applied scent to her elbows, knees, breasts, and ears. A little rubbed along her upper lip, a dab on her thighs and in her navel.

She donned an elegant blue dressing gown, trimmed with lace, and patted her hair, which was perfectly arranged from the evening. She stepped back from the mirror to admire herself. Oh, yes—he'd not resist this easily.

Into the silent corridor she crept, her bare feet making no noise. She passed Madeline's door, and Anna's, and the spare guest room now standing empty and silent in the midnight light.

At Jonathan's room, she paused, aching, wondering if he still waited for her—and if he did, what he wore. Anything? In her mind's eye, she saw his sleek, beautiful body washed in moonlight. A wave of longing so wild it took her breath swept through her. For a long, fiercely painful moment, she wavered. If she did not go to him tonight, it might well be over between them. If he learned what she was doing instead, it would be over.

She swallowed, thinking of Madeline and Lord Esher on that castle tower this afternoon. Madeline was quite massively smitten. Lucien Harrow would have her in his bed in no time unless Juliette took pains to prevent it.

Purposefully, she moved down the hallway and stopped at Lord Esher's door. She scratched the panels. There was no immediate answer, and she scratched again.

All at once, the door was flung open, and a very drunk Lucien Harrow glared at her. "What is it?" he said. Then he saw what Juliette intended, a long bare length of thigh, poking out from between the folds of her gown, and a generous section of unharnessed breast almost carelessly showing. A dark look flooded his eyes, an expression measuring and furious and calculating at once.

Dryly, he said, "What have we here?"

"Whatever you like." She smiled her best smile and smoothed the silk over her body suggestively. "Might I come in and share your port?"

He was shirtless, his hair loose, and Juliette didn't wonder that Madeline was smitten. He wasn't Jonathan of course, but he was beautiful nonetheless. And the darkness in him was exciting. Lazily, he leaned on the doorjamb, bottle in hand, and let his gaze rove over her. Juliette inclined her head, but a flush began on her neck; she could feel it creeping up her face, to her ears. Men did not consider her a bawdy in a whorehouse, but leaped upon her as if she were the choicest morsel at a feast. His slow reluctance shamed her deeply.

"It isn't that I wouldn't like to," he said at last, "but I value my friendship with Jonathan."

Just then, a door opened down the hallway, and Jonathan stepped into the dim corridor. Juliette bolted forward, shoving herself between Lucien and the doorway, scraping her arm rather viciously as she did so. She plastered her back against the inner wall and listened to see if she could tell where her love had gone. Silence echoed back.

"Where did he go?" Juliette whispered.

"Downstairs, I believe," he said. "You've time to get back to your room, I'd guess, or into his—or even to the library."

He'd seemed very drunk a moment ago, but Juliette thought he saw a lot for one as inebriated as he seemed. She looked at him steadily. "Thank you for not giving me away."

He took a breath and lifted the bottle, carelessly gulping it before he answered. "If things were different, Juliette, I'd like nothing better than to devour that beautiful body of yours." He pursed his lips. "But you only offer yourself as sacrifice to save your virgin child, and I find that rather unarousing."

The heat in her neck crept higher. "Am I so transparent? I thought myself a good deal better courtesan than that."

Lucien shook his head. "You needn't worry about Madeline, Juliette. She is only a child, and although she is charming, I have no wish to bed a trembling virgin." He examined the bottle in his hand a moment. "I'd rather have Anna, I think. It would be a pleasant diversion after so many years."

Juliette, flooded with a sense of relief, moved forward and took his hands. "Thank you."

His eyes, dark pools in his haggard face, were unreadable. "Think nothing of it." He gave her a little shove. "Now go find Jonathan before I am tempted to take you myself."

With a brilliant smile, Juliette did just that. Grabbing her wrapper close, she ran for Jonathan's room.

11

In sweet music is such art,
Killing care and grief of heart.
—John Fletcher

For several days, the workmen hammered and sawed and made noises all the day. Madeline flung her attentions into repairing the damage to her garden, thankful in spite of herself for the help of the men hired by Lord Esher.

To her surprise, Lucien even gave help himself, seeming to take great delight in the tasks she assigned him. He worked harder than she would have expected, and came back to the house in the afternoons as covered with grime as Madeline or any of the workmen.

She could not help contemplating the motives of both Lord Esher and the marquess. One wished to marry her—and sent men to fix the windows of the house. The other wanted to seduce her—and sent men to mend her greenhouse, which, while not practical, was the heart of her life. At low moments, Madeline wished Charles had been the one to make the extravagant gesture.

Foolish. What point to repairing the greenhouse unless the house windows had been replaced first? Charles, even more kind in the long run, had provided the necessities, so that Madeline might use whatever other funds she could muster to fix the greenhouse and gardens. Lucien, on the other hand—

Annoyed, she forced herself to stop allowing the squirrels to chase themselves in her brain. One man was practical, the other was pleasure seeking. Not such a difficult tangle.

In spite of everything, she did find herself liking Lucien better for the fact that he was willing to come out to the garden, morning after morning, to work. His hands got as torn and scratched as Madeline's own, and it would not be hard to mistake him from afar as a village farmhand. The fine cut of clothes gave him away up close, of course, but he worked as hard as anyone else. The men liked him as well, for he made jests all the day, his enormous charm drawing them in, his good-natured teasing easing their hard labor.

One morning Madeline commented, "I believe you really enjoy yourself out here, Lord Esher."

He grunted, struggling with a shovel in a stubborn bit of ground. "Yes, I think you're right. Perhaps I've missed my calling."

"It isn't too late. Surely you have estates to tend—perhaps you could use your newfound talent on them."

"There are no beautiful young ladies to seduce at my estates," he countered quickly, a devilish shine in his blue eye. For an instant, Madeline thought that at last he would claim the kiss he held in hock from her, that it would be over with and she could stop wondering when it would come.

Instead, he only put his attention back on the shovel and Madeline drifted away, feeling slightly vexed. She wanted the kiss done. She hated it hanging over her this way. When they were not working together in the garden, she went to great lengths to avoid him entirely.

A new party of guests had come in from London. Madeline finally realized Juliette's genius at work once again. It was far less expensive to maintain this country estate and life, even with the entertaining, than it was to live in London and indulge the round of parties and dances and salons they would be expected to attend and present. By snagging the rather juicy prize of London's most notorious rake in the body of Lucien Harrow, presently under a cloud of great speculation, Juliette had assured a fashionable flow of guests eager to be considered as bon ton as anyone else.

While she found the London set trying—their idle chatter boring, their simpering and flirting coy and unsettling—she was thankful that Lucien was so very popular with them, for it gave him less time to pursue her.

For pursue he did. Relentlessly, cheerfully. And Madeline, drawn to him for reasons she could not name, resisted by hiding herself away.

And for once, Madeline could look for no help from Juliette, for it was plain to all the woman had fallen in love. She and Jonathan were the buzz of the day. They did not leave each other's side, there was a flushed and dewy glow to them, and they disappeared at regular intervals. It was almost embarrassing, Madeline thought, and she heard the mean, pointed comments about the disparity in their ages. Sooner or later, Jonathan would tire of his aging mistress and move along to more supple prey, they said, and fretted over what such an end to the thing would do to the countess.

It was not Madeline's concern. She thought her stepmother was a good sight more resilient than the catty lords and ladies did, for one thing. And Juliette was known to do exactly as she pleased.

No, Madeline didn't worry about Juliette. She worried about herself, and the omnipresent seductive presence of Lucien Harrow. She threw herself into her garden, and prayed Charles would finish his business and return to Whitethorn.

The sooner, the better.

For the most part, the weather cooperated with the workmen, but toward the end of a fortnight, a spell of rainy, windy weather set in. The workmen could not come in from the village; the guests could not go out and ride or walk, but were trapped in the rooms of the house trying to entertain themselves. Cards and books passed the long afternoons and evenings, with one or another often taking up instruments to play and sing. Juliette had a particularly strong voice, and entertained them with bawdy ballads and long, sorrowful folk songs.

The Thursday marking three weeks after the big hailstorm, Madeline was restless by noon. The drinking had gone late the night before, and few were about yet, nor would they be. Often the guests kept to their rooms almost till dinner, nursing hangovers and applying beauty treatments—perhaps even making love; Madeline didn't know.

The only other person prowling about was Lucien. As unsettled as she felt, Madeline didn't want to be anywhere close to him. He was as out of sorts as the rest, and she knew he almost never slept. He went from drinking late in the salon to pacing about in the maze and gardens, to working in the mornings with her. The lack of rest showed in his face a little, though it made him no less handsome—he looked even more dangerously beautiful, as if the frivolous had been whittled from his face.

To escape him, escape her growing attraction to him, Madeline spent long hours in the music room. He never followed her there. Protected by music, Madeline found a measure of peace.

The Marais concerto she was working on defied her every attempt to get it right. There was a trill of notes through the middle she never quite mastered no matter how she practiced, and today she took up the instrument with the intent of doing so. Surely if she just did not give up, the errors would smooth away—she'd be able to understand just what she was doing incorrectly.

She stood before the long, Elizabethan windows of the room, watching a soft gray drizzle wash the landscape clean. The verdant carpets of lush grass were almost painfully bright to look upon, and in combination with the gray sky, somehow poignant. Madeline sighed and tried her piece again, listening carefully for the mistakes she so often repeated. She played it from the beginning, straight through, then practiced the middle section that was proving so frustrating, then started over from the top again.

She was deeply engrossed when a voice came from the doorway, rough and unexpected, startling her. "That is not a flat there."

She turned to find Lucien coming into the room, looking tired but otherwise magnificent. His face was cleanly shaved, his hair brushed into a neat, glossy queue tied with black ribbon. His coat was freshly brushed, his boots polished to a high gleam. In the grayish light, his blue eyes blazed.

"Pardon me?" she said.

He crossed the room and took the bow out of her hand, then the violin. Not a "May I" or "Do you mind," just summarily took it. Madeline frowned at him.

Lucien caught the frown. "It's been weeks you've been massacring this piece, and I never liked it to begin with. If I show you where you're going wrong, perhaps you'll move on, hmm?"

She crossed her arms. "Or perhaps I'll play it all the more."

"No, you won't." He smiled. "I know musicians better than that—no one is ever content to stay with the one they've mastered."

"But as you're too well aware, I'm no musician."

"You're fair," he said. "Unschooled rather than untalented, really. You must come by it from Juliette."

He touched the bow to the strings, lightly, testing, and made an adjustment to the tuning. Rainy light came through the windows, bathing him in translucent, silent beauty. There was in the way he held the instrument an exquisite grace, even with the scratches and marks the work in the garden had left on his hands. His fingers were long and elegant, and perfectly sure. Experimentally, he bowed again, adjusting, frowning, adjusting again. Madeline could barely distinguish the small changes he made.

When it was tuned to his satisfaction, he looked at her. "This is what you're playing," he said, and illustrated, exactly, down to the sour notes she couldn't quite cure. "Do you hear?"

"Yes, of course." It embarrassed her a little, but she had been trying to master it for a long time and was weary of it. She shifted, putting her hands on her hips. "How do I fix it?"

He smiled. "So simple." He showed her, and the change was only a few minor things, adjustments that cleaned and clarified. "You're not quite hitting the notes through this section. Slow down a little. Your left hand is moving too quickly for your right." He played, illustrating, and it was perfect. "You try."

Madeline accepted the instrument back from him and played the song hesitantly, then a little more surely. "Like that?"

He nodded, but she could tell by the hard look around his mouth it was still not quite right. He moved suddenly, and came behind her, putting his hand under her left elbow, another on her spine. "Straighten your back," he said.

She did so, all too vividly aware of his touch. One hand touched her shoulder, and her neck. "Posture is everything with a violin," he said.

Madeline wondered if he heard the deepening of the Russian sound to his voice when he spoke of music, and it gave her a secret pleasure to notice. Probably when he'd spoken of music or been taught, it had not been in English. Knowing something so quietly intimate about him made her relax a little. Madeline let her body straighten, pull into the lines it should have for this.

"Good," he said, and ran a palm over her spine. She tried not to react, but a tiny trembling touched her limbs. He stepped close and kept one hand below her elbow, just barely touching it. The other roamed on her side, on her ribs, very close to her breast. His breath fell on her ear. "Try again."

Madeline ignored his proximity and played. She played it wrong, on purpose, just enough wrong that it seemed she knew what he'd told her and only just missed. He let her go, as she'd known he would, and took the violin from her hands.

"Like this," he said, and played it. The sound rolled from the instrument, rich and vibrant, utterly unlike the small quietness of her own hesitant bowing. She crossed her arms hard across her chest and watched him.

He played the trill of notes that troubled her, then stopped a moment, his gaze on the violin. His face held an odd intensity. For the first time since she'd met him, his attention was wholly fixed on something besides herself. "This violin has a beautiful sound," he commented quietly, more to himself than to Madeline.

She dared say nothing to disturb the moment. He ran an open hand along the curves of neck and body, sweeping around them as sensually as if they belonged to a woman. There was longing in the gesture, a hesitant and pained hunger. Below that, there was more, too—a swelling wildness that frightened her.

"Lucien, perhaps—"

He began to play. The notes were, at first, light and full. Free. Madeline thought of Lucien racing across the lawn the first moment she'd seen him, and that feeling of heedless liberty she'd sensed about him.

He played with the deft, rare control of a natural musician, and in the gray cold light, he seemed a dark flame. The music swirled and danced and doubled back upon itself, changing now, becoming overlaid with something else, something dark and ominous, something terrifying that stomped away the light gaiety of the first section. It roared out now, quick and harsh and overwhelming. Madeline backed up a step.

Lucien did not notice. It was plain he was lost, lost in his music, lost in the power of expressing it, lost in the sorrow and the swelling potency of the emotion he unleashed from the body of her violin.

She heard one section of notes that she recognized—it was the piece he'd thrown in the fire that morning of their picnic.

What happened to his music?

It was here, plucking painful chords within her, circling and swooping and unerringly striking emotions she did not wish, at this moment, to feel. It was stormy, passionate, filled with a rage so vast Madeline wondered how he bore it.

His body became the music, bending, swaying, joining it, until he seemed to become a note, a leap, a sorrow. She thought of him defying the high wall at the ruined castle, and riding his horse too hard, and throwing the paper in the fire, and she understood far, far more than she wished of Lucien Harrow.

There were tears on her cheeks and she held up her hands to cover her ears. "Stop!" she cried.

But the music kept rolling out, a pause, an echo of the first light notes, obliterated by the dark crashing chords, over and over, like a giant's foot stomping out all the life and beauty in the world.

"Stop!" she cried again.

And he finally heard her, finally came back to himself. A fine sheen of perspiration clung to his brow, and she saw his breath came hard, as if he'd been running. He stared at her, the brilliant blue of his eyes almost searing in the gray light. His hair had been shaken loose in his passion, and wisps of it clung to the moisture on his face. In his hands, he held the violin and bow, and he was utterly, utterly still, his posture rigid.

"My God," he said, the words barely a whisper.

Madeline didn't move. She saw his throat move as he swallowed, saw that his hands trembled a little.

"My God," he said again, and moved forward to give the instrument to her. His movements were very controlled, very rigid, as if he were a marionette. He paused, and Madeline moved forward, unsure what she could say to ease that stricken expression on his face.

But his music had burned away all her words, and she couldn't summon any. He stared down at her for a long moment more, and then turned on his heel and left her.

Madeline, holding the bow that still carried the warmth of his fingers, closed her eyes. She was falling in love with him.

That could not happen.

Hastily, she put the violin aside and rushed from the music room to her own chamber. With shaking hands, she pulled a sheet of paper from her desk and dipped her pen. The first effort left a blob of ink on the sheet, and she started again.

My dear Charles, she wrote,

> *I find I am most anxiously looking forward to your return to Whitethorn. You will not believe the amount of work the men have got done on the windows. Nearly all are finished now.*

She hesitated, wondering how to communicate urgency without appearing forward, to hint to him there was danger to their plans if he did not come back to Whitethorn posthaste. Biting her lip, she wrote carefully:

> *Lord Esher generously provided workmen, as well, insisting he wished to help, and that we'd be doing him a great favor by accepting. His men have worked, at his order, almost exclusively on the gardens and greenhouse, which, as you know, are very dear to my heart. You'll scarce recognize them, I daresay.*
>
> *Many of the guests have left, and others come in their places, but Lord Esher and Lord Lanham show no sign of leaving. Perhaps they'll be with us all summer.*
>
> *I do hope to see you soon, and I do hope we needn't wait a long time to be married.*
>
> *Fondly,*
> *Madeline*

Satisfied the marquess would understand her missive, she sealed and posted the letter, feeling much relieved.

By supper, Lucien was quite thoroughly drunk. He'd started on port at noon and steadily made his way through whatever else he might find for the rest of the day. As they waited for supper to be called, he downed two more glasses of wine to be sure food didn't sober him any.

Jonathan noted his state with a lifted brow. "What sorrows can you be drowning in this bucolic setting, Lucien?" He plucked the full glass of wine from Lucien's hands and gave it to the butler, waving him on.

Lucien scowled. "Not all of us have found eternal love and bliss," he said, pleased when the words came out on a perfectly ironic note. "I'm weary of the place. Getting drunk seemed a good tonic."

"Ah."

Jonathan nodded—superciliously to Lucien's way of thinking. A taste of bright rage welled in his throat, and he clamped it back, reaching instead for the dull calm of the port-induced haze. "I'm bored," he said again. "Nothing mysterious about that."

Just then, Madeline came into the salon. Lucien felt a shock of awareness and heat penetrate the fuzzy haze surrounding him. She'd done her hair up in some elaborate pile of pins and jewels and braids. It glittered and shone. Her dark eyes burned in her pale face, and her dress was the green one she'd worn the first night; it showed her creamy shoulders, the luxurious swell of her white breasts, the fragile, graceful line of her collarbone. He stared at her.

As if she sensed his intent gaze, she glanced at him, and it seemed across the room, through all the crowd and noise and milling conversation, that he was again alone with her in the music room, and music was pouring out from him like the waters from a broken dam, and she was stricken and staring and roused—

He tore his gaze away, feeling nauseous from so much wine. There was no headache, which he thought odd, until he remembered the music had been given rein, hadn't it? It made him want to laugh. Instead he caught Jonathan's measuring gaze. "What are you lookin' at?"

"Not a thing," Jonathan replied.

It occurred to Lucien that his friend was completely sober, that he had a mature and calm aspect about him that had not previously been there. "Why are you so full?" he asked, and waved at the butler, who nodded and poured him another glass.

"Full?" Jonathan echoed. "I don't know what you mean."

Lucien noted the calmness again, and the only answer it could be struck him with force. "You can't mean she's going to marry you."

Jonathan ever so slightly smiled. "I believe she will."

"Well." Lucien took only a small sip this time, unwilling to have the glass taken again. "Well," he repeated. "How in the world did you manage it?"

"It isn't settled yet, but she only needed one very rich man to secure Whitethorn. Since Madeline is going to marry the marquess"—Jonathan smiled— "Juliette is free to marry as she chooses."

"Neatly done." Cynically, however, he shook his head. "I wonder Jonathan, if you have any idea how foolhardy you are."

A blaze burned in the bright green eyes. "Watch yourself."

Lucien lifted a hand, waving the comment away. The mistake most often made about Jonathan Child was that his blond, angelic good looks made people underestimate him. "I only speak from long experience," Lucien said. "Juliette and Anna are among the most notorious women in England."

Jonathan said nothing, but a sudden bright expression on his face made it plain the subject of his amour had appeared. Lucien tossed back the port for strength and looked up. Juliette sailed toward them, afloat on her belled skirt. A great, round diamond glittered in the hollow of her delicate throat, and for one minute, Lucien was reminded of Madeline—in this she was like her mother, those delicately beautiful shoulders and arms in contrast to the full breasts.

No, he remembered, fuzzily, they were not blood relations, but stepmother and daughter. Perhaps it was only in the way they displayed their gifts or something in the way Madeline moved. Madeline was sweeter, younger, innocent, so did not have the practiced air about her that Juliette carried, but her mannerisms were much the same.

The butler took his glass. Lucien pinned him with a glare. "Another," he said distinctly.

Juliette joined them, and Jonathan took her gloved hand to kiss. "You look magnificently beautiful, as always," he said.

A shimmer of pure light glowed in her face for a fleeting instant, but Lucien witnessed it with a sense of being thunderstruck; Juliette was in love with Jonathan! In love.

To celebrate, or whatever was appropriate to such a strange event, Lucien had another drink.

Madeline twice thought Lord Esher would claim his kiss during the evening—that sultry gaze he'd given her as she came into the salon seemed to promise it.

The first time was as they were called to dinner. Madeline lost a button on her slipper and sent her partner in ahead. She was grateful for the delay, which would mean Lucien was seated already and she could sit as far away from him as need be. It wasn't as if the table were filled every night, and certainly would not be tonight.

But as she came from the salon, she saw Lucien

coming from the opposite direction. In his pale blue coat, he was the very epitome of elegance and danger, the embodiment of every rake and rogue who'd walked these halls at Whitethorn for two centuries. His eyes were too bright and burned with an unholy light.

"It seems we are both tardy," he said, holding out his arm. "Allow me to escort you in to dinner."

Madeline had no choice but to accept. Gingerly, she put her hand on his elbow. Gloves on her fingers and satin on his coat prevented any tactile sensation, but Madeline could not halt the sudden, vivid picture of him this afternoon, bathed in that clear, cold light of the music room, his arm crooked so naturally, so easily, to play the violin.

He paused outside the dining room. "You are so beautiful. I think we're alone enough right now that I might steal that kiss, are we not?"

She lifted her head, thinking two things at once— *Oh, yes, we are alone and it will be at last finished,* and *No, if you kiss me, I will die.*

She didn't know which one he saw in her eyes, but he said, "No, I think I will wait."

It was only then she realized he was quite rippingly drunk. His breath was thick with the scent of it, and his gait was ever so slightly unsteady as they walked into the room. Juliette looked up as they came in, her eyes holding the faintest . . . what? disapproval? worry? before the serenity of her earlier expression returned. Lucien led Madeline to a seat next to Lady Heath and took his own chair nearby Jonathan.

To her horror, Madeline realized her hands were trembling. She could not, for a moment, even lift her fork.

The countess leaned close. "My dear, I do hope you're not foolishly contemplating a liaison with Lucien Harrow?"

"Of course not!" To prove she was calm and ordinary, Madeline picked up her fork and stabbed a small chunk of tomato on her plate. It skidded and flew into her lap. "Oh, bother," she said with a sigh. "I'm afraid I'm still not used to these silly gloves."

With an annoyed gesture, she yanked one of them off. Some evil part of her looked down the table to where Lucien was leaning back in his chair, a glass of port in his hand, staring back at her—that curious burn in his gaze. Lifting her chin, she tugged the other glove off and let it fall to her lap. Not even the slightest smile broke the gravity of his face.

And once again they were alone, music pouring into the room from the violin, notes of shattering sorrow and terrible power—and Lucien was staring, stricken at what had come from him. Madeline closed her eyes and prayed fervently that Charles would return quickly.

"My dear," the countess said, "run as fast as you can."

Madeline gave a guilty start at her words. Calmly, she said, "I assure you, Countess, you've no need to worry over my virtue." Archly, she looked at her. "If, indeed, it is my *virtue* you worry about."

A spark leaped in the still-beautiful eyes. "You are so young—and need better looking after than Juliette has given."

"I think you regret laughing at the young man he was."

"Not at all, my dear." Anna leaned forward. "You have yet to learn one secret women in our set must know—and that is that a woman must never allow her heart to be touched, else all is lost."

"If her heart is never touched," Madeline countered, "what point is there to anything else?"

Anna shook her head. "So much, Madeline. So much more than you can imagine. Peace and freedom, for one thing. We're never free while we love."

Freedom again. Why did that word keep coming up? Madeline looked at her plate. "I'll keep your advice in mind, Countess. Thank you."

And she managed to be polite for the rest of the meal, even when she was too aware of Lucien at the other end, drinking much and eating little. It was, in a way, a relief. She disliked the attitude that no lord could ever be too drunk. When a man reached this point, she found him singularly unattractive.

She did have to admit to a sneaking admiration of his ability to remain upright, however. Considering all, it verged on the miraculous.

And considering all, she was best off away from him. After supper, she found Juliette and murmured in her ear. "I am most unwell tonight. Forgive me."

But as Madeline was about to exit the salon, Lucien smoothly put himself between her and the door. He said nothing, only gazed down at her with those haunted eyes.

She sighed. "I dislike drunkenness, as I've already told you. Please, excuse me."

"Do you so soon retreat?" he asked. "Did I frighten you so much today?"

Madeline met his piercing look steadily. "Don't play the doomed man with me," she said. "I lack the energy or the interest to save you."

"Oh, it is no game," he said, and there was despair on his face.

Before she could relent, Madeline pushed rudely

by him. He grabbed her elbow as she passed and said against her ear, "Do not forget, Princess, that you owe me a kiss. I intend to claim it."

She yanked from his grip easily and hurried up the stairs.

12

I prithee send me back my heart,
Since I cannot have thine.
—John Suckling

Madeline changed into her night rail and brushed out her long hair. A feeling of restlessness crawled in her limbs, and she wandered toward the long open French doors that led to the balcony beyond. On the stone floor there pattered more rain, and the heady scent of it blew in on a soft breeze, lifting the decorative muslin curtain. From below, she heard the rising flicker of voices and laughter. No doubt everyone would get quite drunk, once more, following Lucien's example.

She sighed. What would it be like when she was mistress of a house? Given the current standards, would she be expected simply to allow the drunkenness to go on? It wearied her—not so much the spirits themselves as the chaos they nurtured. More than once she'd seen the training of a lifetime overthrown when a man or woman indulged in too many glasses of port.

Beyond the window, she thought she heard a noise, a soft scrape or scratch; thinking there might be a cat trying to climb the vines that clung to the wall, Madeline moved forward, putting her brush down on the dressing table as she passed.

"Here puss!" she called softly.

Lucien Harrow appeared in the doorway instead. "Will I do?"

Madeline gasped softly. He was quite thoroughly drenched, his shirt clinging to his flesh, his hair dripping, his face covered with a sheen of moisture. "What do you want?"

He took a step forward. "You."

She backed away. "This is not—you are not to be—" she licked her lips. "Go. I don't know how you got here, but you may take that route back and leave me."

"No." He gave her a slow and stubborn shake of his head, and wiped rain from his face. "No, that I will not do."

A flicker of fear whispered over her spine. In this mood he was reckless. Dangerous.

A single candle burned on her night table. It illuminated his face in strange and exotic ways, shimmering along a cheekbone, skimming the line of mouth, shadowing the breadth of his shoulders, high and broad against the night.

He moved again, forward. Madeline retreated.

And yet, she wanted him. His beautiful face and dark heart. She wanted to touch the skin revealed below the wet cambric that clung to him. One dark flat nipple showed against the cloth, and a pattern of silky hair, and the line of ribs. She swallowed, and closed her eyes.

Her back bumped the bedpost and she startled, instinctively raising a hand to keep him away. Her palm landed on his stomach, and it was unutterably flat and hard and strong. The cold fabric warmed instantly as it sandwiched between her skin and Lucien's. "Go," she repeated, pushing against him.

"No," he said, but he stopped in front of her, and lifted his hands close to her face. He turned them, palm out, so the backs of his fingers and the elegant rise of bones were next to her skin—though not quite touching. His eyes were heavy lidded and lazy, and carried a sultry expression.

His right hand skimmed over her face, so close the path of his fingers disturbed the tiny invisible hairs over her skin. She fisted her hand and turned her face away from that elusive, arousing touch.

Undaunted, he moved his hand down the side of her neck, over her shoulder, down her arm, never quite touching her, but all the nerves in the path he followed were alerted to pleasure and urged her closer to him.

She pushed again with her fist. "You must go, Lucien. Now. I will not have my reputation put in such jeopardy. Do you want me to be poor as a church mouse all of my life?"

"Of course not. I only came for the kiss I hold in hock."

"Tonight?"

"Yes." He bent close, so close his breath swept her lips and made her breasts taut. His mouth hovered over her own. "Would it be so terrible to be kissed, Madeline?"

She clutched the bedpost behind her for strength. He stepped in, and their bodies touched, his stomach against hers, his chest against her breasts, his manhood pressing thickly against her thigh.

For one long dangerous moment, as he moved ever so slightly against her, Madeline ached for him. She wanted to reach for him and put his hands on her body, and tug his head down and have him put his mouth against hers, and taste at last the sweetness his devilish smile promised. He smelled of port and rain and horse, a combination as heady as freshly turned earth. Tighter and tighter Madeline clutched the post, tighter and tighter as his hair fell on her shoulder and his mouth skimmed over her cheek. "One kiss, Madeline. You owe it to me."

She did owe it to him, but tonight, like this, it would not be one kiss. One kiss and she would tumble like a neat stack of dominoes to his allure. And in the morning, she would be ashamed and sorrowful and ruined.

It took all she had to turn her face again away from him. "I am too small to force you to do anything against your will," she said. "But I ask you again to leave me."

Ever so slightly, he moved against her, and he ran his hands over her face, down her arms, his thumbs skimming her breasts. "Please Madeline," he whispered. "One kiss."

"Go, Lucien."

He stood there one more minute. Madeline looked up and caught a fleeting, sultry desire in his eyes before he turned away. "As you wish."

Into the rain and night he went, as suddenly and completely as he'd come. Madeline waited until he was gone to let go of the bedpost, and sank to the floor, trembling violently.

After a long moment, she managed to pull herself into her bed and settle the covers close around her. Please, she thought urgently. Charles, hurry back!

*   *   *

Lucien did not know how he managed the climb back down the vines outside Madeline's room—but then, he didn't much know how he'd managed to climb up, either.

Without conscious thought, he moved over the grounds toward the door that would lead to the stairs that would take him to his chamber. He skirted the salon where gaiety and candles held the line against the night and the weather. He stopped momentarily to watch them all, glittering and resplendent like richly plumed birds, their laughter a bright exotic call. Standing in the rain, Lucien watched them and heard music ringing through him, the same notes— doomed notes—as haunted him in Madeline's garden, in her greenhouse, and in her room, just now, blazing and loud and undrowned even in however many bottles of port he'd drunk now. He'd lost count.

Unmoving, unmindful of the rain drenching him, he stared at them, remembering another time when he'd stood on the outside—had he not always been on the outside?—and watched the dancing, hearing music like knives in his veins, tearing him to pieces.

His mother had seen the music in him, and nurtured it, giving him ways to find his way inside it. She gave him Russia, and Saint Petersburg, and finally Vienna, where it was no shame to hear music and play it and be consumed with it; she'd given him teachers who heard it, too, and helped him leash the sounds. For nine years, from the time he was six until he was fifteen, he'd been on the inside, been a part of something larger than himself.

The joy of those years seemed all the more rare for

the way they were wrenched from him. Lucien's
mother died. His father, probably grief stricken and
not altogether reasonable, had forbidden Lucien to
play or compose his music, and beat him severely
when he did. Such pursuits, the earl said, were the
realm of foreigners and men of unnatural tastes. It
was time Lucien took his place as an Englishman, and
the future earl of Monthart.

Had he been even a year or two older, Lucien
might have been able to resist the change that he'd
known, vaguely, would destroy him. But at fifteen,
dizzied by his mother's death, needing desperately to
find a new place for himself, he capitulated to his
father's wishes. Bitterly, but completely. When the
music seduced him, he squashed it with derision or
drowned it with liquor.

And to his surprise, he learned he had another talent—women loved him. He learned to flirt and flat-
ter, to dance and tease, to kiss and caress. If not for
the countess of Heath, he might have gone on quite
happily debauched for years.

The memory galled. Rain streamed over his face as
he stared at her, remembering the painful lust that
had consumed him. He'd thought himself so very
sophisticated and polished, all grown and experienced at the age of nineteen. She was older, more
experienced, and taught him all manner of new and
astounding things. For one whole winter, they were
inseparable, and quite the talk of the town.

Much as Jonathan and Juliette were now.

Love made Lucien's music live. He composed for
her—sonatas and ballads, light and lively little pieces
he played in private. It amused her.

Inside the salon at Whitethorn now, she danced

with one of the squires come in for the evening from the outlying farms in the district. Her powdered face was as flawless now as it had been when Lucien was nineteen, and her body as dangerously curved, but Lucien felt only hatred when he looked at her. The memory of her betrayal stung deeply—his earnest composing, her laughter when he dared to give tribute in public.

Even ten years later, the emotions lingered. He'd been humiliated and pained, and even though he understood now that she'd been trying to calm her husband, the facts gave no help for the damage she'd wrought. It didn't help that he'd further humiliated himself with a challenge to duel her husband, who'd managed to just graze the flesh of an overwrought boy.

It didn't bear thinking on. That night, his music had died—he'd stuffed it deep into a reinforced trunk in his mind and left it there. And there it had stayed, with rare outbursts of need that he wrote deep in his cups and burned before he slept.

Until now. Until Madeline and her blasted gardens and her blasted eyes.

With a soft whooshing roar, the rain doubled in intensity and Lucien was driven within. He took the stairs to his chamber, stripped off his sodden boots, and dried his hair.

The music that had been dancing at the edges of his mind now rushed forward, as if to torment him, loud and insistent—and beautiful. So beautiful and seductive and sorrowful. He slammed a fist on the table and buried his head, covering his ears to shut out the sound, but it came from within and did not cease.

Sweet and light, so easy at first, then darker and

darker it grew, until the light moments were blotted out, as if stomped, squashed—

With a groan, he found his pen and sharpened it roughly, and began to write, humming, dreaming, listening. Once he gave in, the pressure in his chest eased and he could breathe, and his head did not ache. But he wrote with sorrow, wrote the sound of the last days of Pompeii, so light, then dark, and at last destroyed in a great, inescapable violence. Pompeii. Pompeii.

He wrote until dawn crept into the room. He filled page after page with the notes he could not escape. When the first full fingers of sunlight broke over the eastern horizon and splashed onto his composition, Lucien halted in surprise. All night he'd written. All night. There was in his body a curious lightness, as if he were unwell, and he stared at the dawn with a feeling of confusion. All night.

With a sigh, he stood and gathered the sheaves of paper and carried them to the fire. It had fallen to embers, but they burned well enough once he stirred them. The paper caught with a satisfying blaze.

Suddenly into his daze broke the memory of Madeline standing in this room, humming the notes she'd read on the paper, fighting with him to keep the papers out of the fire—and the taste of her a few moments later, heated and unwilling, aroused and furious. He had been almost mad with want of her in those moments, and yet she had resisted him. There was an immovable integrity about her he wondered if he could crack. He wondered if he would, after all, be able to seduce her.

Idly, he poked the sheaf of burning paper, smelling the acrid scent with a sense of relief.

And with the audible click that so marked inspiration, he saw the answer that had been eluding him all along—music was the key to seducing Madeline. It was the only tool against which she had no defense. He frowned, thinking of her face as he'd played her violin yesterday—overwrought, overwhelmed, wide open.

Yes. He pursed his lips. Yes, music would woo her to his bed—even against her own will. But could he do it? Could he twist even that to his lust? Was he willing to sacrifice his last holiness? He knew with utter certainty that it would also destroy him. And that he would do it anyway.

Madeline worked in the gardens the next morning. No one joined her, for it was Sunday and the workmen did not come. Nor did Lucien appear, which was no terrible surprise, considering how deep in his cups he'd been the night before. She doubted he'd leave his bed at all today.

It was a relief. Mainly. A tiny shudder passed through her every time she remembered the look of him last night in her room—tall and soaked and wild. He was so fierce and free. It was almost impossible to imagine such a life. She wondered, as she weeded, if he appreciated it.

By the time the scents of breakfast began to tease her, Madeline had finished a considerable amount of weeding. All four of the lace beds were now cleared and properly trimmed. She admired the yellow daisies blooming amid circles of silvery lamb's ears. Exquisite.

Beyond the lace gardens and the tall dark edges of the maze, the rose gardens, too, were neater than they'd been two weeks before. She—with Lucien's men and his own hard work—had made much progress.

Walking now back to the house, she puzzled over that. Why he bothered. The obvious, that he meant to seduce her, was only a part of it. He seemed to take great pleasure in doing, in being busy, challenging himself. He possessed an almost inhuman level of energy, which was a large part of his charm.

Her stomach flipped. Charm. Yes. He had more than his fair share.

Last night there had been one terrible, illuminating moment in which she wondered if it would really be such a disaster if she allowed him to have his way with her.

The thought made her feel vaguely faint and flushed. She saw a sizzling memory of his cambric shirt clinging, wet and thin, to his chest, and his dark male nipple showing through.

It didn't bear thinking of. To touch Lucien Harrow, to let him touch her in return, would mean betraying Charles in a most vile manner. She would not do it.

In the safety of her room, she washed her face. The troublesome attraction she felt toward Lord Esher and the alarming moment at which she'd nearly capitulated to his seduction might not have been so terrible if it hadn't been for Charles, actually. She'd never been married to virtue for the sake of virtue; it just seemed the liaisons she'd witnessed were unclean somehow, distressing in ways she didn't really understand.

Charles would be a good husband to her, a man she could trust. One on whom she could depend not to be out on the town or in a carefully appointed

house with his mistress, or chasing opera dancers.
Madeline could not bear a life like that.

So, until Charles returned, she had to stay as far
from Lucien Harrow as possible—which might, considering his persistence, mean hiding if necessary. It
could not be much longer, after all. Perhaps she
ought even contract some vague illness and take to
her bed until Lord Esher was gone or Charles
returned.

No. That was too cowardly. She'd simply avoid
him.

This sensible plan seemed reinforced when a footman gave her a letter as she entered the dining room.
It was from Charles. Because it was still not yet eight,
there was no one else about. Madeline settled in a delicate chair by the long Elizabethan windows, in the
good light. The windows the hail had broken were
now replaced, and the clear light coming through was
ideal for reading. She broke the seal.

> *My dear Madeline,*
>
> *I cannot express the Joy your letter gave. If it
> were my choice, I'd rush back to you this very
> instant, instead of sending my man with this let-
> ter, but I fear I am obliged to stay here. The
> hailstorm devastated our Fields, as well as
> many homes and other buildings. I am quite
> desperately needed here for the moment.*
>
> *If you were another sort of woman, I'd worry
> that you might misunderstand my values, but
> you are too close to the Land yourself to hold
> this against my suit, Nor I think would I be the
> man I am if I did not stay here. Unlike Lords
> Esher and Lanham, I have already taken the*

*reins of my Responsibilities and cannot turn my
back on them.*

*As soon as my Business is complete, I will
return post haste to Whitethorn, and we can
then discuss our plans for the Future.*

> *Yrs ever,*
>> *Charles Devon*

Blinking back stinging disappointment, Madeline
folded the letter aright and stared dismally at the gardens. Behind her came the clink and shuffling of
another breakfaster, but Madeline didn't dare glance
at whoever it was just yet.

Oh, Charles, she thought. I need your help!

She didn't know why she was so reluctant to go to
Juliette for assistance and advice. How difficult could
it be, after all? She'd simply mention she didn't care
for Lord Esher, that she thought him a lecher, and
Juliette would send him away.

And yet, Lord Esher had proved to be a most valu-
able draw, and the longer they stayed in the country,
the longer they could avoid the horrendous expenses
of London. Madeline probably owed her stepmother
that much; especially as she'd sold so many of her
jewels to finance the clothes Madeline wore now, and
to have these parties so Madeline might make a good
marriage.

In sudden decision, she stood up, filled with purpose, and nearly slammed into Jonathan. "Oh, I am so
sorry," she cried, catching his arm.

"Quite all right." He looked at her intently, brushing
a scattering of fine crumbs from his satin sleeve. "Are
you feeling well? You look a bit peaked."

"I'm fine," Madeline replied, as brightly as she

could manage. Unaccountably, she held up her letter from Charles. "I've only just heard the marquess will not be returning to Whitethorn as soon as I'd hoped."

"Ah."

Madeline frowned. "Ah?"

Jonathan settled himself before he spoke, adjusting lace cuffs just so, crossing his leg—ankle against knee—pursing his lips as if he pondered the wisdom of his words. "None of us have missed the way you look at Lucien, my dear."

He sounded like a man much older, as if he were gaining wrinkles in his smooth skin, losing the bright wheat color of his hair. Madeline knew he'd like nothing better, but that didn't mean it was true. He was far closer to her own age than Juliette's, however he tried to hide it, and she disliked the superior attitude he adopted with her.

"Is that so?" she said. "If it's anything more than gratitude you see, Jonathan, I'm afraid your own love has clouded your vision."

"No, I don't think so." He paused to eat a strawberry, freshly plucked from the kitchen gardens and dusted with sugar. "It's nothing to be embarrassed about—I'm afraid the man has had more than his share of women since he returned from Vienna—but you should know he's quite dangerous when he makes up his mind to have a woman."

Madeline narrowed her eyes. "What possible motive could you have in telling me this?" she asked. "I should think you a very poor sort of friend."

"Or perhaps a loyal lover." Carefully, he placed his fork on the china plate and dabbed his lips with a napkin. He looked at her. "A lover who most earnestly requires your help."

"Mine?" Madeline echoed. "I can't think what I could offer you."

"Knowledge." His eyes were almost iridescently green in the bright cloudy light. "I vow I am quite at my wit's end to convince your stepmother to marry me."

Taken aback, Madeline said, "Oh, I see."

Jonathan leaned forward. "I warned you about Lucien with the most noble intentions, you see. He is my dearest friend, but I have seen him ruin many a maid—noble and not. You seem so well matched with the marquess, I dislike to see you spoiled."

A frission of irritation swept her nerves, but she stamped it down. "Have you offered for her?" she asked cautiously, knowing Juliette had little use for marriage.

His smile was self-mocking. "Oh, yes. More times than I care to admit."

"Well, she certainly can't think you a fortune hunter."

"No." He shook his head. "Her only excuse is that she wishes no husband at all."

Gently, Madeline asked, "Can you blame her?"

He looked up, a little startled. "I had not thought. I am no man to bully her or make her choose some life she does not like—" He broke off and jumped up to pace. Restlessly, he moved from doors to table and back again. "I cannot find a way to her heart, Madeline, and I am without shame enough to ask you if there are keys I've not yet thought to use." With a sigh, he paused at the window, glancing over his shoulder. "Foolish, is it not?"

Touched, Madeline went to him, earnestly, putting her hand on his arm. "Oh, no. I am quite moved."

With a rueful smile, he turned to cover her hands

with his own. "You're an extraordinary young woman, Madeline. Do think on it?"

"Of course."

From the doorway came a voice, sharply sarcastic. "How quaint," Lord Esher said, coming into the room. "Doing mother and daughter both, Jonathan? No wonder I could make no progress with the girl."

In a blind flash of rage, Madeline crossed the small space to him and slapped his face. "How dare you!"

Lucien touched his face, his mouth hard, his eyes averted. Madeline saw fleetingly that he'd shaved properly and he smelled of fresh bathing instead of rain and port, as he had last night.

"Forgive me," he said in a low voice.

"He's only jealous, Madeline. Not such a pleasant emotion is it, my friend?" With a quirk of his brow, Jonathan nodded at Madeline. "Excuse me." He left them.

Madeline waited, aware that her breath came too fast, that her cheeks were hot. And Lucien did nothing for interminable moments.

At last, he lifted his head and looked at her. "I deserved that, as much for last night as this morning. I've forgotten how to behave like a man instead of some wild dog." He reached for and captured her fingers. "Forgive me."

Before he could press his full, rich lips against her flesh, Madeline pulled her hand away. "It was nothing," she said. She gripped her hands together, tightly, and backed away, noticing with one tiny part of her mind that her finger marks burned red against his freshly shaved cheek. She hadn't intended to hit him quite so hard.

But he had deserved it.

Only now did she realize how intently he gazed at her, how the dangerous light had brightened in his eyes. "I think," he said quietly, taking a slow step forward, "that you'd like better some other things than hitting me, wouldn't you?"

Madeline panicked. Before he could take one more step, she bolted, running through the French doors and down the steps to her garden, heading for the maze. In her clumsy skirts and wretched corsets and panniers, she was hobbled. On a good day, in the right clothes, she might have outrun him in a footrace. Not today.

And it *was* a race. He loped behind her, as graceful as a tiger, confident of his conquest, noiseless but for the faint clink of coins in his coat pocket hitting against his thigh. He didn't call out, and Madeline had no idea what he would do when he caught her— or what she would do.

She ducked into the maze.

13

Kiss me, dear, before my dying,
Kiss me once, and ease my pain.
　　　　　　　　—John Dryden

The day was warm and overcast. When Madeline turned into the maze, its silence engulfed her, and for one instant, she paused to catch her breath. A pain filled her chest, part fear, part exhilaration—she was on her own ground now. In the maze, she could outsmart him.

She took the left side, for it was more complicated, and Lucien could not know it well enough to find her if she chose her hiding place well. She'd find a place and wait him out. Soon or late, he'd tire of this strange chase, and she would sneak back to the house and hide in her room.

And pray Charles would soon return to Whitethorn.

Lifting her skirts, she kicked out of her slippers and started off at a quick run once again. She realized very quickly how loud the sound of her clothing was, brushing here and there against the shrubbery, the panniers rattling in their wooden harness; even her jewelry jingled on her arms. She halted, and began to move very silently through the narrow paths. Behind her, she heard Lucien call out her name, teasing and assured. He thought he had her trapped.

At the first *claire-voie*, she eased up to it and peeked around the edge—and a sword went through her heart, for there he was, waiting, as if he'd known she'd look for him. A cunning smile curled his beautiful mouth, giving his eyes an exaggerated slant like a big cat. He simply stood there, three small turns of the maze from her, watching her.

She ducked down and passed below the *claire-voie*, and lifted her skirts to run again. Lucien began to whistle, and the easy sound twisted and floated and broke eerily as she turned this way and that, deliberately taking a wrong turn into a dead end with a hidden bench and small garden of herbs. Ducking behind the wall, she pulled her skirts in tight and sat on the ground, forcing herself to breathe as silently as possible.

He would not find this place, she was sure. Not even Juliette knew how to find it consistently. It was Madeline's own, hidden and cool, down a singularly slim path.

In a singsong voice, still teasing, Lucien called, "Oh, Madeline, where are you, love?" His voice carried easily, and it was impossible to tell by the sound of it just where he was. Not far away, but not very close yet either. "Come out, come out where ever you are!"

She hugged her knees. And waited.

Lucien circled through and through, wandering clear to the center the first time before he doubled back and more carefully sought Madeline's secret spots. He followed the intricate turns in and back, whistling, calling out, teasing her. There was no response.

He had not really expected one.

By the third time through, there was a kind of madness in his blood. His frustration grew. He started back in and suddenly realized he would not find her by making noise.

He fell silent. This time he turned at each opening, following it clear to its dead end each time, peeking behind the false walls to the benches behind, taking care to keep his step light. Again, he wandered to the center of the maze without finding her, and with a curse, he slapped his thigh. Where the devil had she gone?

Faintly, he heard a meow, and lifted his head to listen. It came again, a faint, demanding cry. He smiled. Moving back the way he'd come, he stopped periodically to listen for the meow. It got louder, closer, the plaintive, chatty tomcat making conversation with the woman who cared for him.

At last, behind an illusory wall, he found an opening he'd never before seen. Stepping as lightly as he was able, he moved down the path. The meow, satisfied now, rattled out. And at the end of the path, Lucien spied a swatch of pale blue fabric—her skirt.

In the path, he stopped, then doubled back the way he'd come and edged along the parallel way until he could hear her breath on the other side of the living green wall. Through dense leaves he could see tiny swaths of her dress, a blur of darkness that he knew to be her hair.

Quietly, firmly, he quoted, "'As the empty bee, that lately bore / Into the common treasure all her store / Deflowering the fresh virgins of the spring, / So will I rifle all the sweets that dwell / In my delicious paradise, and swell / My bag with honey, drawn forth by the power / Of fervent kisses.'"

He heard her quick, sobbing breath—a sharp intake of panic. But to her credit, she didn't speak. He smiled, opening his hands to touch the leaves that separated them. Quickly, for he wished to take her by surprise, he ran to the end, and down the short path to the hidden bench. Deliberately, he put his foot on her hem, and spoke from behind her, "'I'll seize the rosebuds in their perfumed bed, / The violet knots, like curious mazes spread / O'er all the garden, taste the ripened cherry, / The warm, firm apple, tipped with coral berry.'"

A soft, tiny cry sounded in the stillness behind his low recitation. Lucien peeked around the wall. Madeline clutched her skirts in her fists, and her eyes were closed, her head thrown back so that the whole of her white, smooth throat showed. Her breast rose and fell quickly, and he knew she was as aroused as he.

With a deft, practiced movement, he captured her in his arms, finding only token protest. He pulled her into his lap, against that roused and aching place, and she molded to him as if she were made to his specifications. "I've come for my kiss, Madeline," and opened his mouth over the sweet plumpness of her innocent lips.

She gave a low cry, the sound deep in her throat, and her mouth opened to his, hot and fluid, her tongue seeking his. Lucien pulled her closer and groaned.

He held her, his hands open against her long, slim back, and kissed her. Kissed her as he'd been dreaming of kissing, wet and sliding kisses, deft and nibbling, slow and twirling kisses. His head was filled with music, clear and distinct, as it never was unless he was drunk. But perhaps he was drunk now on Madeline, on

the nectar of her flesh, on the smell of her hair, on the
tiny aroused sounds that fell from her lips. He felt
swept from himself, and he spoke her name, and the
word was ragged. He kissed her collarbone and the
upper swell of her creamy breasts. He opened his eyes.

She looked at him with the dazed hunger of a
woman at her limit. His breath was unsteady and he
found he could speak no more but only gaze up at her
face, and slowly he opened his hands and touched her
breasts lightly, curling his fingers over the cool flesh
above her bodice. They gasped together, surprised at
the sensation. Lucien didn't move for fear she'd bolt,
only touched her there and looked at her. He told
himself it was so that the passion would grow in her
until she could not leave here without fulfillment, so
it would seem to her her own choice, but the weighty
hunger in his groin, his belly, trebled at the feeling of
her supple flesh against his fingers.

In his imagination, this had gone this way, just this
way, until the next moment, when Madeline braced
her body against his and lifted her hands to his face.
She smoothed her fingers over his cheekbones, his
jaw, his nose and lips and eyes, touching him the way
she touched her flowers, as if his face were a precious
thing, as if she had never explored anything so won-
drous. Her lips parted a little, and pressing into him
tightly, she bent and kissed him.

It was an inexpert kiss, a little awkwardly fit at
first until she thought to shift a little and slant their
mouths tightly together. Lucien felt the kiss from his
forehead to his knees, her simple soft movements, her
tongue darting out to seek his own, her full, hot
mouth open and hungry—

He groaned, and pulled her tight, shifting their

bodies so that Madeline lay in the thick, cool grass, her skirts scattering over the lawn. He kissed her in return, teasing and showing her how to move, how to join, to dart and retreat, to play. Kissing her was a thing unto itself, and he had not ever known that it could be such a big thing, so satisfying, so arousing all by itself.

Violins and flutes and cellos rang in his mind; the colors danced and threaded together, and Lucien was suddenly afraid. What if he could not escape the music any longer? What if he could never sleep again for it? What if all he could do was write it and burn it and write it and burn it, forever?

In anger and fear, he grew rough. This little innocent had so overridden his senses that he could not even properly ravish her. Not that he made a habit of ravishment, but this moment seemed to call for it. Harshly, he yanked her dress from her shoulder, pushing at the fabric to expose her breasts.

She cried out, "No!" and grasped at the fabric in a rush.

He paused and held her, kissed her again, leaving her breast uncovered but touched only by the naked air as it never had been, left it open to the kiss of his gaze. He lifted his head, his arousal almost painfully acute now, and looked at her—a full round plumpness tipped with coral, like a flower—hearing the swirl of violins swell in his head.

He touched the point with one finger only. Her breath caught. The flesh beaded tightly and he gently moved to take the dress from her, so her shoulders and breasts were bare and open to his eyes and his touch and the sensual caress of wind.

Looking at her, Lucien touched her nipples with

his thumbs, then bent and suckled her, deep and hard. She cried out—a bright cry that burst into the day with surprising and erotic force. Her fingers clutched his arms. "I want to touch you."

He turned her and unlaced the dress and pushed the fabric off her arms, so she was naked to the waist in the thick green grass, and he wore all his clothes, and that didn't seem fair. She sat up, purpose in her eyes, and reached for the ribbon in his hair, and plunged her hands into it. She straddled him boldly and bent her head to his, and kissed him. Lucien groaned and touched the long smooth stretch of her back, her sides, her waist. He squeezed gently at her buttocks, and bit her mouth with light nips.

Her movements were restless, her fingers combing through his hair, over his face, down his back. She pressed closer and closer to him, as if she didn't know . . .

Of course she didn't know. With a great burst of joy and arousal, Lucien realized he would enjoy the pleasure of teaching her for the first time all the secrets of her responsive body.

He broke away from her lips and kissed a path down her chin, over her throat, slowly, slowly, all the while stroking the sides of her soft—oh, soft!— breasts. When he kissed the high round swell of flesh, she pushed at his shoulder again, only a little, her protest dying in the space of a breath, for he knew what she would like, and he did it—he opened his mouth and covered her nipple, and suckled lovingly until she near melted, a sound like pain coming from her throat.

Lost in his own passion, Lucien reached for her skirts, and pulled them up and touched her leg, just above the knees, and skimmed his hand upward to her hip. He ached for her, and a hard ragged sigh came from him at the tenderness of that hidden skin. He moved his fingers on her—

Madeline bolted. "No!" she cried, shoving at him with impossible strength. "No."

He captured her once more. "Shhh," he said, and kissed her—or tried. She fought hard, pushing against him, her clothes askew. Her work had made her incredibly strong, and he could not keep hold of her long enough to coax her back to softness.

"I love you, Madeline!" he blurted out in desperation. "Don't go!"

It startled her, he could see that, but not for long. She pushed away, pulling her clothes around her. She stumbled to her feet. Her hair had come loose and a lock of darkness fell down to touch one white breast.

A blaze of need bolted through him at the sight, and he jumped up. "Madeline," he said roughly, bending to capture her mouth, holding her face in his hands. Against his sleeves, he felt her breasts, against the sides of his wrists, but he did not touch her again, not like that. He held her face as lightly as he could and kissed her, letting himself fall adrift on the taste of her tongue and the fullness of her lips and the softness of her hair.

"Madeline," he whispered, and kissed her face, her eyes, her bare shoulders. "I love you, let me love you. Let me show you."

She shoved him, hard, and he stumbled backward. Angrily, she pushed her hair off her face. "Love." She spat out the word. "You wouldn't know love if it killed you."

"Madeline—"

She struggled with the dress, trying with a flush on her cheeks to cover herself. She turned her back to him. "Go away, Lucien!" she cried.

The sight of the small white rise of bones in her back pierced him. Stabbed with uncommon guilt, he reached for her sleeve, and before she could shove him away, tugged it into place. "Madeline—"

"'They that are rich in words in words discover that they are poor in that which makes a lover,'" she quoted softly. "Go, Lucien. Can't you see I'm not like you? Seduce some other woman."

"I don't want another woman," he said.

She looked at him. "You'll destroy me."

Music ripped through his brain, bright and loud and sorrowful. Without a word, he turned on his heel and left her. She was right—he was a coward and a rake and he had no business dragging her down with him.

With a kind of lost desperation, he headed for the stables.

Juliette thought the weather oppressive, and it had grown worse by evening, when it should have been cooling off. Instead of soothing breezes blowing in from the water, there was a thick humid stillness weighting the air. It affected the guests adversely, making them quarrelsome. Madeline had snapped at her, and Anna bit the head off three maids, sending one after the other down the stairs in tears. In exasperation, Juliette herself had stopped by the countess's room, on a thin errand, to help her dress. Anna complained about this and that, but it was plain she was pouting because she wanted Lucien, and Lucien didn't return her lust at all.

"I'd watch him, Juliette," Anna said as they went downstairs. "I can't think how you'd let such an incendiary sort in the same house as your unmarried daughter."

Juliette laughed that off. "Madeline is quite able to take care of herself."

"Perhaps," Anna said with a flick of her fan, "but perhaps you've simply forgotten what it is to be young."

She sailed off.

Juliette made a face at the haughty, retreating back. Under her breath, she said, "Perhaps you've forgotten!" She turned to examine herself in the long mirror on the wall. Her neck, though not so taut as it once had been, showed no crepeyness, and her eyes were as bright and clear as they'd ever been. But weren't there a few more lines around her lips now? And a little dry look around her eyes? At thirty-six, she was bound to show some of the years she'd lived, but had it marred her?

So deeply did she examine her face that she did not hear Jonathan's approach, and she startled when he slipped his arms around her waist, meeting her eyes in the mirror. "Why do you frown so, beautiful lady?"

A rush of thick warmth filled her. Together they were so beautiful a pair—he so tall and elegantly slim and blond; she smaller, rounder, but just as blond. She lifted a hand and touched his jaw, admiring him in the reflection. "I was only wishing to be younger," she said, and ruefully smiled.

He bent his head and kissed the side of her neck. "Do not change even one thread of yourself. I adore you as you are."

The crown of his head, showing hair smoothed back from his high, aristocratic forehead, aroused her oddly, and she turned her face to meet the kiss he had waiting, reaching behind her to touch him boldly. "I hope you'll not dally this night, my love," she said with a throaty laugh. "I have something I think you'll like very much."

"Oh?"

"You'll see."

A discreet cough from a footman broke them apart. Juliette smoothed her coif and sailed regally into the dining room, wickedly glancing over her shoulder at Jonathan, who struggled to right his clothes. He winked at her. She flipped open her fan and laughed.

Anna was only jealous.

Or was she? One of the first people Juliette spied as she came into the salon was Lucien, dressed elegantly in black. He leaned insouciantly against the wall, a glass of port in his hand. Looking at him, Juliette felt a clutch of fear.

He burned. The fire lay bright on his features, lighting them from within, giving his face a haunted, brilliant cast. The restless heat was in his form, as taut and poised as a cat about to spring, and in the careless, deliberate flame of his movements.

But it was mostly in his gaze, in the burning look he sent across the room. Juliette touched her ribs, knowing who would be at the end of that fevered blue gaze, who would be the subject of that pointed and urgent passion.

Madeline.

Who sat to one side by herself as she tried to ignore that sizzling look. Tonight she wore a gown of turquoise silk that accented her olive-toned skin and dark hair. The color pointed up the natural red of her lips, the rosiness of her flushed cheeks—and what girl could help being flushed when pinned by such an intense perusal?—the depth of her dark-lashed eyes.

Juliette, seeing Madeline through Lucien's eyes, was quite startled by the hitherto unseen sensuality of the girl's movements, in the tilt of her head, the rise of her breasts over the low-cut gown, in the nervous way she sucked lightly on her lower lip and let it go.

Dear God.

For a long terrible moment, Juliette was paralyzed by all the things she'd not observed because she'd been swept into such a state by her affair with Jonathan. A taste of bile rose in her throat. She looked from Lucien to Madeline and back again. Madeline carefully sipped her port, settled her hands back in her lap. She looked up at Lucien, and Juliette clamped her teeth together to catch the cry that nearly tore out of her throat, because for one bright, shattering moment, Juliette saw that Madeline was most desperately in love. She probably didn't even know it.

Anna sidled up next to her. "Nothing to worry over, is it?" she said slyly, and laughed.

With a steely calm that had served her well for more than twenty years, Juliette smiled at her long-time friend and competitor. "Nothing at all," she said, and flicked open her fan with an arch of one perfect brow. "Now you'll see what a master might do, my dear."

But as she sailed confidently toward Lucien, her heart slowly shredded. It had been a most expensive and delectable luxury to fall in love with Jonathan—she had known that. She had not known it would cost her heart, her love, and her daughter.

Her only hope of saving Madeline lay in successful seduction of Lucien Harrow, and preferably, in fla-grante, so all the world knew.

Including Jonathan. Including Madeline. Who would both, she had no doubt, hate her when it was revealed.

But Juliette had not risen from the life of a dress-maker's daughter to the status of countess by whining over the cost of sacrifices. With a determined and glittering smile, she bore down on Lucien Harrow.

He roused himself to greet her, and she saw with alarm that he'd grown thinner these past weeks, as if the fire were consuming him from within. What a ter-rible waste if such a man had consumption.

But no, there was none of the telltale weakness about him. Indeed, it seemed as if he never slept. Perhaps he had only been indulging too much in the wrong things. "Good evening, Lucien," she said, flicking open her fan.

"Good evening." Quite automatically, he paid trib-ute to the beauty of her bosom with his eyes, and to her lips, and to her hair—no wonder he was so suc-cessful with women, Juliette thought—how many men really looked at a woman that way?

With a coquettish smile, she inclined her head. "I wonder if you'd play a little game with me," she said.

"A game?" He lifted an amused brow.

"Yes. Close your eyes."

He obliged her. Juliette noticed distantly that he had astonishingly long lashes, and they fanned like a child's over his high cheekbones when he closed his eyes. It gave his gaunt face a curiously touching and vulnerable look.

"I've a bet with Lady Heath," Juliette said, "that

you can name the dress color of every woman in this room, and I'll win a sovereign more if you can tell me their jewels, as well."

Lucien smiled. "You wear yellow with garnets. Lady Heath is wearing royal blue brocade and sapphire and diamond ear drops with a long necklace upon her breast."

"Lovely!" Juliette crowed. There was no bet of course, but men could not resist showing off. It was one of the kernels of knowledge that served her best all these years. "Squire McKinnley's wife? And Lady Roake?"

"A green satin with diamonds. Lady Roake is wearing a ghastly robe of brown with—" He frowned. "I can't think of her jewels—the dress was so appallingly made. Ah, she is wearing topazes, unfortunately. The whole outfit is unfortunate."

"And Lady Madeline?"

His eyes opened. "I don't recall."

Juliette shivered at the burning in the vibrantly colored irises. "Oh, surely you remember something."

"No," he said, and lifted his glass of port. "As I've said, I do not care for innocence, Countess, but much prefer"—he lifted that sardonic brow and let his eyes drop, once again, to her mouth—"more experienced beauties."

"Ah," Juliette said, smiling through her knowledge that he lied as baldly as it was possible to lie. "Perhaps then you will dance with such beauty after supper?"

He bowed. "It would be my pleasure."

As he wandered off, Juliette felt a clutch of foreboding. No good would come of any of this. She could feel it in her bones.

14

But my kisses bring again, bring again,
Seals of love, but seal'd in vain, seal'd in vain.
                                    —Shakespeare

The evening was sheer misery for Madeline. She'd tried to get out of dinner altogether, but Juliette had seen through her ruse and ordered her to dress and come down to eat. As a hostess of Whitethorn, Madeline had a duty to be present at all evening gatherings unless she were quite desperately ill. Which anyone with half an eye could see she was not.

Not in body, anyway. But didn't an illness of the heart or spirit come to the same discomfort? Madeline was so ashamed of herself she could barely lift her head. Since she could not share that emotion with her stepmother, Juliette was immovable.

So it was that Madeline, disturbed and sulky, swollen with a thousand emotions she didn't dare examine, suffered through supper. Suffered the silly conversations and the gossip and the mean-spirited barbs that masqueraded as wit. Suffered the cloying presence of Lady Heath, who seemed not to leave Madeline's side for even a tiny moment all evening.

And suffered most of all the intent and invasive gaze of Lucien Harrow, who overtly and broodingly watched her all evening.

But why not? He had nothing to lose—his reputation would only be enhanced if he succeeded in tumbling her, and he'd told her that first night that he would do whatever was necessary.

Even tell her he loved her. That sinfully false declaration of love bothered her most. For one long, shimmering instant, Madeline had wanted with all her being to believe him.

Shame pulsed in her, a heated wash that touched her in the places he had touched her, filling her with a yearning and revulsion she could not reconcile. How could she, after so many years of observing the habits of lazy rakes and their women, have fallen under his spell so violently? Lord Esher, by his own admission, was a most accomplished seducer.

But in the maze this afternoon, it had been his despair that moved her, the hopelessness burning in his eyes—a sorrow so vast she couldn't begin to understand it, an unhealed grief so long buried it festered like a maltreated wound.

Thinking of it gave her an odd feeling in her stomach, a breathlessness. His mouth, so close to her own, had been too inviting to resist. His face, so beautiful and haunted, had seemed to beg for her caress. So she had touched and kissed, and—

No, she would not think of the rest.

There was dancing after supper, line dances that thankfully kept her apart from the narcotic presence of Lord Esher, who seemed busy enough with other women anyway that she needn't have worried.

He didn't speak to her. After supper, he didn't

look at her anymore either, and disappeared for a long time. Jonathan came up to her as she drank a cup of punch, hoping to find oblivion in the potent brew.

"Have you seen your stepmother?" he asked.

Madeline shook her head. "Nor do I care if I ever do again."

He chuckled. "Don't be so sulky, my dear. She wants only what's best for you."

"I have the headache," she said crossly. "I am weary of guests and dinner parties and music. I want silence and my old country life."

"Come." He held out his arm. "A little air will no doubt clear your mind."

With a sigh, Madeline took his proffered elbow and allowed herself to be led into the night. Skimmers of clouds drifted over the stars, and only the smallest of moons illuminated the night. It was very dark.

"Isn't that better?" Jonathan asked, as they moved away from the house and all the noise, moving down the newly raked gravel path that led to the rose gardens.

She nodded. "I fear I was not made for these times. Perhaps I would have been better born when there were no carriages clattering down the roads, and so many people in one place."

"There is no shame in wishing for a quiet life, Madeline. It suits you, and you should pursue it."

"Yes." She thought of Charles, and regret crippled her again. How could she have been so wanton with another man after promising herself to him? How could she betray him so? With effort, she said, "I believe I will find that life with the marquess."

"I've no doubt at all."

They circled the graveled paths and headed back to the house. The sulky meanness she'd been feeling eased, along with the muscles in her shoulders and neck. Perhaps she had been foolish today, but it was not the end of the world. Charles need never know she'd nearly been ravished by a rake—and resisted. She had to remember that: in spite of her wanton arousal, her very deep wish to do with Lucien whatever he wished, Madeline had not succumbed. In spite of her traitorous body, her spirit and will had resisted him.

With a smile, she said, "This has helped immensely, Lord Lanham. Thank you."

"My pleasure."

As they moved over the lawn to the house, there came a cry and a groan from a hidden spot. Madeline froze, looking urgently up at Jonathan for direction. If they continued forward, they ran the risk of exposing lovers in the act. Just now, Madeline could not manage even the thought of it.

Jonathan seemed to read her plea. Putting a single finger to his lips, he melted into the shadows of a great, old elm and pulled her with him. In the shadows, they crouched.

"It's Lucien, you know," he whispered in her ear. "There is no other man at this party who'd consider a midnight seduction in the garden."

A pain as violent as a knife rendered Madeline without speech. She wanted to cover her ears so she would not hear the sounds, but instead pressed her hands to her mouth. Why did it wound that he should have found someone else to ease his carnal hungers? Had she not just congratulated herself upon resisting such advances?

But wound it did—the gash deep and sharp. She thought of his face this afternoon, bathed in the still cloudy light, so beautiful and fragile and vulnerable, thought of his mouth, so rich and—

Foolish, foolish woman!

In the cover of bushes, the rising and falling of voices seemed to go on forever. Urgent, then softer, then argumentative and soothing. Male and female, weaving together, pausing, starting.

At last, the sounds ceased and a pair of shadows emerged. Madeline recognized Lucien's elegant figure, graceful as a cat even at night in the shadows.

She also recognized the woman with him. With sorrow, looked up to Jonathan, who went utterly rigid. A choking sound escaped his throat and for a moment, she wasn't sure what he was going to do. Rush from the bushes to demand a duel? Faint? Kill them both?

Lucien shook off Juliette's hand on his arm and stalked away, obviously angry. Juliette laughed, and the sound carried an edge. She let Lucien go, and stood a moment in the darkness, rearranging her gown. It was plain it had been unlaced, and Juliette could not seem to catch the strings.

Without a second thought, Madeline moved from the shadows to her stepmother. "Whatever are you doing?" Madeline asked, as if she'd only just come upon her. "Let me help you."

"Thank you, my dear," Juliette said smoothly. "I fear I rather got carried away." Her voice fairly purred with lush satisfaction. "Lord Esher is a talented fellow."

A pounding beat in Madeline's throat, and she yanked the laces tight. She thought of Jonathan, in the trees. She wished she could slap a hand over Juliette's mouth, but the damage had been done.

Juliette, oblivious, chattered archly. After a moment, Madeline thought Juliette sounded brittle, almost to the point of breaking, and when she looked at her, she saw there were tears making sticky trails through the powder on her face, like a river cutting new tributaries.

"Mama!" she cried. "Did he hurt you?

"Ah, child, you've not called me that for many years," Juliette said, and started to cough. "No," she said, waving away Madeline's concern. "He didn't hurt me."

Madeline heard the hesitation in her voice, and thought of the argumentative sounds she'd heard from the bushes.

Jonathan. Madeline glanced over her shoulder, but the place where he'd hidden was empty. "Juliette, what about Jonathan? He loves you."

With the weariest expression Madeline had ever seen, Juliette looked at her. "He'll love another." Leaning on Madeline, she said, "Take me to my room. I am most unwell."

Lucien had shed his shirt and stood in his breeches and boots when the door to his chamber slammed open. Madeline stood there, furious, if he were to judge by the high spots of color on her cheeks.

"You are disgusting," she said, and her voice was low and breathless. "You accuse Jonathan of—of—"

"Doing mother and daughter?" he drawled.

"Yes! And you're the one attempting it!"

He smiled bitterly. "Not that I expect you to believe me, but I have not touched your stepmother."

"I saw you."

Carefully, he turned, narrowing his eyes. A tendril of her dark hair trailed over her shoulder, making a line he could follow with his mouth over her collarbone, down the slope of her chest, and swaying into a curl on the white swell of her breast. His chest tightened. "Be careful what you think, Madeline. Thinking you see and really seeing are not the same."

Her gray eyes blazed, made bright by the flush on her cheekbones. Her agitation was not entirely anger, and if he wished to be truly relentless, he would press his advantage now. She'd tumble to her emotions in this moment, tumble to him, thrash and cry out—

"I wish you would leave Whitethorn," she said.

He stared at her, willing her to remember what had passed between them this afternoon. He thought of her breasts, plump and round and tipped with coral. Her mouth softened, the slightest bit. Lucien turned away to hide his arousal. "I know."

She waited another moment, but when he did not turn, she slammed the door. Lucien lifted a bottle and drank. It was better that she believed he seduced both mother and daughter. It was evidently what Juliette wanted the girl to believe, and he had to applaud her cunning. She had followed him from the salon and stalked him until he paused in a quiet place, and proceeded to seduce him. Her dress came loose and she stood naked to the waist in the dark, cloudy night, and he had to admit the sight had been a splendid one.

But not even the slightest twinge of arousal had moved him. That had shamed her. They'd argued.

And Lucien had made a mortal enemy.

It was, perhaps, best if he left Whitethorn before things grew more complicated. He'd leave Madeline to her marquess, Juliette to Jonathan, his music in oblivion.

But just now he was driven to the paper, to the ink. In the humid, close night, he heard a transition that had eluded him, and he scribbled it down. Just now, he had to catch that little turn at the end of the fourth bar. Just now . . .

Shirtless, barefoot, with a bottle of port, a fat tallow candle, and a pot of ink at his elbow, Lucien sat in his chair and wrote.

Juliette waited for Jonathan. She left a candle burning on her night table and sat on the chaise longe nearby the door to the balcony, dressed in a diaphanous wrapper he liked. Her hair she left dressed, as he also liked, and her maid had repaired the mussed powder on her face.

She felt unwell, sick at heart, with a thick weight of sorrow and shame in her chest, a weight utterly unfamiliar. It had been so humiliating to offer herself so boldly to Lucien and have him refuse. It had never happened—no man had ever turned her down.

Which only meant she must be, after all, getting old.

Wearily, she leaned her head on a pillow, closing her eyes for only a moment. How lucky she'd been to find Jonathan! Perhaps, after all, she should take him up on his offer of marriage. If society chuckled at her behind its hand, how would it be different than the whispers she'd endured as the dressmaker's daughter?

Except she'd grown used to a certain deference, both to her beauty and her power.

These thoughts chased themselves in her mind,

like squirrels after their tails. She smiled as she
thought of the tiny gray squirrel babies she'd fed all
spring from her window. Squirrels.

She started awake much later, feeling the stiffness
in her neck and wrists from such an awkward posi-
tion. The candle spluttered, nearly out, and she could
hear no sounds from the rest of the house. Blinking,
stiff, coughing, she sat up and peered at the clock on
her mantel. It was past three.

With considerable effort she got to her feet and
padded over to the mirror, the damp cough rattling
her lungs as she bent to examine the damage her nap
had done her face. Remarkably little. She pushed a
curl from her forehead.

Odd Jonathan had not come to her. With a wash of
fear, she wondered if he'd somehow learned of her
attempt to dally with Lord Esher. Although she had
been prepared to lose him to save Madeline's virtue,
the disastrous seduction attempt had proved nothing.
What a dreadful irony if she lost him over it.

Refreshed by her little nap, she donned a silk
dressing gown and took up a candle to guide her way
through the halls to Jonathan's room. She scratched
at the door and waited, noticing with a small part of
her mind that there was noise yet coming from Lord
Esher's chamber—the man never slept!

There was no answer at Jonathan's door, so Juliette
pushed in. He wasn't there. Had not been there at all,
she guessed. With a trill of worry, she backed out and
headed downstairs, looking for him.

He was not in the drawing room or library. She
asked of the footman dozing by the door where he
might have gone, and he, befuddled, shrugged. A gentleman had gone to town, but he'd returned long since.

Juliette lifted her skirts to once again climb the stairs. She coughed but could not dislodge the tight feeling in her chest. Fear. As she moved back to her room, she tried to recall when she'd last seen him—if he'd been anywhere about when she followed Lucien out to the garden.

No. She was simply tired and overwrought from the events of the day. There was likely some perfectly reasonable excuse for his absence, and she'd hear it in the morning and laugh at her dread this evening.

In the morning, when she'd had some rest, she would laugh.

If dinner had been trying, the next day was worse, Madeline thought the next afternoon. A relentless drizzle poured from a dark sky all day long, trapping everyone indoors with their roiling emotions. Madeline stayed as long as she was able in the greenhouse, but even she had to eat eventually.

Reluctantly, she wandered into the salon, hoping to snag a few little cakes to nestle in her apron, and perhaps some buttered bread. She didn't intend to issue protest tonight—she simply would not appear for supper. Nor would she allow Juliette to bully her into it. To that end, she didn't bother to change her gown before joining the guests, but went looking for tea wearing the faded muslin she worked in.

The salon was a large room, facing the same view of lawns, maze, and drive as the dining and music rooms. Two sets of French doors complemented the row of long mullioned windows, letting in all possible light. The walls were painted light blue and accented in gold. Carved chairs and amoires and delicate sofas were scattered about the room; crystal and brass and enamel tastefully anointed surfaces.

It was Juliette's room, light and airy and gay, as she was. The blue of the walls and the patterned carpet reflected the blue of her eyes; the copious light romped over her flawless skin—and made parody of her imitators' every flaws.

This afternoon, not even the long windows could chase away the gloom; Madeline was struck by the chill the glass allowed when she entered, and tugged her shawl around her more closely. A quick glance at the room showed a knot of guests playing cards to one side, and one of the squire's wives embroidering serenely nearby a window. Ubiquitous servants lingered nearby the tables set for tea, ready to pour and serve the tasty bits of food provided. Madeline made her way to them, hoping to escape without having to converse with anyone.

The hope was futile. As she took a small warm bun from a basket, Juliette's voice pinned her, "Madeline, come here, darling."

Madeline sighed at the footman, who took her bun back with only the faintest trace of amusement, and turned, bracing herself for whatever politics there were to manage today.

The four lords and ladies, as she'd come to think of them, Juliette, Anna, Jonathan, and Lucien, were arranged around a small low table. It looked as if they were playing a game, but Madeline didn't recognize the arrangement of cards laid out on the table.

She tried not to see Lord Esher, but her gaze tripped on his long legs, encased in dark green breeches that fit the hard shape altogether too well. A feeling of heat filled her mouth. He ignored her, his gaze fixed on something beyond the windows. Stung, Madeline ignored him, too. "I'm sorry, Mama," she said. "I've much work to do and cannot stay. I only stopped to get a cup of tea."

Juliette sat in a darker place than usual, and when Madeline came close, she was appalled at her appearance. Not even her thick powder could hide the ravaged look of her face, the hollows under her eyes and cheekbones. Her eyes were faintly red and a bit swollen, as if she'd been weeping or had not slept. Juliette was so vain, Madeline could not believe she had even allowed herself to be seen in such a state, and that worried her more. Moving forward in concern, she began, "Mama—"

Lucien leaped up quickly, and took her arm. "I'm so glad you've come," he said in a smooth tone. "Show me the pastry we discussed, will you? I'd so like to take it to my cook in London."

Nonplussed, she looked up at him, and he tugged her elbow. "Please," he said, but the word was an order.

Her anger and feeling of betrayal flooded back, and Madeline less than politely removed her arm from his grip. Planning to ignore him entirely, she turned back to the little group, about to speak. It was only then that she registered the strange tension emanating from the trio at the table. Jonathan sat very close to Lady Heath, who fanned herself lazily, a triumphant expression on her face. Jonathan's face held no expression as he met her gaze, but she knew he'd had his revenge.

Madeline swallowed and looked up at Lucien. She nodded.

They strolled to the pastry tables, hands folded tightly, Lucien's behind his back, Madeline's locked at her waist. He looked better this morning, and there was even something radiant about him somehow. "I vow I did not touch her," he said. "It matters little to me if you believe it, but I'm loath to lose my oldest friend over any woman."

"And I, sir," she parried, "care little for the friendship of rogues, but very much for the feelings of my stepmother."

His tone was cool, his eyes emotionless, so much so that Madeline wondered if she had dreamed the passionate interlude in the maze. "Well, then, we have a common purpose."

"It will not matter." Madeline looked over her shoulder at the trio. Juliette looked disturbingly dull. "I pity them both."

"Do you?" he said, and now the voice was dangerous, low, resonant. "Why?"

Madeline worried her fingers, aware that Lucien had moved closer. She fixed her eyes on his coat sleeve and remembered with a sudden flush how that fabric had felt against her naked flesh. "They love too deeply."

"As I love you?"

Madeline lifted her eyes. Anger filled her. "Do not begin again, my lord. You are a shallow, shallow man with no knowledge of love at all."

"How can you be so sure?" he asked. "How can you profess to know what is in my heart?"

The aloof amusement in his gaze infuriated her. "I'll not discuss it," she said with a voice so level she gave herself a mental cheer. Impossible to stand so close to him without smelling that elusive man-note that was his alone; without sensing the heat of his skin. She forced herself to meet his impudent gaze, so dark and seductive as he smiled down at her.

"What *will* you discuss, my little plum?" He bent close to say into her ear, "Or perhaps we should not talk at all."

Madeline ducked her head and pushed by him, unwilling to fall under his spell again.

He grabbed her arm. "See to your stepmother, Madeline. I feel she's made herself quite ill with regret. I dislike seeing her so distraught."

The unexpected compassion seared her. Without looking at him, she hurried back to the table and bent over Juliette's chair. "I hope you both will forgive us," she said to Jonathan and Lady Heath, "but I require the Countess and her clear eye in my chamber."

"Of course," Anna cooed.

"We'll see you at dinner, I hope?" Jonathan said, rising. His gaze burned toward Juliette, but Madeline shielded her stepmother with her body. "Both of you?"

"Yes."

But once Madeline had helped Juliette to her dark chamber, she doubted Juliette would be doing anything for the rest of the day. Her flesh burned with fever, and a deep cough erupted from her lungs as Madeline pulled off her gown and unlaced her undergarments. Her body, always thin but for the weight of breasts, had grown almost scrawny. Madeline wondered how long she had been losing weight.

"I don't feel very well," she said as Madeline tucked her in. "It must be a summer cold."

Madeline frowned. "I'll bring some tea. Shall I send for a doctor?"

"No." The word was adamant.

As she lay back, she started to cough violently. Madeline gathered several pillows and propped her up halfway, her mind whirling. There was something she felt she was overlooking, something important. She touched Juliette's brow, and her hand came away with a thick coating of powder. With a frown, she went to the pitcher and bowl on the washstand nearby the window, dipped a cloth into the water, and brought it back to the bed.

"You'll have to rest upright like this until that cough clears a little." Gently, Madeline washed the beautiful face. Below the white powder, the flesh was very pale. "I wish you'd wear a little less powder. It hides you."

"A woman my age cannot afford to go out unpainted," Juliette replied wearily. She coughed again and turned her face away. Madeline, to her chagrin, saw tears. "Oh, do not weep!" she cried, putting her hand on Juliette's thin arm. "Nothing matters so much as that!"

"He's gone," she said. "I've lost him."

"No," Madeline said, soothing. "No, he loves you. He came to me for advice on how to win your hand— did you know?"

"Really?"

"Yes, just a few days ago. I told him I'd think about it, but perhaps I need not. All you need do is give him your love, freely and steadfastly, and all will be well."

"I am so weary," Juliette said. "So weary."

"Go to sleep, then." Madeline stroked her brow, humming quietly under her breath. Juliette fell asleep. For a long while, Madeline sat with her, listening to the rattling exhalations.

When it was plain Juliette had slipped into the deep rest of exhaustion, Madeline left her to get ready for supper, her hopes of an evening cloaked off to herself completely ruined. At the kitchen, she stopped to have a special tea prepared for Juliette's cough, and insisted one of the younger maids should be allowed to go upstairs to sit with Juliette.

Then, with a strange sense of impending doom, Madeline dressed for supper.

15

*The thirst that from the soul doth rise
Doth ask a drink divine.*

—Ben Jonson

After the little scene in the salon, Lucien spent the remainder of the day riding, in spite of the annoying drizzle. It didn't bother his horse, nor did it bother him, and they had the meadows and lanes to themselves. It was quiet and refreshing.

He had nearly decided to leave Whitethorn, and the afternoon's odd events tipped the balance. In the morning, he would go back to London. Surely the boy so intent on defending Herotica's honor had learned the truth about her by now and wouldn't be so quick to run Lucien through. He was getting too old for duels and skipping town. He hadn't the heart for it anymore.

Without really intending to do it, he rode out to the ruins of the castle. Hobbling the horse under a sheltering spread of branches, he shed his coat and made his way through the ruins to the crumbling tower.

It would have been certain suicide to attempt the climb along the wall in the rain; instead he took the steps to the top of the tower and gazed out around him. A timeworn embrasure provided a convenient seat, and Lucien leaned against it. It looked serene— the vibrant treetops, the rolling stretch of meadows, the deserted lanes, all obscured and softened by the drizzling rain. Whitethorn was a beautiful estate, one to be proud of. Lucien understood why Madeline wanted to fight for it.

A clump of grass grew in the crack of the embrasure. Idly, Lucien plucked a stalk and chewed it, taking pleasure in the dusky taste on his tongue when he bit it.

In the landscape, he saw her. There, that newly plowed stretch of dark earth, was her hair. And the undulating meadows, rising and falling in such womanly splendor, were her body. The sky, pale and smooth, was her flesh—that flower, so red, her lips.

Even in fancy, even in such an abstract way, the thought of her aroused him. He could not bear leaving Whitethorn until he'd bedded her. If he could coax her into his bed for one long night, he could walk away. It was the chase that consumed him. Once conquered, women were all alike.

How to accomplish it, though? She was a perplexingly resistant woman. Even when she was nearly mad with need the other day in the maze, she'd managed to halt him. Of course, his own lust had been so engaged he had less finesse than usual, too. Ordinarily, he didn't lose his head until the conquest was assured.

He frowned, watching a pair of starlings flitter around an overhang. That was part of his trouble. Madeline made him forget himself, so he forgot everything he'd learned about how to seduce women, how to wear down their defenses, and immersed himself in the feeling of Madeline around him, against him, kissing him. He lost himself in her, and no matter how he resolved to maintain his control, it all evaporated when he touched her.

He had to have her. Soon. He would create with his music a moment when she was vulnerable, when there would be nothing to interfere with her losing control, nothing to bring her back to herself. Together, they would lose themselves.

A shiver walked his spine at the thought.

Afterward, when dawn broke and their night was done, Lucien would walk away without complaint and bear her hatred as the inevitable price. The marquess was so besotted he'd care little whether Madeline was virgin or not, and they'd go on with their lives as planned. In odd moments, Madeline would remember that single, stunning night.

His heart felt tight as he imagined it. What would he be doing while she had her serene life and thought of him? Would he think of her? Would he be at last the earl of Monthart and live a life of some usefulness? His father was a cruel man, stiff-lipped and disapproving. He made life hell for his dependents, not only his son, but all the local labor, the people in the town, anyone who had to look to him for compassion. He had none.

Lucien didn't know how his mother had married such a man. Perhaps he'd not seemed so cruel in Russia. He didn't know and expected he never would.

The notion of running those vast estates had very little appeal for Lucien. He would do it, of course, because he bore a responsibility to the land and the people on it. He had a legacy to fulfill. He supposed, in

the end, he'd even find a maleable wife and beget sons
to whom he would eventually deed the title and lands.

A sense of strangling overtook him. Was there
nothing else? Only land and children and obligations? Was there never joy? True fulfillment?

What point was there to living at all?

In that dark mood, he returned to the house. As he
walked back from the stables, his mood as black as
the sky, Jonathan came out of the greenhouse door
and strode purposefully toward him. A murderous
fury made a twisted mask of his face.

Seeing it, Lucien knew he was going to have to
fight. With a weary sigh, he tried to forestall it.
"Jonathan, not—"

"You bastard!"

Jonathan hit him. A cold, hard chop to the jaw,
with enough power behind it that it sent Lucien backward a step, involuntarily lifting a hand to the place.

He dropped the coat he carried and ducked his
head down, swinging his fists up. A breaking sense of
relief surged through him—the pain blistering his lip,
sending wild feeling through his numbness. He swung
hard.

And felt the bruising impact as his fist landed
solidly against bone. He ducked as Jonathan rallied,
threw a left, and then landed one in Lucien's belly.
Air *whooshed* from him, but he dipped and swung
himself, landing another bruisingly solid left to
Jonathan's face. The impact sent Jonathan reeling
backward, and Lucien pressed his advantage, leaping
into the air to tackle the other man before he could
recover again.

Jonathan moved, slimmer and a tad shorter than
Luicen, but no less powerful. They were almost

exactly matched—what Jonathan lacked in finesse, he made up for in speed; what Lucien lacked in speed he made up for in sheer power. As they tumbled, a single blow landed against Lucien's mouth and he tasted blood. It enraged him.

They struggled in the mud, grunting and gasping for Lucien didn't know how long. Long enough Lucien felt aches all over him, long enough he grew reluctant to swing his bruised fists again.

Long enough.

All at once, a shocking blast of icy water froze them both in shock. They halted, gasping for breath, pulling away, trying to decide what had happened.

Lucien recovered first. Madeline stood above them, her dinner gown marred with splotches of mud, her hems ruined. "I don't know what you think you're doing, but I'll have you tied up in the stables if you try it again. And you'll both leave this house with first light. Is that clear?"

Neither man spoke, but Lucien touched his lip and shifted. She threw the bucket down beside them and headed back inside, her back stiff. Lucien watched her go with a sinking feeling.

Jonathan staggered to his feet. "I have never been so evilly betrayed in all my life."

"It was your woman who betrayed you, not me," Lucien protested. "She followed me out there—"

Wrong choice of words. Jonathan kicked him. Lucien was on his feet in a trice, and this time, his slight edge in size served him well, for Jonathan was a London man, and without endurance. Lucien shoved him against the brick wall of the stables. "If you attack me again, I'll kill you." He lifted his lip. "I tried to tell you they're all worthless, but you wouldn't listen."

In disgust, Lucien shoved him away and wiped a dirty hand over his cut lip. "I will regret this disaster always, Jonathan, and hope only that you will one day see reason."

He stalked into the house, heart heavy. What was there for him anywhere? At the moment, he'd welcome the explosion of Vesuvius, blotting out his life.

As if to underscore the thought, he heard a mournful explosion of low-pitched strings in his mind. Stunning. Wild and mournful, the end of everything. Pompeii forever obliterated.

Yes.

Madeline furiously stalked back to her room to change her gown, and found the only one available was a silk brocade of darkest rose she had not been able to bring herself to wear. The color veritably hummed, and Madeline felt it too loud, though both the maids and Juliette had insisted it was not.

And as her maid helped her don it now, she realized it was not loud by itself, but it seemed to exaggerate every detail of her person. Her waist looked extraordinarily small, her hair particularly dark. The bodice framed her breasts as if they were ripe fruit, ready for the tasting, and not even the fichu she tucked into the edges seemed to ease that impression. She tried on several necklaces, hoping to find something that might break the wide, inviting slope of skin, but everything seemed only to point up the neckline even more. Better to leave it bare.

Both Jonathan and Lucien were in the salon by the time she had cleaned up and changed. She supposed men had fewer clothes to bother with. Jonathan, his face only showing a slight mark on one cheekbone, stood in a corner with Lady Heath, stood too close, too obviously, so everyone should know he was sleeping with her, or soon would. Lady Heath simpered under the attention. Jonathan somehow managed to look as elegantly dapper as always.

In contrast, Lucien looked as if he'd been brawling for weeks. A tender-looking cut swelled his lower lip, and one eyelid was blackening. A red mark marred his jaw near his ear. As if to dare anyone to say anything, he had brushed his dark hair straight back from his face. Not even the severe style or the bruises could make him look unattractive, however. Madeline glanced away.

Because Juliette didn't come down, Madeline took her place at the head of the table, with Lucien to her right, Jonathan to her left. Lady Heath was far down the table.

As she settled herself, Madeline said to the men on either side, "I trust we'll have a calm meal, gentlemen?"

They muttered assent.

And in truth, it was the least notable dinner that had been served since the men had arrived so many weeks earlier. There were the usual bawdy jokes extended, and the shrill laughter of Lady Heath, and the predictable dark glances over the table, but all in all, Madeline couldn't have asked for anything simpler.

She desperately wanted to excuse herself then, but she did not. Earlier, she'd conferred with the musicians and asked them to play after supper. A concert with soothing tones—something rather dull, so everyone would get sleepy and go to bed.

But to her disappointment, one of the violinists had been unable to play. He'd injured his hand in a boating accident and could not come back to work. "Can't you play with only three of you?" Madeline asked, eyeing the guests as they milled into the music room.

"No," said the leader. "Impossible. We can play perhaps a little dancing music, but not a concert as you requested."

More cards then, and brittle gossip, while some of the guests danced and others made fun of their styles. "Very well," she said irritably. "Move into the salon."

So into the salon they all went. It was stuffy with humid air lying flat in the room, and Madeline ordered the French doors opened. Instantly, the scent of rain and freshly turned earth filled the room, easing the tensions.

They danced. They played cards. Jonathan insisted Madeline should dance with him, and she could not refuse. In his arms, however, she realized he'd had quite a lot to drink. He held her too close, and his hands roved too freely.

It made her angry. "Lord Lanham," she said firmly, stepping away, "you do us both ill favor by acting this way. You're trying to make jealous a man who cannot feel, and a woman who only gloats."

"Am I?" he said, and moved against her. "Do you not wish to punish them all sometimes? Your stepmother sells you to the highest bidder, London's worst rake is determined to bed you at any cost—but isn't adverse to taking your stepmother on the side—and the man you want to marry can't be bothered to rescue you."

She shoved at his shoulders, but his grip was surprisingly strong. "I am not a vindictive sort," she protested. "Let me go."

"Stop pushing and I will."

She relaxed, and he surprised her by pulling her close and planting a kiss to her shoulder. At her sound of annoyance, he laughed and let her go.

Earnestly, she stepped forward. "Jonathan, I know you're hurt, but you mustn't ruin your life in the bargain. Juliette meant to keep me from Lucien Harrow, that's all. She loves you." Madeline frowned. "She's made herself quite ill with regret."

His gaze was full of despair. "If she could act in such a way and profess to love me, then no more fickle woman was ever born."

"Jonathan—!"

"Nothing you say will salve this wound." He moved away.

The musicians finished their piece and moved restlessly. Madeline nodded to the leader, and they took a break to stretch.

As if she were a general at a most critical point in the battle, Madeline scanned the room for the principal players. There was Jonathan, pouring a glass of port. And Lucien glowered in the shadows by the door, his attention fixed upon Madeline. She flushed but steadfastly ignored him. Tomorrow he would be gone. Tomorrow, all of this would be finished.

Lady Heath sidled up beside her. "What a lovely gown, my dear. You must give me the name of your dressmaker."

Self-consciously, Madeline put a hand to her bosom and hated herself for it immediately. "You'll have to ask Juliette."

"Quite inflamed Jonathan, didn't you?" A hard thread of jealousy wound through her words. "But then, what man could resist nearly naked breasts?"

Madeline's temper flared. "As it's the ploy you've most often used yourself, I suppose you would know."

"He bedded me last night, you know—not your stepmother."

Madeline looked at her, dredging from some hidden resource the most withering look she could. Then she moved away, or tried. The countess caught her elbow in a firm, almost pinching grip.

"Oh, do stay. This will be interesting. Watch." With a sweet little whistle, she called the attention of the party to her. "I have a wonderful announcement to make," she said, smiling beneficently. "Lord Esher is going to give one of his rare performances. Isn't that right, Lucien? What has it been, ten years?"

Madeline sucked in her breath. He wouldn't do it, of course, but his fury was deep and without outlet to this point–she knew how he hated the countess.

He moved out of the shadows, and his cheekbone looked even more bruised, giving him an extraordinarily dangerous look. "More than that," he said. There was barely leashed power in his movements, in the deceptively lazy way he crossed the room. "It was while you were yet young."

Amused murmurs met his comment. A stir of expectancy rustled the room. Lucien halted before the countess, who still held on to Madeline's elbow. "I must have accompaniment from Lady Madeline," he said.

Panic welled in Madeline's chest. "No! It would be impossible. I am too—"

"Any woman in this room might play accompaniment, Lord Esher," said the countess. "Madeline does not wish to do it. Choose someone else."

He looked at Madeline, and his eyes burned. "I don't want another woman."

Only she knew the words had been said before, in a private place, with both of them disheveled from passion. "I'd really rather not," she said, but the words were almost whispery, insubstantial.

He brushed them away. "But you alone have seen the work. It is you I must have."

Madeline looked wildly at the countess, who'd been outmaneuvered and showed an apoplectic flush, though Madeline knew she tried to control it. The countess was not sympathetic. She gave Madeline a mean little shove. "So go to it, my dear. You are the hostess after all—you can hardly refuse."

The shove put her up close to Lucien and she put out a hand to halt herself. Her palm landed against his stomach, and she felt the rigid muscles below his clothes, and remembered—

She raised her eyes, pleading. He alone knew why she did not wish to do this; he alone had seen the effect his music had upon her. He alone knew what had passed between them, and knew he had the power to destroy her. "Please," she whispered.

His nostrils flared. For a moment, she thought he was going to relent. A ripple of relief swept her, cool and refreshing.

Then he grabbed her hand and tugged, striding across the room to where the instruments were assembled. He settled her at the clavichord and took up the violin. There was something wild about him tonight, something barely leashed as he tuned the strings. And his mood seemed to infect the guests. She felt their expectation as a palpable thing, alive and entwined with Lucien's rashness.

He nodded at her to get ready and she lifted her hands. A thready terror beat in her chest, making her fingers damp, and she didn't know what she was afraid of—it was only music, wasn't it, and music couldn't do anything to you.

But afraid she was nonetheless, and the terror trebled when he gave her a few bars of introduction, an introduction that hinted at all there was. It was the piece she'd seen scattered under his hands that morning she went into his room, the pages he'd tossed into the fire after they struggled together. And as the pages burned, he'd kissed her so brutally, so passionately, that she thought she'd die of it.

Bowing her head, she tried to breathe clean air into her chest, to clear her mind. Her fingers rested on the keys, aching to try to play the counterpoint he played now, patiently, waiting for her to pick it up. He played, and waited, and played.

And of their own accord, Madeline's fingers moved on the keys, and she picked up the simple accompaniment he wished from her. And her eyes, of their will, turned to him so she could watch for changes.

And he stared at her, his blue eyes alive in a way she'd never seen, alive and burning and unbearably beautiful in his wounded, bruised face. He began to play, very softly. Madeline stared at him, noticing with one part of her mind how graceful his hands were, the hands of a musician, but masculine, too, dark and strong, powerful against the delicate instrument.

The power of the music lay not in anything overt, but in the simplicity of his phrasings, in the deceptively sweet repetitions, in the building horror and trauma and terror that then settled in, collapsed upon itself. Somehow she managed to follow him, building, playing counterpoint.

Lucien's face took on a luminosity she'd never seen upon it, as if the music were light, and he only lived as long as it glowed within him. She saw an almost painful joy in his movements. He bowed and moved and bent into the notes, and once again, as she'd seen before, Lucien was the music—it shaped his body or his body shaped the music, she didn't know.

The piece flittered down, softened, slowed, and Madeline found her hands ceasing, to allow the last dying breaths of the concerto to fade.

His breath came hard as he allowed the bow to drop, his gaze upon Madeline. And she knew he'd played it for her, he'd let it come from him, at some terrible cost to himself. Truimph and hunger shone in his face, and Madeline realized her face was awash with tears she'd not known she'd shed, and behind her, the gathered guests were stunned into silence.

It was the first round of clapping, followed by more and more, and shouts of approval, that shook Madeline into life. She grabbed her skirts and stumbled away, running out of the room before he could touch her, before she betrayed herself completely.

She fell against the balustrade beyond the windows, feeling thin sprays of cool rain on her skin. Wind, ungentle and carrying threats of damage, swept over her.

And then, Lucien was behind her, his hand against her nape, the backs of his fingers sliding over the bones there, down and down, to edge the back of her dress. "Madeline," he said, "look at me."

Her breath came in quick, short bits, and she

gripped the stone balustrade. "I have never been so moved in all my life," she whispered. "The music is beautiful."

Lucien stepped closer, and she smelled his man-scent, heady as newly turned earth. Along her back, she felt his heat, and his mouth fell on her shoulder. "Never again will it be played, Madeline. Only tonight, for you, because I have no other gift to give you."

At the press of his lips to her skin, Madeline's knees nearly buckled.

"Look at me, Madeline," he commanded, and this time, she turned.

His breath, too, came quickly. He touched her face, the tracks of her tears. "You move me," he said, as if helpless to resist. He touched her mouth. With more gentleness than she would have believed him capable of, he bent and pressed the most delicate of kisses to her lips. "Tomorrow, I leave you, Madeline, but you have changed my life." Another soft, delicate kiss, to the corner of her mouth, to her cheek, her eyelid.

She could not resist him. Waves of longing pulled through her, irresistible as the moon's call upon the sea. She trembled, waiting for him, her hands frozen behind her on the balustrade.

He let his hands slide into her hair. "You're so beautiful, Madeline." He bent to kiss her, and rubbed her cheekbones with his thumbs. And kissed her again, moving closer. And again, closer yet, until her bottom was against the balustrade, his body against hers from shoulder to ankle.

She raised her hands, intending to pull his hands from her face and escape. Instead, she gripped his wrists, sinewy and strong. "Lucien, please go away."

"Not tonight, Madeline. Not this time." He opened his mouth now, and covered her own, and without knowing she would, Madeline opened her lips to him, letting his tongue in to flitter against her own, rousing her. She swayed, and he caught her close with an arm around her shoulders.

"Tonight, I will be your lover." He pulled her tight and she let go of a small moan of protest. "Say yes," he whispered, and bent to press his mouth to her throat.

Trembling against him, swept into the need he kindled in her, Madeline pressed her cheek into his hand.

"Say yes," he repeated, and suckled her ear. A rocking shiver moved through her. "Come salve my wounds and heal my heart. Let me love you." His hand teased her breast through layers and layers of clothing. "Say yes."

She opened her eyes and looked up into his face. A hand of wind seemed to give him help, for it brushed a lock of his dark hair over his face, easing the hard lines. His mouth was wet from hers, and a sultry darkness changed his eyes to a liquid beauty unlike anything she'd ever seen.

All the rest of her life, she would make love to the marquess, happily and easily. For tonight only, she would give herself the pleasure of sex with a man who knew what it meant to give and receive pleasure of this sort. For tonight, she could no longer resist him.

"Yes," she whispered, and kissed him, her mouth wide open.

A low burning cry came from his throat, and he scooped her into his arms, as if he were afraid she would change her mind. "Oh, God, Madeline," he whispered, and kissed her again even as he moved, striding down the promenade with her in his arms, his grip fierce. He kicked the door into the hallway, and swept up the stairs, kissing her almost helplessly.

Madeline clung to him, her arms around his neck. With a wildness she did not know she possessed, she gave into the feelings that claimed her, and kissed his jaw and his throat, and the underside of his chin.

In her room, he put her down and closed the door, but instead of moving away, he pushed her against the wall, kissing her as he shed his coat and waist-coat, and started on hers. "I'm mad with want for you," he said.

And it was so with Madeline, too. She pushed her hands under his shirt to touch the skin that so tantalized her, and heard him groan. The sound made her bold, and she left his skin to smooth her hands down his buttocks, over the outside of his thighs. "I've wanted so often to touch you," she whispered.

He groaned. "Touch as you wish, my sweet." He pulled her hand around to put it against his organ, and at first Madeline was shocked. It was hot, even through his breeches, and instinctively she moved her hand over it. He made a low, almost pained sound, grabbing her fiercely, sucking at her mouth as if he would inhale her. The wild Lucien, she thought, comletely under her power. It thrilled her.

"I've wanted to touch you," he said, reaching behind her to unlace her dress, which came free under his expert touch. He peeled it from her arms and pushed it down. The pannier Madeline unbuckled, still kissing him. It clattered to the floor, and Lucien held her hand as she stepped out of it. She tripped, her toes tangling in the wooden bracing for her skirts, and he caught her, lifting her again to put her on the bed.

Only the softest light came through the windows, but it was enough. Madeline lay on her familiar bed, watching as Lucien shed his shirt, then his boots, then his breeches. Her heart stumbled at the magnificence of his body, at the wide expanse of his shoulders, the narrowness of his hips, at his strong thighs, furred with hair.

He came to her, kneeling on the bed to unlace her corset and chemise, helping her out of them one by one. Her hair came loose a little and he reached up to pull free the pins, one at a time, until her hair tumbled all around her naked form. She knelt before him and lifted her arms to the ribbon that held his hair in a queue and took it out. When she touched his hair, her naked breasts touched his naked chest. The feeling was almost unbearably exquisite, and she moved forward to touch him so again.

He pushed her back, gently, into the pillows, and stretched out over her, letting his body brush hers, their thighs and knees tangled. He moved his arm over her stomach and breasts. And kissed her.

Naked body to naked body made a kiss a different thing. Madeline felt an almost immobilizing tremble invade her. Lucien moved his hand on her body, lifting her breast, rubbing his thumb over the aching point, drawing circles around her navel, and lower, into the dark curls at her thighs.

The shock of that feeling made her cry out, and he quickly covered her lips with his own to capture the sound. Not that anyone would hear.

It made her feel odd to have him touching her that way, and she moved restlessly. He bent and touched his mouth to her breast, and at the same time moved his hand into the folds of her. She stroked his back, moving restlessly, unable to bear the welling sensation that filled her. He kissed her breasts and belly, her throat and lips, and the feeling built in her as wild as a storm, almost arriving and not yet there—

He took his hand away, and she cried out in protest, but then he was over her, his lips on her own, his hand in her hair. With one strong thigh, he parted her willing legs and settled himself between them, just for a moment staying just like that, with the heated weight she had stroked nudging the darkest, most secret center of her body. She moved, arching instinctively to put her body against his.

Then somehow, he was filling her, filling and filling, the feeling deeper than all the oceans. He paused for a moment, and reached between them and touched her and Madeline felt two things—a wild swelling breaking thing, rippling pleasure so deep and encompassing she could not dream it was real, and a sharp tugging pain from deep within her. Together the pain and the pleasure engulfed her, rippling and tumbling, wave after wave, and she heard a low sound, long and sustained, and knew it was her own voice.

When she thought she could not bear another instant, the pain ceased and there was only Lucien, filling her all the way, wrapping her with himself, kissing her, touching her. His body was against her belly and legs, and under her hands. She found herself smoothing his long, muscled back and touching his firm buttocks, clasping him closer as he cried her name in a hoarse voice and moved against her, inside of her, his hands tight on her shoulders. A cry left him and he went still and she felt the shudders of his body.

And again her body responded to his and she shattered, holding him close, relishing his presence, knowing it could never last.

With all that she was, she wished that it could.

16

In delights our pains shall cease,
And our war be cur'd by peace;
We will count our griefs with blisses,
Thousand torments, thousand kisses.
—Sir Edward Sherburne

Lucien could not breathe her in closely enough. As the waves of intense pleasure subsided, he put his face against Madeline's neck, tasting there salty sweat and the nectar of her flesh, a unique and heady flavor. He touched his mouth to the hollow of her throat and the curve of her chin, tasting, inhaling her.

He didn't want to leave her. Wanted to hold her this way, their bodies linked, all night. Bracing himself on his elbows to take some of his weight from her, he lifted his head and placed a kiss on her mouth. It gave him a twinge where the cut was still so tender, but that did not matter. Her full lips, firm and giving, nestled against his perfectly. Sweetly.

"You taste of rainbows," he murmured, "Of all things, of all the colors in the world. I could kiss you forever." He angled his mouth and illustrated, kissing her deeply, slowly.

When he lifted his head, she gave a whispery little

sigh and arched ever so slightly into him. Impossibly, he found himself growing hard again, inside of her, a feat he'd not known since raging youth. He willed himself to be utterly still, willed it to go away, knowing no matter how much care he took, she would be sore in the morning. And yet . . .

She opened her eyes and pushed his loose hair away from his face. In the quiet light, her face showed only in round highlights and arched shadows, her eyes pools of unreadable darkness, but her hands spoke for her, pushing the handfuls of hair from his face, stroking his jaw, smoothing her fingers over his chin. "I'll never regret this night, Lucien. Never." She swallowed, and lifted her hips and he groaned at the heat all around him.

There was no way she could know what he wanted then, and yet instinctively, she moved. Her breasts teased his ribs, and she lifted her heels to lock him close to her. He rotated his hips, and now it was she who cried out, and he was amazed that she could feel something, too, so much. So much.

She grabbed his head and kissed him, violently, so violently the cut on his lips split open and he tasted fresh blood between them, falling on her tongue, on his own. Unable to control his urges at all now, Lucien dug his hands into her smooth, taut buttocks and hauled her as tightly as he could against him. And this time, it wasn't slow. It was wild and violent, rocking hard, with the kind of savage need he thought impossible.

Her cry, so sudden and surprised and abandoned, sent him over the edge, rolling into her once more, and his cry joined hers, and they plummeted together into that landscape without end or beginning, where they alone existed.

Lucien exploded into her and died, and came back to life, music alive and dancing all through him, his soul as black as a tar pit. His soul, which would languish always in eternal hell, because for his own purpose, he had used music to have a woman who would not have fallen to any other seduction. He had broken his only inviolable rule, a rule as holy as prayers to another man, and he would suffer for it.

And yet, it was done. He kissed her breasts, and her neck, and her mouth, and vowed he would make his damnation worthwhile.

Madeline did not know there were so many things a man and a woman could do to pleasure each other. Nor did she dream there could be so much touching in so few hours, or that she would welcome the many touches with such wonder and joy.

He kissed her—how he kissed her!—from forehead to toes, and she found there were places that made her shudder and squirm that were perfectly normal most of the time: the back of her neck, the soft indentation in her back above her hips, the circle of her navel, the inner part of her wrist. And elsewhere, too, he put his mouth and tongue, until she nearly wept with the feelings he stirred, the pleasure he gave.

In return, she learned the tastes and smells of Lucien, learned what to do to draw from him the soft groans and choked cries she found so erotic. His body, too, provided a plethora of surprises—it was lean and curved and hard all at once, and smelled in the very pores of that scent she found so rich. His organ was silky to the touch, the sacs below as intriguing as a new flower. Her very examination appeared to surprise and arouse him. "Is it unseemly for me to look closely?" she asked.

He swallowed and touched her hair. "Uncommon. Not unseemly." And he brought her close to him again.

Exhausted at last, they fell together in a tangle of sleep. When Madeline awakened, it was dawn, and yellow fingers of sunlight fell into the room, onto the bed, splashing into her eyes. She did not remember at first what had happened; it was only odd that the curtains were not drawn around her bed and the sunlight came in so rudely.

With a frown she shifted a little, and felt her nakedness, and smelled her lover, and she opened her eyes.

Lucien knelt beside her, naked, gazing down at her with a boiling in his eyes. She lay on her back, her hair scattered below her, over her, around one shoulder. He lifted a hand and pulled away some that covered her breasts, exposing her body to his eyes. His gaze, serious and heated, touched her breasts and belly and thighs, sweeping down, then up.

Madeline didn't move, but her mouth went dry at the probing heat of his gaze. Her nipples tightened, almost as if he'd touched her.

In the night, she had learned the feeling of him, and the scent, and the taste. Now she drank of him, as he drank of her, with the gift of sight. His body was beautiful, sinewy and long and lean. The face, bruised and battered, and shadowed now with dark bristles along his jaw, stirred her deeply: the high sweep of bones, the tender firmness of his mouth, the black frame of lashes and winged eyebrows.

He opened his hand and touched her breast with the very tips of his fingers. "Cinnamon," he said, and his hand slid into the hollow between her breasts. "And cream." He touched her lips. "Strawberry and," he skimmed down to the tuft of hair between her legs, "chocolate."

Madeline would have thought it impossible that he could make her feel anything again. She would have said her body was too tired. But as he brought his hands forward and cupped her breasts into his palms, and gazed at her nakedness, she clutched the sheets into her fists. When he bent his head over her, she knew she could never look at him again without thinking of the sight: the crown of his dark head, the slope of his nose, his mouth on her breast, his hands scooping her flesh into reach.

And she touched him, seeing her hands on his body so she wouldn't forget. Her slim hand on his flat, muscular belly, on his naked thigh, on the urgently pointed organ.

Face-to-face, eyes open, they joined again. He came into her slowly, a tiny thrust forward each time, so as not to irritate her tender skin, his own tenderness. When he was fully sheathed, he paused. Lucien turned them to their sides and held her against him. "Don't move," he said.

Madeline stared at him. "No," she whispered.

They stared at each other, his blue eyes as vivid as a summer sky, the pain smoothed from his forehead. She kissed the place at the bridge of his nose where a line was beginning to form. The movement jolted their hips and gave Madeline a bright, hot shock of sensation.

"Promise you will not forget this night," he said, and his voice was oddly raw. He stroked her face with the backs of his fingers. "Promise."

"I won't forget." His mouth was too close to resist.

She moved forward and touched her tongue to the wounded place, very lightly. "I could not forget," she whispered. A tiny, almost indiscernible pulsing began deep within her, and Lucien shifted a little, just once, jolting the sensation. She made a soft, quiet sound.

"Nor will I," he said, and Madeline almost believed the night had been as shattering for him as it had for her. He kissed her gently, and his hands moved on her back, down to her buttocks, where he curved and cupped the flesh, then smoothed his hand down the back of her ticklish thighs. She wiggled and the growing pulse jumped another notch in her groin, but still he didn't move, though she felt his fingers curl into her flesh almost painfully for an instant. His tongue swirled around her mouth, lazily and boldly. He moved his hand upward once more, and rested the heavy, broad palm on her shoulder, and kissed her and kissed her and kissed her—

And the welling in her built into shivering, deep pulses, higher and higher, and she could not help moving ever so slightly. He grabbed her shoulder and his body went utterly taut, and there was again just the savage pleasure he gave, and she took, and his mouth on hers, and the taste of his cut again broken, and his arms suddenly tight around her, his face in her neck. "Never forget," he whispered.

"Never."

He held her so closely she could barely breathe, and there was a trembling in his powerful arms. "Lucien," she whispered. "I will never forget."

He kissed her temple and hugged her close, and she tasted his hair on her mouth, and his flesh, and knew he was shattering, and there was nothing she could do to stop it.

*   *   *

Juliette was far, far improved in the morning. The heavy weight in her chest had evaporated, and her cough, which had been a long time with her, had returned to its usual dry, ticklish annoyance.

It might have been the sun that so cheered her, after so many days of dark gloominess. Or the deep rest she'd known for two days. She took chocolate in her room, and answered several letters she'd neglected, all by eight in the morning. The strange energy amused her—perhaps her daughter's habits had infected her.

She peered hopefully toward the gardens several times, but there was no sign of Madeline. Juliette supposed it had been a long few days for her daughter, too. It couldn't be easy, balancing all the conflicting emotions of the principal players in the house the past few weeks. And yet, with her usual practical attitudes, Madeline had managed to keep everyone and everything on a firm keel.

What a fine wife she would make the marquess! What a fine, calm life they would find together.

A small mental disturbance rustled the sunny mood. Jonathan. He had not come to her last night, either, but it wasn't surprising. He was punishing her—and perhaps Juliette even deserved it. She knew he'd spent the last two nights in Anna's bed, not out of any kind of lust, but because he'd chosen the one lover Juliette would find most loathsome to forgive.

But forgive she would, galling as it was. And Jonathan surely knew it. They would heal this rift, and go on as they had been, so blissfully happy.

A warning nudged her. What if he would not forgive her?

She paced toward the open French door, gazing out upon the sun-gilded landscape. A horse and rider came up the drive. If Jonathan was not inclined to forgive, she would simply do her best to forget him. Given the choice between her lover and her daughter's well-being, Juliette had made the only choice she could make.

The rider cantered up the drive and stopped before the wide front steps of the house. With a bright sense of relief, Juliette recognized Charles Devon, dressed in a pale blue coat. For once, he'd left his hair alone, and it shone a bright chestnut in the morning sun. In spite of his rotund figure, he moved with confidence, dismounting and taking the steps lightly.

Happily, Juliette went down to meet him in the hall. She kissed his red cheek, realizing he was a rather commanding figure after all, like a general, in spite of bearish looks. "We did not expect you back so soon!" Juliette said, taking his hands. "George, bring us chocolate to the salon."

"I'm afraid I cannot stay," he said. "I've more urgent business in London this afternoon, but I could not bear to ride so close without greeting Lady Madeline at least in passing." He gave a quick look toward the gardens. "May I go look for her?"

"She's not about yet," Juliette replied. "It's been rather busy here, and I'm afraid I ran the poor girl into exhaustion. I can't even remember the last time she slept so late!"

"I see." It was plain he was very disappointed. "I haven't time to linger. Please tell her I stopped in and will be back in a few days when my London business is concluded."

"Oh, no!" Juliette protested, and took his hand.

"She'll be very disappointed if you don't at least say hello."

The marquess held back, gazing toward the stairs as if they might be the path to heaven—or hell. "No, thank you, Countess, but I'll—"

"Nonsense." Firmly, she dragged him toward the stairs, her skirts in one hand. "One moment to say hello. She can wave at you sleepily and then you can be on your way. What will it hurt?" she asked over her shoulder. "I know she'll be dreadfully disappointed if she hears you've been here and she was asleep."

She kept up a steady patter all the way to Madeline's door. Without even a little scratch, she opened the door.

And froze. Beside her, the marquess, too, froze in silence and shock.

From the windows streamed bright lemon-colored sunshine, that fell over the floor, touching the carpet and the wooden bedposts and the gathered, undrawn curtains around the bed. On that bed, tangled and naked and sound asleep against the white sheets, were Lucien Harrow and Madeline.

For one searing moment, Juliette stared, thinking how beautiful they were, their long youthful limbs entwined, Madeline's head on his shoulder, his arms wrapped closely around her as if he would not let her go. Long black hair fell from two heads and tangled around them. "Oh, my God," Juliette said, stunned, and covered her mouth to keep from screaming the words.

Next to her, the marquess took her arm and tried to lead her away from the sight. "You couldn't have known," he said kindly, and tugged on her arm.

Oblivious, Lucien and Madeline slept on.

"No!" With a cry, Juliette roared across the room. The sound roused the lovers, but their fog was deep and they didn't untangle very quickly. Not quickly enough. Juliette grabbed a slipper from the floor and swung it down with all her might on Lucien's leg. "Get up, you fools!" she screamed. "You've been found out! Rise up and take your punishment!"

Lucien came to awareness first, and he turned to hide Madeline from view, blocking her with his body until he could cover her with the quilt bunched at the foot of the bed. Juliette beat him as he moved, and he didn't wince at all, only blocked the worst of her mean blows as he took care of Madeline.

And from behind Juliette came strong arms— Charles Devon, calm as ever—lifting her from her feet, holding her flailing hands close to her body.

Lucien dragged a sheet from the bed and wrapped it around his waist as if there was nothing amiss. "Take her to the salon, Charles," he said. "I will be there momentarily."

"No, you bastard!" Juliette cried. "No! You'll be gone from here, or I'll kill you myself. You despoiled my daughter! In my house!"

Now, servants and guests, drawn by the noise, had begun to peek around the doorway, and Charles held Juliette close. "Hush before you wake everyone," he said in a stern voice. "The moment can be salvaged if you will be still."

Stunned, shaking, Juliette let the shoe drop. When Charles let her go, she looked over her shoulder at Madeline, mussed and ruddy cheeked and weeping. "I am so ashamed of you," she said darkly, and left the room with as much dignity as she could muster.

*　　　*　　　*

In the dead silence that followed the wild scene, Lucien pulled on his clothes. Madeline huddled in the bed, her back to him, the sheet drawn to her breasts. Long, long streamers of loose, hip-length hair half covered, half exposed her, and he felt himself grow aroused once more. Impossible.

Emotions welled in him—tenderness and regret and hunger and sorrow. He no more wanted to leave her now than to cut off a leg, but there was no choice. Against her flesh, the bones of her spine stuck out, and he bent over to kiss it, smoothing a hand over her hair. "Madeline," he said helplessly, and pressed his forehead against her nape. "Look at me."

She buried her face into the pillows, a low keening sound coming from her. One hand was curled into a fist against her ear, and the knuckles were white.

Guilt joined the other emotions in his heart, and he pulled her around, pulled her beautiful, naked, precious form into his embrace and rocked her, smoothing that long hair all around her. "Somehow it will all work out, Madeline, I swear it. Right now, I'll go and tell them I seduced you, that it was none of your doing." He swallowed, thinking of the night. So perfectly had they meshed! "I'll offer for you, but Juliette would rather murder me, I'm sure."

Her weeping slowed as she nested close. He touched her thigh. Her breasts, so inviting, pressed into his coat, and he ached have her again. How could he contemplate never holding her again? With a great effort of will, he put her away from him and took a breath. "I'll make it all right."

From the bed, she looked up at him, her eyes full

of regret and sorrow. She touched his face. "Never forget," she whispered.

With a groan, he fell on her, body to body once more, even if his was sheathed in clothes, and kissed her with all the passion he knew. "Never," he said.

Then somehow, he stood up and straightened his clothes, donned his jacket and smoothed his hair. And marched out of her room, knowing he would never be allowed within thirty yards of her again.

Not as long as he lived.

17

The pleasure of possessing
Surpasses all expressing,
But 'tis too short a blessing,
And love too long a pain.
—John Dryden

For long moments after Lucien left her, Madeline huddled in the bed. It seemed to her that she should never move again, that if she simply stayed where she was, time could not progress and there would be no consequences.

But that was the act of a coward, to hide. She'd been a willing participant in her own seduction. She had not sent him from her. She had joined with him eagerly—and now she would pay the price.

Not for the world would she have wished to so disappoint Charles. He was a good man and deserved better. Madeline had thought herself as high-natured as he, but she'd been proved wrong. Perhaps her blood had been infected by simply living in this house all these years, watching parades of lovers trailing by.

Nor would Madeline have wished Juliette to learn of her fall to temptation. Juliette, who'd done so much to capture the attention of the marquess for her; who'd sold her precious jewels and silks to buy gowns to make Madeline beautiful and give a party to which the marquess could come. Juliette had even tried to seduce Lucien and lost her own lover, just to divert Lucien's attention.

It was a gross betrayal Madeline had indulged.

As she washed, carefully, for her body was very tender, she wondered how it was that something done in the dark could seem so right, and when it was examined in the bright morning, all the seams and perfidy showed.

Except—oh, how beautiful Lucien had been at dawn!

She would not think of that.

With as much dignity as she could muster, she went down to the library. Only Juliette still remained, and Madeline wondered if she'd taken too long getting dressed. Juliette stood beneath the stained glass window that celebrated the Virgin Mary. The soothing browns of her robes fell into the room to spill onto the carpet. Madeline entered and stood still, waiting for Juliette to take notice of her.

At last, Juliette turned. Her face was tired, her eyes weary. "I awakened this morn feeling more alive than I have in years," she said conversationally, plucking absently at a fall of lace on her sleeve. "I was so happy to see the marquess—we were so happy to go find you—"

Madeline held up a hand. "Please," she protested.

"How could you? After all we've done? All you've done? It's so unlike you!"

"I don't know," she whispered, her head bowed. "I have no defense." She looked at Juliette. "I don't know."

With a cry, Juliette gestured wildly, shoving everything from the top of the small secretary onto the floor. A bottle of ink broke with a tinkle, and big brass statues crashed to the floor. "You are an ungrateful child!"

Madeline winced, and lowered her head, clasping her arms around her chest. A vast, yearning loneliness engulfed her—always Juliette had been her rock of stability. "I am so sorry," she said. "If it will please you, I will go to London and try to find another husband."

"No." Juliette paced toward the desk, her wrapper trailing behind her, and paused. "Only God knows how you snagged so wise and humble a man when you are so filled with treachery, but the marquess still wishes to marry you, if you are willing."

Madeline stared. "He does?"

"He is aware of Lord Esher's reputation. You are not the first young woman he's ruined, you know."

The statement, and its attendant reality, crushed her. "No," she whispered. "I don't suppose I am."

"I've sent him packing, and his two-timing friend as well. Even Lady Heath will be gone by nightfall, and she'll not soon darken my doorway, either, I can tell you."

Crushed, stunned, overwhelmed, Madeline only looked at her stepmother. Two bright patches of color burned on her cheekbones.

"I will ride to the earl of Monthart's estate this afternoon. Lord Esher has felled his last virgin."

"What will you do?" Madeline asked, fearful.

"I intend to see him disowned."

"No." The word was simple and strong. "He did not come to my room and storm the door. I am not without blame."

"No, you are not," Juliette agreed. "But you will

pay in ways you have yet to discover. He will not, unless I seek vengeance."

"Please don't."

Juliette gave her a brittle glance. "For a girl who has so betrayed everyone around her, you are bold."

She bowed her head. "Perhaps it is better if I do not marry the marquess. He surely deserves better."

"Never say that again," Juliette said. She crossed the room and took Madeline's chin in her hand. "You have erred, surely, but you are still a good woman and will make a good wife to him." Juliette peered into her face. "Will you be all right, my dear?"

Madeline blinked back a furious wash of tears that filled her eyes then. "Yes," she choked out. But she wasn't at all sure it was true.

Letting her go, Juliette donned a brisk attitude. "As I said I ride to the earl of Monthart today. Jonathan and Lucien have been ordered to collect their things and go immediately back to London. The marquess will return tonight to hear your answer. I will have an intimate meal prepared for the pair of you, and you'll do your best to put things right."

Wordless, Madeline nodded.

Before she could humiliate herself by bursting into tears of grief and shame, Madeline tore away from Juliette and ran from the room. In her own chamber, she found the maid stripping the sheets from her bed, and she wanted to cry out *"No!"*

Instead, as calmly as she could, she turned around and took the back stairs to the greenhouse. Here she could be alone. Here she could grieve and make sense of all the days ahead. Days she would spend without Lucien.

She wept away the agony in her heart. She allowed

every moment of their night together to filter into her mind, where she looked at it carefully, smelled it and tasted it, and, like an outgrown gown, folded it away. When the whole night had been thus examined, she closed the trunk lid and locked it up.

Lucien Harrow was a rake and ne'er-do-well who would likely die drunk or in a duel, or possibly both. Like some beautiful animal that wandered in from the wild to be fed and then wandered back, he was not a creature meant for domestication, for dogs and rides and children.

In one night, he'd given her the best of his sexual expertise. He'd shown her the mysteries of love as only a well-practiced rake could show them, and for that, Madeline was grateful. She would take what she'd learned and use it to make her union with the marquess a happier one. She had learned very much about how to pleasure a man, and it was useful material.

Drying her eyes, she straightened. A hip bath to wash her hair and the smell of Lucien from her, a nap to rest her weary heart, and she'd be ready to greet the marquess this evening.

Calmly, she went in search of a maid.

Honed with purpose, Juliette bustled about, ordering her carriage and the proper accompaniment, choosing her gown—a rich brown velvet, she decided, embroidered simply and fit close to her figure. It was a little loose around the waist, but fit nicely against her bosom. It never hurt to be dazzling when one was outraged. She'd never met the earl of Monthart, but he was a man like any other, she was sure. And he'd sired Lucien Harrow, had he not?

There was a bright fire in her as she traveled. A hot bright flame that burned away the sorrows she'd known this day, that meant her life would be forever changed. Madeline had betrayed her trust. Her long friendship with Lady Heath was finished, for Juliette would not forgive Anna's theft of Jonathan.

Jonathan. Even the sound of his name, echoing in her brain, hurt. When she'd ordered him from the grounds of Whitethorn, his expression had been one of extreme ennui. She'd thought he might protest, that he might finally realize what was going to happen to them if he did not relent.

She was proud of herself. She'd matched his aloofness with arrogance of her own, masking her sorrow well. If he was gone from her, so be it. There would be other lovers—for both of them. She wasn't the sort of woman to sit around bemoaning the fate of a love affair.

But the true fuel in her ability to maintain a sane facade was her fury with Lucien Harrow. She said his name under her breath, and the very syllables seemed made of poison.

How dare he boldly deflower her daughter in her own house while he was full on her food and wine? How dare he take her daughter—pure and strong and good—and foul her like a whore in a brothel?

How dare he?

He had come into the library this morning without even a tinge of regret on his face. She saw the rough red marks on his neck, and once again her rage had been so violent, she threw a book at him. He ducked and the book smashed into the far wall.

With his usual grace, he stood up. "I would most earnestly like to make your daughter my wife," he said.

"No," Juliette said.

"No," Charles said.

Lucien's eyes blazed and he didn't speak at all to Juliette, but to Charles, who was pouring brandy in a glass. He put it in Juliette's hand and bade her drink it. With shaking hands, she'd lifted it to her lips.

"My lord," Lucien said in a low voice, "if I were a gentleman, I'd not have the reputation I've made for myself. If you wish to run me through, I shouldn't be surprised."

"Dueling is a foolish and absurd way to manage grievances," the marquess said stiffly. He met Lucien's eyes steadily. "I'll thank you to leave here now, however, and do not return. I'm sure honor is quite beyond you, but perhaps you might find it in yourself to be kind and leave her alone henceforth."

"Very well." With a quick bow, he turned away. "My best wishes to you both."

"Oh, no, you don't!" Juliette cried. "You won't get away that easily!" She rushed in front of him and put herself in the doorway. "I will ruin you, Lucien Harrow. I warned you I would not be content with cutting you at parties and all the rest of that foolishness. I'll see you ruined from the source."

He gave her a disdainful glance. "Do your worst," he said, and left.

He didn't think she could do it, Juliette knew. Carefully she patted her skirts. Wouldn't he be surprised to learn just how far her sphere of influence reached?

It was the only joy she could find in the day at all.

Madeline allowed herself to be dressed and brushed and powdered for her supper with Charles. She stared at herself in the mirror, wondering if she

looked different to anyone other than herself. She
wore the same green gown in which she'd met both
Lucien and Charles—only a few weeks before!—and
it seemed to her that she looked very different. There
was no shine in her eyes tonight, no matter how she
attempted to appear cheerful. Her smile was as false
as Lord Moorhead's wooden teeth, and she was still,
in spite of her nap, very tired. Her body was sore all
over, in private, unnamable places, and each time one
place or another gave her a twinge, she thought of
Lucien's hands or mouth or body upon her.

It was not the best state in which to greet the marquess. When the maids had finished, she waved them
outside and sat down at her dressing table to catch
her breath. Beyond the long Elizabethan windows of
her room she saw a line of clouds coming in, blotting
out the rays of sunlight on the western horizon. A
storm tonight. Good.

She didn't know what she should do—act as if
nothing had happened? No. That seemed to insult the
intelligence of them both. Hang her head apologeti-
cally? The very idea made her cringe.

The truth was, she had behaved very, very badly
and nothing would make it better. Dithering would
do the least good of all. Steeling herself with a deep
breath, Madeline went down.

She found the marquess in the small salon. He,
too, wore green—a pale green satin coat and a silk
brocade waistcoat in the same color. His stockings
were clean and white, his red-heeled shoes quite dapper. Against the gold-and-white baroque room, he
looked at home, and in full possession of his world.

He heard her, and turned, his hands clasped
behind his back. The sherry-colored eyes were

unreadable, very calm in his simple English face. "Good evening," he said.

Madeline felt rooted to her spot. Her feet would not move. "Good evening."

A bewigged and liveried footman poured a glass of wine from a crystal decanter and put it on a silver tray he carried toward Madeline. She took it gratefully and sipped some. Still she couldn't move. Her gaze darted to the table, small and intimate, that servants had moved to sit before a pair of glass doors open to the stray summer breezes coming from the garden. Had it been only last night, Madeline thought, that Lucien had kissed her against that very balustrade?

The thought made her blush. "Charles—"

At the same moment, he said, "I don't wish—"

They stopped. Charles lifted a hand and indicated she should state her mind first. She bit her lip. "I am not very good at pretending things are all right when they clearly are not." At last her feet unstuck themselves and she moved toward him. "Honestly, I don't know what to say or how to act."

His face was sober. "Nor do I, Madeline."

"So will we stand here and stare at each other?"

"No." He cleared his throat as discreetly as possible. "My wish is to make you comfortable enough that I might make my own apology."

"You apologize? For what, pray tell?"

"For ignoring your veiled but very clear call for help." He frowned. "I am not sure what I thought when I read that letter, Madeline—perhaps that you were more sophisticated than you are. That you were a calm and sensible woman—"

"Stop," she whispered. Shame moved through her in great waves.

He took her free hand. "I mean only to say that I should have come when you requested my help. It was not my place to judge whether you really needed me or not—if you thought you did, I owed it to you to be here to lean on."

She looked at him. "It's a very noble attempt to shoulder the blame, my lord." She smiled. "But you were right to tend to your farms."

"It's only—oh, this is all so bloody awkward." He let her hand go and gestured toward the footman, then paced a little forward, a little back. "It should be said between us, that's all. You fell under the wiles of a notorious rake, Madeline. It has happened a thousand times, and will a thousand more."

At her attempt to cut in, he held up a hand. "Let me finish. What I want to know is whether you wish to love Lord Esher, or if you feel you can make a true and faithful marriage to me."

Quietly, with as much certainty as she could press into five small words, she said, "I wish to marry you."

"I'll not forgive a wife what I forgave today," he warned. "I am not a worldly man and will expect you to be faithful to me."

"As I would wish faithfulness in a husband, I can deliver no less."

He paused, measuring her. "If you will recall, I asked that you consider what a life with me might be like. I am not an exciting man, Madeline. I'll likely grow fat before my time is finished. I love my archaeology and my dogs and my estates. Can you envision a life such as that?"

"Yes. I can imagine, and I hope very much to still be able to share it with you." She looked away, a blush heating her cheeks. "In spite of all, it was never my intention to do otherwise."

For another long moment, he looked at her, as if he were not sure. Then he seemed to come to some decision. "What I would most like is to forget all this and have supper—we need not decide the fate of our lives tonight in this very moment."

"I don't suppose we do."

The footman discreetly pulled out Madeline's chair. She sat down and settled her skirts. Charles sat down opposite.

"There is one thing I would ask, Madeline."

"Yes?"

"If you find, upon reflection, that your feelings run deeper than you expected for Lord Esher, I would like to know it."

A stab of regret and sorrow and a hunger so wild she nearly could not breathe came into her chest. As evenly as possible, she looked at Charles and said carefully, "If there comes a time when my feelings for Lord Esher compete in any way with my wish to marry you and make a home, I will tell you."

His expression was serious, as if he understood that she'd chosen her phrasing very carefully. "I can ask no more than that."

Stabbed with guilt, she leaned forward. "When I look at you, and imagine our life, I see children and warmth and happy festivals." She paused and crossed her hands, and continued earnestly. "I have ever wished for a stable life, where I am free to explore my own pursuits and live quietly and modestly."

A singularly pleased expression crossed his face. He covered her hand with his own, and she liked the solidity of his wide palm. "Those things I can give."

"And in return, Charles, what do I offer you?"

He lifted her hand to his mouth, and pressed a kiss to her knuckle. "I am fortunate enough to have chosen a wife for love."

Looking at him, with candlelight gleaming on the chestnut fall of his hair, seeing the firm resolve in his eyes and the determination in his jaw, Madeline wondered that she'd ever thought him a weak or passive sort. There was nothing at all flashy about him, but he would be a good companion and a good friend, and she might even one day love him.

Giving him her best smile, Madeline said, "Shall we eat and talk of happy things, then? And I must show you how much work your men have done!"

"I'll look forward to it."

18

It is one who from thy sight
Being ah! exiled, disdaineth
Every other vulgar light.
                    —Sir Philip Sidney

For three days after his return to London, Lucien did not emerge from his rooms. He kept an apartment in London, a rather elegant set of rooms overlooking Saint James's Park. He liked the freedom of keeping a set of rooms in town without the bother of a full-time staff. One man and his wife provided for his needs when he was in the city, cooking and cleaning as necessary, screening visitors, keeping his wardrobe in good repair and helping him dress.

Generally he had female help for the undressing.

One of the things he most liked about the spacious rooms was the view of the park, the verdant treetops hiding all the hustle and hurry below. From his study he could walk out on a small balcony and watch young girls and their mamas scuttle out to buy hats and stockings and heaven knew what else. A bakery at the end of the block scented the air with the aroma of fresh bread and cinnamon buns, and one of his favorite pubs was just down the street. He could see the sign—the Cross and Sword—from his bedroom.

For three days he did not go out, but sat in his study hour after hour, drinking port and brooding. His music was dead, as he'd known it would be, and the silence nearly drove him mad.

The price of seducing Madeline had been high indeed.

When he could not bear the silence any longer, he finally pulled himself together to go out. The view was obscured by a steady, dreary rain. The streets turned to rivers of filth and the mamas and daughters had mostly chosen to stay indoors for the afternoon.

Which left the pub and a willing woman to chase away the cobwebs from his brain. A good helping of debauchery was bound to improve his mood somewhat.

At the pub, he was rather warily greeted, and outright rebuffed by the owner. The bartender, Tom, the owner's son-in-law, was a little friendlier and served him with a scowl toward his father-in-law, who walked away muttering.

Lucien found it odd—Juliette had barely had time to begin her supposed campaign to ruin him. He asked after Jonathan, however, and learned his erstwhile friend had recently left after spending the afternoon drinking. "Piss-poor spirits he was in, too," said Tom. "Said you'd ruined his life once again, and this time he'd have your head."

"I ruined his life!" Lucien exclaimed. "That shedevil who tossed us out more likely."

"All the same, he told us what ya done, man." Censure bloomed in the bright blue eyes. "Weren't fittin' to spoil a virgin."

Lucien, stunned that Jonathan should speak so poorly

and loudly of his life, stared mutely at the barkeep for the space of thirty seconds. "Is that what he said?"

"Aye—told us her name, too—the countess Whitethorn's daughter."

With a cry, Lucien slammed his tankard on the bar and grabbed the man by the front of his shirt. "You tell my 'friend' that if he says another word to sully her name, I'll kill him with the weapon of his choice."

"I just though' you ought to know."

Lucien released him, his hands shaking. He stalked out.

If he'd gone in those moments to Jonathan's town house, Lucien would have killed him. Instead, he prowled the streets, stopping in here and again at favorite spots, seeking out old friends.

Everyone had heard the story. Jonathan had left no corner undisturbed.

So Lucien was not surprised when the usual invitations did not arrive. He was not surprised when former acquaintances cut him at the clubs; not surprised when Jonathan would not receive him.

He was surprised, however, when he found himself unable to get credit anywhere—not with the butcher or the vinter or even the tavern where he'd been drinking since he came to London fourteen years ago. The bartender shrugged when Lucien probed. He was only following instructions.

But Lucien knew. He knew.

Juliette had made it to his father.

Juliette and Madeline rode into London on a dark, humid day. They rode in Juliette's well-appointed carriage, with the velveteen seats and ballooned curtains, but all the luxury in the world could not ease Madeline's mood.

"I do wish you'd stop your sulking, Madeline," Juliette commented. Dressed in a glorious yellow traveling suit with a tightly fitting bodice and a dashing hat festooned with a tumble of silk daisies, Juliette looked like a ray of sunshine. Madeline wondered if she'd done it on purpose.

"I'm not sulking," she said. "I'm only tired and I dislike London. I do not see why I must make the rounds of all these silly parties. It's only going to be more expense."

Juliette gave her a curled, catlike smile. "Well, the expense is something you needn't worry about, since Charles has so generously—"

"Extravagantly," Madeline inserted.

"*Generously*," Juliette repeated, "provided for a new wardrobe for your trousseau." With a *tsk,* she took a lace-edged handkerchief and blotted her face. "Honestly, Madeline, most girls would be positively swooning at the thought of shopping for all those new gowns."

"I loathe shopping," Madeline replied, staring out at a field of yellow grass—probably wheat—being cut by a family of sturdy farmers. A little boy about three, barefoot and blond, chased a butterfly, leaping and running behind it with vigor. She smiled to herself. It would be so much better if she could simply marry the marquess in a quiet ceremony, perhaps in the garden at Whitethorn, and then together they could set out for Italy, alone but for a small number of servants.

Instead, Juliette, upon returning from her successful and malicious errand to see the earl of Monthart, had plunged directly into the planning of an enormous wedding for Madeline and Charles. At first she was a little dismayed at their timing—it would have been so nice to have had a proper spring wedding!—but there wasn't time to lose. In case of other trouble, namely a child, they had to make up their minds and marry quickly.

In Madeline's opinion, Juliette had always been a little too set on having her own way. She'd always done whatever she pleased, ordered the lives around her as if she were the only one with any sense at all.

For years, Madeline had lived with it, but now she found herself ready to snap. Juliette had decided upon an autumn afternoon for the ceremony—a Saturday in September. Juliette had decided the bride should wear topazes and garnets in honor of the approaching season. Juliette had decided that since both of them loved Italy so, they should honeymoon there.

The marquess, wisely, departed for his estates, giving Madeline only a rueful apology. She understood and forgave him. What man ever enjoyed wedding preparations? And certainly none would enjoy the bossiness of this particular mother-in-law to be.

Juliette coughed, bringing Madeline back to the stuffy environs of the coach. Madeline looked at her stepmother a little guiltily. She was a trifle flushed, her upper lip beading with perspiration as soon as she blotted it away. Her breath made a soft whistling sound when she exhaled.

"Perhaps we might wait a few days," Madeline said, as kindly as she could. "You need to rest."

"Nonsense," Juliette said, but gave again a moist cough into her handkerchief.

With a sigh, Madeline reached over and touched Juliette's cheek, then her forehead. Too warm. "Well, I'm afraid I'll insist upon it. The past months have been wearing and you were very ill only a week ago. I you want my company on shopping expeditions, you'll take a day to lie abed."

"All right, my dear." Juliette took her hand, smiling. "You take such good care of me."

Madeline brushed away a lock of her stepmother's hair, pressing it back into place below the sunny bonnet. "I do appreciate all you've done, for me, and if I could enjoy shopping, I would."

"Perhaps this is better. The world is changing." She turned her head, and Madeline thought there was something sad in the curve of her jaw. "You'll be a part of the new world."

"So will you."

Juliette only nodded abstractedly, and Madeline allowed her a moment of private reminiscence. For all that she'd not said a single word, Madeline knew Juliette missed Jonathan desperately, that she mourned the end of the affair as fiercely as she'd mourned her husband twelve years before. A great deal of this celebration and display was designed to attract Jonathan's attention.

Madeline almost wished Juliette would share her sorrow, so then Madeline too might say, "Oh, yes, I am so filled with longing at times that there is no room for breath in my body."

But of course she could not. Even if Juliette could speak her sorrow, Madeline could not. It would infuriate the older woman once again, and Madeline couldn't bear it. As long as she could remember, this beautiful, witty, and sharp-natured woman had been her guardian angel and protector; her champion and her friend.

Impulsively, Madeline leaned forward and touched Juliette's hands. "I was very lucky my father married you," she said. "I could not have asked for a more dedicated mother."

To Madeline's surprise, Juliette's eyes brightened with tears. "And I could not have asked for more in a child, my dear. We were well matched."

For Juliette, who had worked so hard to track down an ethical and honorable man to be her husband, Madeline could marry without love. For the gardens at Whitethorn, she could marry. For the sake of the children she would bear, Madeline could marry a man who might be a true father to them.

Even if her heart burned all the rest of her days for the man who'd awakened her soul.

She would try not to think about that.

Upon their arrival at their London town house, Juliette took to her bed all too readily. She found, once she tumbled into the cocoon of coverlets, that she was most opposed to activity of any kind. Her chest again grew congested and she had no desire to eat, and there was in her limbs a weariness so deep it seemed an effort even to breathe.

Madeline had wished for her to rest one day, but that one turned by degrees to several, and still Juliette could not rouse herself enough to do the necessary shopping. At last she told Madeline to go on without her, to do what she must and bring her purchases in to show her.

Worried, Madeline wanted to send for the doctor, but Juliette would not hear of it. The very notion of doctors, with their razors and leeches, gave her hives. "No doctor," she said. "But send to the apothecary for my peppermint drops and some camomile tea."

Still, she did not particularly improve. Madeline brought her dresses in as they were delivered, and modeled them with a light and pleasantly mocking attitude. She brought tempting morsels of food, too—chocolate drops and croissants freshly baked by the rotund little man nearby the theater district; specially brewed coffee, thick with milk and sugar; cakes and exotic fruits fresh from Africa; newly plucked raspberries, shining with water.

Juliette pretended to take great pleasure in the food, but in truth, it disgusted her. She could see she'd lost weight again, but she simply could not force the food down her throat. Madeline's tidbits seemed to help stir her a little, but she more often than not had her maid dispose of the food when Madeline left.

Nights were the worst. She found her fever rose, and with it, her sense of futility and despair. Her mind was filled with visions of her own mother, coughing and gray and covered with the tiny marks leeches made on her neck. Woven in with the visions of her mother were visions of Jonathan, loving her so tenderly, his blond hair tumbling around his beautiful face. How could their love be gone? How could he let it go?

She wondered, in the grip of those fevers, what point there was to anything, to any life, if one never attained happiness or peace.

But one night, after a brutal bout of coughing that left her weak and trembling and overheated, Juliette knew there had been a point to her life, to everything she had done. She sent urgently for Madeline to come to her.

The maid protested gently, "My lady, it is very late."

"I must see her now. Wake her if needs be."

"Aye." The woman bobbed crisply and left, and brought back Madeline. She wore a flowing white night rail with a gauzy white wrapper, tied with ribbons, and her dark hair fell around her shoulders and down her back like a river. She carried a brush and had a ribbon tied around her wrist, so Juliette knew she had been in the midst of her bedtime routine, but not yet abed. "Are you all right?" Madeline asked, taking Juliette's hand.

"Yes," she said, her voice soft and quavery like an old woman's. "I just want to talk to you."

The maid left them, and Juliette urged Madeline to sit on the side of the bed. "Let me watch you brush your hair," Juliette said. "You are such a beautiful girl."

Madeline smiled. "Thank you. You're rather a beautiful lady."

"Have you done most of the shopping now?"

Madeline took a breath. "I have another fitting with Madame General tomorrow." She giggled, like a young girl, at the name she and her maid had given the dressmaker. "Then nothing more until they finish the wedding dress next week."

Juliette nodded. "You have not seen Lord Esher, have you?"

"No!" Madeline looked stricken and Juliette regretted her impulsive words. "Why would I?"

"He's bound to be in London. His father will have cut him off by now, and wouldn't allow him to go to the house at Monthart."

"What you did was wrong."

"You will understand one day, sweeting." Juliette took a breath. "I called you in so I might tell you something, my dear. It is not easy for me to say it, but I need for you to know."

"What?" A quizzical and worried look creased Madeline's smooth white brow, and for one blazing minute she so resembled Juliette's mother that she could not breathe.

"An old, old secret that you may keep or tell as you choose." Juliette took the brush and bade Madeline turn so she could braid the hip-length tresses for her. "I met your father, the earl, outside a bakery. I had an armload of three new dresses I was delivering to a lady nearby Saint James's Park, and he was off to some engagement. Neither of us were looking where we were going, and he knocked me down. I fell face first into the gutter—skinned both elbows and my chin, and ruined the dresses."

Madeline glanced over her shoulder. "I've heard about the dresses. I didn't know about the elbows."

"Oh, yes. Your father was beside himself. He was not a young man anymore, even then." She smiled, thinking the earl had been about her own age now—thirty-six—but she'd thought him very old indeed. "I burst into tears when I looked at the dresses—it's hard for you to imagine it, but the disaster might have ruined us. My mother had died shortly before and I was working morning till night trying to make enough for us to eat."

So, so long ago, but Juliette remembered every detail with a clarity made sharp by sweetness. That accidental meeting had changed her life. "He was quite handsome, and he was contrite at the mistake—and without vanity, I think I can say that at fourteen I was an extraordinary beauty, although I did not know it truly until the earl became so besotted."

Ordinarily, she stopped the story there, moving lightly over the intervening months when the earl had seduced her, given her more money than she'd seen in her life, fed her until her skin smoothed and her body filled out. Her father looked the other way, seeing a way out of their poverty, but it had not sat well with him, a God-fearing Christian man.

"I found myself with child," she said quietly, pulling the brush through Madeline's dark tresses, willing her not to turn around until she could finish. "As did the earl's wife. He cared for us both, tending to her needs as well as mine. He established rooms for me, and a midwife, and a girl to come in and help. I was to be his mistress, you see, and I was quite willing."

"His mistress, and pregnant," Madeline repeated.

"Yes." Over and over she brushed, watching candlelight shimmer in Madeline's hair. "And each of us gave birth to a child, mine a little sooner than hers. We both had daughters with a lot of hair."

Madeline turned, her expression very sober.

Juliette met her gaze. "The countess of Whitethorn died in childbed. Her baby lived only hours."

"You are my mother?" Madeline asked and touched her eye.

"Yes." Juliette swallowed. "You must understand how deeply the earl and I loved. It was a risk, but we both knew it was worth taking. His wife and daughter were buried together, but all thought the babe was well. He fetched you and gave you to the wet nurse. Within months, I, too, lived at Whitethorn, as wife—not mistress."

Madeline closed her eyes and swayed forward to put her head against Juliette's bony shoulder. "You are my mother."

Juliette clasped her close, smelling in with gratitude the scent of her thick hair. "Yes." After a moment, she asked, "Do you mind?"

"No."

A vast, enveloping weariness filled Juliette, mingled with relief. Her whole body began to tremble with the effort of holding herself upright, and she gently released Madeline. "I must rest again," she said. "Perhaps tomorrow I'll feel well enough to go abroad with you."

Madeline rose. She tucked the quilts closely around Juliette, and pressed a kiss to her brow. "'Night, Mama," she whispered.

Juliette, her heart unburdened, slept.

19

Our passions are most like to floods and streams,
The shallow murmur, but the deep are dumb.

—Sir Walter Ralegh

Lucien, having no choice, let his rooms go.
He would have let the servants Delwin and Harriet
Green go, too, but they cornered him on his last day
in the apartment.

It was a dark, hot day, humid and oppressive.
Lucien thought, looking over the unmoving treetops,
the day fit his mood. The oppressive stillness without
reflected the dead silence within. Even when he was
drunk, his music did not stir.

He could not remember a summer that had been
so dark and wet and gloomy as this one. He'd hoped
August would be better, but it showed no signs of
improvement yet.

His neck prickled with perspiration and he
scratched at it irritably, packing his favored books—
things he'd not allow another soul to transport for
him—into wooden boxes. There were pages and
pages of music here, written by friends and by great
masters and some even by Lucien himself as a youth.

Carefully, he sheaved it together, wrapping it in a layer of fabric before putting it away in the boxes. The music itself meant nothing, but there was some sentimental value in the pages, in the days he'd spent in Vienna. They had been, after all, the only days in his life that he ever felt happy or whole or as if he belonged somewhere.

Not like London. He shook his head. If one wanted to laze around and drink and play cards, London was a fair-enough place to light. Lucien's trouble had always been a higher than usual level of energy, and it drove him mad to be idle. He could only sit long enough to play cards if he'd had enough exercise the rest of the day. He liked the robust feeling walking gave him, and riding his horse. He had, much to his surprise, also enjoyed the work in the gardens at Whitethorn. It was a satisfying activity—something you could *see* at the end of a day.

And now it seemed he would have his chance to learn how the world lived, for he would not, as he'd always imagined, be the next earl of Monthart, but only henceforth Lucien Esher, modest holder of a handful of properties in outflung areas of England, and a little land in Russia that was willed to him through his mother. He also owned outright a small house with a walled garden, Rosewood, on the outskirts of the city, that he'd purchased for his liaison with Lady Heath so many years ago. The lot of it would give him a few hundred pounds a year; enough to live comfortably but not richly—not as a lord.

Delwin crept into the room about three. "Would ye like some tea, milord?"

Wryly, Lucien smiled. "Were you thinking of brewing the paper here?" His supplies had dwindled rapidly, and the first rents would not come in till September. Until then, he'd be hard pressed even to buy food—all the more reason, he supposed, to find some way back into society. For a few weeks, he could let the countesses and ladies of London feed him. If he could find one to invite him, the rest would quickly forgive him.

And too, he'd heard Madeline and the countess were in town, making preparations for the wedding. The wedding. He lifted his head and focused on the trees standing at attention beyond his window, breathing carefully and slowly until the knot in his lungs broke up and moved away. He just wanted another single glimpse of Madeline before she married. One glimpse.

He'd forgotten Delwin until the servant spoke. "Er, no sir, we brought some tea from home," Delwin said. "And Harriet baked some cookies, too. She didn't want ye going out on such a dank day without something in yer stomach."

Lucien straightened, and rested his hands on his hips, taking the man's measure. Delwin was in his late fifties, still tall and relatively trim. He'd have the Englishman's jowls in another few years, but just now, the flesh was merely soft. Behind him, his wife of thirty-odd years poked her head around the corner, eyes open and curious. "Well," Lucien said. "Brought it from home, hmm?"

"Yes sir."

"Well," he said again, and waved at Harriet. "Bring it in then, but only if you'll both share it with me."

"Yes, milord. We'd like a word with ye."

Too surprised to make a protest, Lucien sat down with the pair and listened to their plea. They'd been out to Rosewood twice to cart his belongings, and he'd noticed then their murmurings as they tromped off into the wooded glade that led to the meadows and ponds, and examined the two-story stable. He had a hunch he knew what they were about to say. "I'll tell you honestly I've no blunt to keep you on. 'Tis a sorry fact, but my father's cut me off and I haven't a farthing without him."

"Beggin' yer pardon, milord, but ye do," Delwin said. "Have a farthing, that is."

"Pardon me?"

Delwin nodded at his wife, and she placed a box on the table, and lifted its lid. Within was a sizeable pile of coins. Gaping, Lucien asked, "Where did it come from?"

"It's yours, milord. You dropped it here and there, out of your purse at night, most like, and in your shoe—" he glanced at his wife. "We allus figured the shoes were gambling winnings ye hadn't wanted to claim. Sometimes, there was a fair piece o' change in there."

Lucien laughed at the acuity of this observation. And he'd simply forgotten it most of the time. It seemed decadent to him, now that his circumstances were so reduced, that he could ever have been so careless. He swore, wiping a hand over his face.

"Weren't just you, neither," Delwin confessed. "Yer friends and the, er, ladies left a bit here and there, too. We've just been scooping it up and saving it all this time, to use in case of emergency or suchlike. I reckon there's a few hundred pounds."

Lucien narrowed his eyes and touched the pile of coins. "No one gave it to you and bade you give it to me?" He would hate it if someone pitied him to that degree.

Delwin frowned. "I tell ye it's as I've just said. Ye dropped it all over the place when ye were in yer cups. We just collected it proper."

Stunned to silence, Lucien stared at the money. Was it possible he and his friends could carelessly drop this much money over the course of ten years? With his index finger, he poked the pile, gauging the amount to be more than three hundred pounds.

Incredible they hadn't even missed it.

He looked at the earnest pair. "Considering all you've endured at my hands these many years, I believe you should keep this money yourself."

Harriet gave her husband a beatific smile. It was smug.

"She said you'd say that, milord," Delwin said, "but we ain't interested in the cash as such. We'd like to come with ye to Rosewood and live in the rooms above the stables. Aren't many that treats folk the way ye do, and we'll work for room and board till yer back on your feet."

Shamed by their devotion when he'd been nothing but a drunken lout most of the time they'd known him, Lucien nodded. From the box he grabbed a handful of coins and held them for a moment, gauging what they would buy—meat for poor children for months; gin for a working man for a year; a roof for a family . . .

Or a single pair of gloves for a society girl like Madeline. With an odd sense of freedom, he smiled. "I think I'm glad to be done with the lot of them," he said, and put the money into Delwin's hand. "You take this and put it away, and you may come to Rosewood with me."

So it was he went to live at the picturesque but tumbledown cottage of Rosewood. The Greens spent their days cleaning and fixing the stable, while Lucien chopped the wild growth out of the garden, which was, of course, filled with roses. There was one blooming that was the exact vivid shade of the one he'd plucked at Whitethorn—that impossibly intense magenta—that glowed against the gray morning. He touched it to his nose and breathed in the musky sweet smell. At the power of it, he closed his eyes . . .

And was filled with a sense of Madeline, all around him. Her skin, like the petals of the rose that he rubbed over his mouth. Her hair, smelling of sunshine and earth and roses, her laughter, surprisingly robust. He thought of her struggling with the violin, and thought of her struck dumb in the hall as Juliette and Jonathan made love in the library. He thought of her in a thousand ways, a thousand lights, a thousand moods.

He could not move while the longing washed through him. Under his feet the earth gave out the moist, rich smell of possibility, and he scented dew on grasses and heard the bright twittering of hidden birds—finches and sparrows, tiny and industrious, seeking their breakfasts. Caught in the silence of his soul, with hunger so deep, he knew he had to see her.

Lucien Harrow, late the worst rake in all of London, had fallen in love.

Too late.

One August morning filled with damp and heat, Madeline peeked in on Juliette. She slept quietly, her breath rasping as she exhaled, the sound rattling in the quiet. Madeline left her alone. Her condition was improving, but Madeline didn't want to risk tiring her with the exhausting work of fittings and tussling with the dressmaker.

Instead, Madeline took a plump maid with her on her errands, a young girl improbably named Electra. When Madeline asked her about the unusual name, the girl shrugged. "Me mum is a great reader," she said, obviously not indulging the same pastime herself.

For a while Madeline wondered about explaining the myth to the girl, but the task seemed unbearably wearying and she did not.

A light drizzle fell from a very dark sky as they set out for the dressmaker. "We'd best get back early," Madeline commented, eyeing the clouds. "I expect there will be more than just this muzzy rain before much longer."

"I expect yer right, mum."

Perhaps then, Madeline thought, she might be able to find an hour to visit Mr. Redding, with whom she'd been corresponding for several years regarding her experimental plants. He had a great conservatory attached to his house and had extended a standing invitation to her when he heard she was in London— she was welcome to visit. He did his gardening in the early afternoons, if she'd care to come then.

She cared. The thought of going to the conservatory, even for a few hours, held promise of refreshment. A feeling of defeat dogged her days, and she couldn't understand it. Hadn't she triumphed? Wasn't Juliette her real mother? Weren't the gardens to be saved?

But from some hidden place a voice cried out, *LucienLucienLucien.* Madeline had given up on silencing it. All day and all night, it chanted there, a small voice crying his name. She had no hope it would ever cease.

As the carriage pulled to a stop in front of the dressmaker's, Madeline saw from the corner of her eye a man who looked remarkably like Lucien. Her heart jumped and she turned her head quickly, peering into the milling crowd on the street, the men in their top hats, the women in their cloaks. A sea of umbrellas moved in the gray mist, obscuring faces. Madeline peered anxiously at them for a moment, but the man she thought had been Lucien did not appear.

Only her foolish imagination.

With a sense of loss, she allowed Electra to lead her into the shop. The last group of dresses was to be fitted today. At least there was that comfort—she needn't be burdened with the task anymore.

As they were about to enter the shop, Madeline spied in the glass the reflection of a tall figure on a horse; a man with black hair pulled into a queue, his limbs lean and long, his face—

She whirled, but the man was gone.

"Are ye feeling all right, milady?"

Frowning, Madeline turned. "Yes, I'm fine."

They went in. The dressmaker bustled over, exclaiming happily about the gowns. Madeline was led into a curtained alcove where two young girls stripped her of her day dress and settled a soft green baize over her body. The color lit her complexion, and the fabric felt pleasant against her skin. It fit exactly right, not too low at the bust, skimming her waist, clasping her arms. Examining herself, Madeline said, "This will do nicely, but you must remove these flowers." In illustration, she tugged at the silk flowers festooning the bodice and waist.

"But Madame will—"

Madeline had heard this before. She waved it

away. "Madame may put flowers on other women's dresses. Not on mine."

She didn't miss the repressed smile one of the girls gave the other. Was she one of those horrendously bossy and difficult customers who'd so embarrassed her as a child when she'd tagged behind Juliette on fittings? No. What she'd not understood as a child was the great expense of such gowns. She had every right to see they were made to her exact specifications.

Beyond the curtain was a small stir, but Madeline paid it little mind as the girls carefully lifted the dress over her head and hung it up. One reached for Madeline's wedding gown, a glorious creation of silk and beadwork, almost too fragile to be borne. If there were fairies, Madeline thought, allowing them to settle the gown around her, this was surely what they wore. Delicate beadwork edged the bodice, embracing her breasts with an elegantly seductive hand. Silk swathed her waist and tumbled over her legs. It was in the new style, not a saque or braced with panniers, but more closely fit.

It was more beautiful than anything Madeline had ever seen. As the girls tied the laces, Madeline touched the beadwork over her body, taking a strange pleasure in the cool glass beads over her warm flesh.

An alarmed voice from beyond made Madeline lift her head curiously. "Sir!" cried Madame. "My lord! You must not go in there—"

Something hot and expectant whispered over Madeline's heart and she turned. One of the girls dropped a scissors and she stooped to pick it up; a shoulder of the dress fell down Madeline's arm.

"Sir, I really must insist—"

The curtain was flung aside. Lucien stood there,

holding the fabric parted like a conquering captain. He wore a black cloak and dark breeches, and his hair was damp from the rain. His boots were muddy. Madeline stared at him, her heart pounding, and curled her fingers into her palms so she would not reach for him.

He stared at her, and there had never been such a burning in his eyes. They seemed to glow with some unholy light, the color a blue so vivid it almost pulsed. He had not shaved in a few days, and the grim shadow of a beard added to his rakish look. Hollows marked his eyes and the space below his cheekbones, and Madeline thought wildly that he was dying.

LucienLucienLucien said the voice. Madeline backed up a step.

"My God," he said, dropping the curtain to move toward her. With one hand, he touched her ear, and with the other he reached for her. She jerked away, but not quickly enough; his palm fell on her bared shoulder and the stunning pleasure, the weight and heat and size of his hand on her skin, nearly made her swoon.

Unable to speak, pinned to the spot with his loose grasp of her shoulder, Madeline stared at him. Her hands were curled at her sides, tight enough to hurt her wrists. He drank her in with his eyes—there was no other word for it—his gaze washed over her face, over her breasts, her hair and hands, with a devouring intensity Madeline had never known. Her breath came quickly.

"You are light itself, like the moon," he said, and gently touched her cheek with the backs of his fingers. "So uncommonly beautiful one cannot even find the words to express it."

With a wild sense of the absurd, Madeline wondered

why no one moved. There were five women, only one man, and yet they were all as frozen as Madeline. He had cast some spell, that was it. A spell to capture them all in his web.

He kissed her. His mouth, so dear and lost, shattered her terror. She opened her mouth to him, hearing herself make a soft, low noise as his tongue swirled against her mouth and within.

LucienLucienLucien

A joy as thick as honey moved in her, and she touched his face, touched his hair, kissed his neck. It was his groan that brought her around.

"No!" she cried and broke away. "No, I am engaged!" She backed into the wall, grasping the skirt of her dress in her hands. "This is my wedding dress!"

Lucien only stared at her, his breath coming hard. Brilliant lights played over his jeweled irises. Emotions stirred on his mobile mouth. Madeline thought he was going to leave her.

But instead, he made a sudden move and snared her in his arms. "No, you will not marry."

He lifted her easily, and Madeline wanted to weep at the pleasure of his touch, at the mastery in his command, but she knew, too, that she was wrong to go with him. "Lucien, no! Juliette will kill you!"

She struggled hard and he nearly dropped her. It seemed to inflame him. With an abrupt turn, he pushed her against the wall and kissed her again, using his knee and the wall to brace her so he could hold her chin. "Tell me you do not want me and I will let you go," he said, and kissed her again. "Tell me."

He tasted of loneliness and forgotten songs and rain. She alone could ease that sorrow—not to save him, but to ease his descent. She closed her eyes. "I cannot."

Noise broke behind them, and he shifted again, stalking with her through the shop. As he flung open the door and carried her into the rain, Madame and her girls and even Electra—the spell broken with Lucien's departure—cried out behind them.

Setting her atop his waiting horse, he mounted behind her. He clasped her into his lap with one strong arm, and flung his cloak around them both. Thus enveloped, they rode into the dark rain.

And with his breath on her ear, with his arm around her body, Madeline knew a terrible thing— there would be no other man in her heart. Not as long as she lived. Lucien Harrow had claimed her the first time he looked at her, and she would forever belong to him. She turned and put her face against his neck, breathing in the precious scent of his skin.

Once they were out of the teeming streets of London, he rode beneath the sheltering arms of a birch tree and lifted her face and kissed her. And on his lips she tasted his love of her, his need that was as wild and great as her own.

"This is wrong, Lucien," Madeline whispered. "I am promised to the marquess."

"Yes." He clasped her face. "But the music is in me when I hold you," he said, and his voice seemed unutterably tired. "I only need to hear it one more time."

"I am to be married in three weeks," she said, but didn't turn her face from his touch. Her heart swelled near to bursting when he bent and touched his lips to hers, gently, and his eyes closed. A soft sigh came from his mouth.

"Only come with me a little while," he said. "Only a little while and I vow I'll not bother you again."

"Yes," she whispered.

With an exhausted sigh, he pulled her close and bent his head to put his cheek against her neck. "I have missed you." His fingers tightened on her back. "So much."

"Yes," she said again, and they rode on.

"What?"

Electra, the little maid Juliette had hired to be a companion to Madeline, stood by the hearth, shivering in her wet clothes. "He just took her, mum. There wasn't anything we could do."

Juliette had been strong enough to sit in the salon downstairs most of the day. The crackling fire gave cheer against the dark day, but now it seemed extraordinarily loud. Juliette could not quite take in what Electra was telling her. "He *kidnapped* her?"

A troubled frown flickered over the girl's face. "I don't know as I'd say so exactly. She went willing enough."

Juliette let go of a wordless, furious cry. Then she called the housekeeper. "Mrs. Reed!"

She flung off the blankets she'd been wrapped in and stood up. For a brief moment, blackness fuzzed the edges of her vision, but it cleared quickly. Anger, she thought, was a very good cure.

The housekeeper came in. "My lady! What are you doing?"

"My daughter," she said distinctly, "has run off with that bloody rake Lucien Harrow, and I mean to find her and drag her home—by the roots of her hair if necessary." She straightened, coughing only a little. "Don't just stand there, Electra. Help me upstairs—I must be dressed. Send another girl to help us, Mrs.

Reed, and see that my carriage is brought around immediately."

"But, my lady—"

"Do as I say."

She was dressed in record time, a wig covering her hair, a quick dusting of powder obscuring the hollows under her eyes. The dress she wore was too loose across the bust and in the waist, and Juliette simply shrugged off the corsets. They made it hard to breathe anyway.

Outside, in the dark day, she had one spell of coughing she thought might never end. She clung to the door of the coach, unable to catch her breath for long moments. The housekeeper stood nearby, wringing her hands. "My lady, let me send someone else! This'll be the death of you."

"No." Juliette straightened with as much dignity as she could muster. "I must do it myself."

Mrs. Reed gestured to a footman. "Stay with her."

He stepped forward. Juliette accepted his strong assistance with gratitude and settled in her velveteen seat, smoothing her skirt. To the driver she gave Jonathan's address.

At his house, she paused a moment, nerves shivering in her limbs. She had missed Jonathan most desperately, and didn't know how she would feel, looking at him again.

As she stepped out of the carriage, she saw the draperies in an upper room shift, and a quiver passed through her. Nerves and fury and longing tangled so tightly she thought she'd swoon. For a single moment, she clung to the footman, steadying herself.

Then she donned her haughtiest attitude to confront the butler, a pinch-mouthed man she'd never liked. "I must see Lord Lanham," she said. "Now."

"He is not in, my lady. I will tell him you called."

"This will not wait," she said, and pushed by him. "Jonathan!" she called from the central hallway. Stairs circled overhead, five flights up. "Jonathan, I must speak to you regarding Madeline and Lord Esher!"

"My lady!" the butler protested, taking Juliette's arm. "I tell you—"

She shook him off. "Jonathan!" she cried. "He's kidnapped her!"

From above came the sound of a door. Juliette gave the butler a triumphant little smile. Jonathan appeared on the second floor, leaning over the balcony. "What are you yelling?"

Juliette looked up, and her heart caught. His thick butter-colored hair was loose on his shoulders, shoulders that were bare, as were his feet. He wore only a pair of very wrinkled breeches, and bore around his mouth the very distinct look of a man engaged in sex. Juliette felt weak, indeed, and for the beat of a few seconds, she could not think why she'd come. "Jonathan."

His lips pursed. He bent over the rail and leaned his arms on the railing. "What do you want, Juliette?"

The posture put his arms into high relief, showing the curve of bicep, the concave stretch of stomach, the firm round of his hip. "I, er . . . I came . . ."

She felt dizzy and without breath. With one gloved hand she touched her forehead, trying to pull herself together.

For one long moment, Jonathan met Juliette's gaze. The sardonic look left his face. His green eyes were bleak, without joy. Juliette ached to go up the stairs. Her heart felt thrice its usual size. His gaze wavered.

"What do you want?"

Pride reasserted itself. Juliette lifted her chin. "Do you know where Lucien Harrow might have taken my daughter?"

He looked at her, as if considering. "You can't save her, Juliette. She's in love—strange as that may be for one of your ilk to understand. And the terrible thing is, Lucien thinks he loves her."

"I don't care if they love each other as passionately as Romeo and Juliet. She is marrying the marquess in three weeks." Heat and dizziness enveloped her. "I will not allow her to ruin her life."

"As you've ruined yours?"

Juliette refused to be baited. "You left me, Jonathan."

"You deserved it."

"Did I? True love forgives sins made for love," she said, and a sense of peace filled her. "She is my blood, my only child, and I'll not sacrifice her to the whims of a rake." She narrowed her eyes. "Do you know where he'd take her?"

For a moment, it didn't seem he'd answer. She saw the war in his green eyes. At last he said, "He might have gone to a cottage called Rosewood."

Juliette smiled. "Thank you." For one minute, she allowed herself to inhale the scent of him that lingered in the foyer, allowed herself to impress the unbearably sexy sight of him against the railing in her mind. She would not see him again, not even if he wished it.

Somehow the truth had come clear to her. The nagging cough was not some ailment brought on by overexertion or any of those other things she'd been telling herself. Like her mother before her, she had contracted consumption. And judging by the feeling in her chest, there was not much time left to her. Calmly, she said, "I'll never forget you, Jonathan."

She went again into the dark wet day. There was one stop more she had to make before she sought out this cottage. She would see the earl of Monthart and be certain he knew what his son had done now: kidnapped the daughter of a peer, in broad daylight from a dress shop!

For she did not want Lucien Harrow simply destitute now. Nothing would do but that he be dead or exiled forever. It was the only way Madeline would be safe from him.

20

For love all love of other sights controls,
And makes one little room an everywhere.
—John Donne

Under the shelter of an overgrown arbor from which dripped yellow roses in heavy, wet, profusion, Lucien dismounted and held up a hand for Madeline. She allowed herself to be assisted, then stepped away, an expression of wonder on her face as she looked at the cottage and the roses surrounding it.

Lucien stared at her hungrily, his eyes as starved for the look of her as his hands were for her skin, his mouth for her lips, his ears for the sound of her voice.

Her hair clung in long wet tendrils to her neck, and one lock trailed over her breasts to disappear within her bodice. The magnificent gown was ruined, but the white silk clung to her body with elegant caress, the beads glinting whenever she took a breath. Behind her, as if designed to be a backdrop for her dark loveliness, the yellow roses cascaded over trellises and crept over the drive. Even in the rain their fragrance was pervasive. She lifted a hand to touch one, and the gesture put her form in perfect outline.

A tiny protesting voice sounded in his mind—what if this action of his ruined her life? What if she did not marry the marquess after all? What if she could not be forgiven this second transgression? What if—

She turned her head and looked up at him. The dress slipped on her shoulder once again, and Lucien could not breathe for need. He stepped forward and bent to kiss that naked shoulder, that swell of breast, those perfect lips. A soft, anguished cry came from her. He carried her inside.

It was warm within, a fire burning well on the hearth. He smelled meat and bread, but there was only Madeline in his arms, Madeline against his body, Madeline's kiss on his mouth, Madeline's hair on his hands. He kicked the door shut behind him. "I cannot breathe for needing you," he said, and put her on the bed.

He shed his shirt and his boots, but waited on his breeches, for Madeline shivered on the quilts in the wet silk, her wet hair a tangle. With a single gesture, he flipped the quilt over her, and covered her with himself, holding her quilts and all against him.

He kissed her brow, lingering between her eyebrows, sliding down her nose, at last claiming her mouth. She worked her arms from the blankets and pulled him closer, her hands splaying against his back. He shifted, putting himself against her leg, letting her feel the need he had for her, the need to be deeply embraced. At his movement, she made a low, longing sound.

He kissed her mouth and her chin and her ear. He tasted the long white column of her throat and opened his mouth to draw circles on the swell of her breast with his tongue. The dress, though loose on the shoulders, was too tight to pull down and Lucien was impatient to wring from her the cry he longed to hear. Bracing himself on his elbows, he gathered her breasts into his hands and settled his hot mouth over the cold, wet fabric, the cold beads, and found the flesh already risen to a point below the silk.

He moved his tongue against that rigidness, and the cry he awaited came from her throat. Low and hungry.

There was no waiting then, not after so many nights of longing, so much time wanting. Lucien hauled her into his lap so he could reach the laces of her dress. Her thighs embraced his hips, and he felt the nakedness of her heat against his erection. He fumbled with the laces. He managed to unknot them and tugged at them expertly, and the bodice slid down, showing her chemise, which he pulled from her shoulders in a hard tug. There was a sound of tearing fabric, and a small cry from Madeline, but then her naked arms were free and she wrapped them around his neck, her tender inner elbow against his ear. Her breasts brushed his chest, and he lowered his head to suckle there even as he shoved up the skirts to take her buttocks in his hands.

And somehow, at last, his manhood was free and he was sliding his heat into the depths of her, and they were joined, truly and completely, her dress bunched around her waist, her legs sprawled around them, his breeches only nominally out of the way. Her hair was pinned and not pinned, tumbling halfway on one side.

Nothing mattered but Madeline, staring solemnly into his eyes, her hands on his face, her fingers touching his lips now, and now tracing his chin, and now his nose. Slowly he moved within her. Slowly she moved her hands on his face. Slowly she put her fingers on his mouth and kissed between them, her tongue a light and exploratory thing against his.

And in his inner ear, there was music, the music of Madeline inside of him, all her colors woven into a brilliant tapestry of singular beauty—a sound of violins and violas and a tumble of surprising harps. It danced in him, the music, as Madeline urged him into quicker pace. Their mouths locked in a deep kiss, their bodies joined deeply, and all at once, he felt the explosion building between them.

With suddenness and power, she began to tremble and pulse around him. In response, his own body shattered. They fell together to the bed, shivering, trembling.

She curled into him. "How can this be wrong, Lucien? How can it be—"

Urgently, Lucien covered her mouth with his own, wishing he had not told her that day in the maze that he loved her. It had been a game that day, another tool in his arsenal. Now he wanted the words back, so he could whisper them softly to her when they were real.

He loved her. For the first time in his miserable life, he'd fallen in love. And if he'd not been so intent upon dishonor, he could have taken her to wife, saved her gardens, lived like a normal man in a normal way.

Instead he'd flung his blessings to the winds, letting whoever would carry them take them away. He tossed away sex, riches, time, and the title that was his by right. He'd refused his music and sulked for the loss of it.

Lying now in Madeline's embrace, it seemed to him the whole society was twisted—it let men squander the best part of themselves, their youth and energy, while awaiting lands and titles. It encouraged waste and decadence.

Music pulsed in him. He pressed his cheek to hers, wishing he could say he loved her.

Tonight, as Madeline slept in his bed, he would write. He would set the music free, and this time he would not burn it. He would give it to Madeline instead of the words he'd uttered too soon.

Beyond the small cottage, a violent storm raged. Madeline heard the howling wind and furious rain with a strange sense of distance. She liked it—there was no going anywhere as long as it raged. Thunder and lightning boomed and flashed through the heavens, and it rained and rained and rained.

Lucien had found a simple loose muslin night rail for her to put on. It barely covered her, so thin was the fabric, but there was something tantalizing about the high neck and long sleeves covering her and not covering her. It made her feel richly seductive.

She didn't ask whom it belonged to, nor did he volunteer. Instead, they lazed on the bed, touching each other, eating, drinking, kissing. He ladled soup into bowls for them and cut bread, which Madeline spread with butter. From a jug they drank cider as cold and crisp as a stream.

Madeline drifted off to sleep. When she awoke, he was writing, the quill in his left hand. His right hand stroked her thigh, but absently, as if he only did it to comfort himself. It was oddly arousing for Madeline, however, those long fingers stroking up and down, up and down restlessly, sometimes curling into the crook of her knee, sometimes sliding all the way to her ankle.

His pen flew over the page, making notations, dipping into the ink, flying again. And as he wrote, he hummed, almost tonelessly. Madeline heard a pattern or rhythm rather than true notes. Every so often, he paused, and he stared into space, and the humming grew louder and he touched her belly or stroked her breast without even seeming to realize he did it.

Madeline simply looked at him, touched by the small details that made him. Over his ear, his hair grew in soft curls, like a child's, giving the harsh aspect of his face a curiously vulnerable look. She had not realized he was left-handed, either, but it seemed somehow fitting.

His right hand dipped over her waist, slid down her hip, moved back upward again. His head bobbed ever so slightly, and he inclined his head, as if he were listening. Which of course he was.

Restlessly his hand moved on her body. Quite erotic, actually, she thought, scooting over to touch him. She didn't speak because he was so passionately engrossed, but she had a strong need to touch him. With light fingers she traced the lines of his ribs and the dip in his spine. Lucien scribbled, his pen scratching against the page, and his hand circled her belly. Again he wrote and his fingers stroked her breast.

All at once, he put down his pen, shoved up her gown and put his mouth on her thigh, where he'd been stroking. The sensation was sharp and stabbing, and she cried out.

"I am mad," he said raggedly. "I am mad."

She pulled him to her and held his face. "I love you, Lucien," she said.

He did not answer, only kissed her again, and again. Madeline tasted his desperation and gave herself to him fully, hoping to ease his sorrows. It was the last chance she would have.

*　　　*　　　*

Juliette was feverish by the time she reached the earl's town house. Even she could feel it.

The earl of Monthart received her in his study on the second floor. A fire burned in the grate. He stood nearby it, his hands clasped behind his back. A heavily powdered wig sat on his head, immaculately coiffed, as were his clothes. He was a grim-faced man and Juliette had no doubt he could be cruel. Gossip said he'd forcibly taken his bride from a party in Russia, so smitten he was with her beauty.

Typical.

As he turned to greet her, Juliette saw he looked ashen, his mouth a peculiar shade. He blotted his lips before he spoke, and she knew a pang of conscience— perhaps she ought return when he was not so plainly unwell. "Good afternoon, Lady Whitethorn," he said. "How may I be of service?"

As if to remind her of her own precarious health, Juliette felt a wheezing sense of airlessness. "Your son has kidnapped my daughter," she said distinctly. "You must do something."

"What can I do? He's cut off. I sign the papers in the morning. As far as I am concerned, my son is dead." No emotion showed on his face. "It should have been done long ago."

"Nothing else?" Juliette cried, coming forward. There was a fishwife sound to her voice she ordinarily tried to control. Tonight, she didn't care. "He has ruined her, sir, and I will have compensation."

"Greedy wench, aren't you?"

Juliette slapped him. He didn't move, but she saw the flash of danger in his eye. Again he blotted his lips. "Go, now, my lady. I no longer wish your company."

But as she turned, he made a strange choking noise, and when she turned back, he was crumpling to the floor, that blue in his lips more pronounced than ever.

He was dead before he hit the floor. Juliette had seen enough death to recognize it. In horror, she stared at his lifeless form, her thoughts whirling dizzily.

"No!" she cried, remembering what he'd said. In the morning, he would sign the papers cutting off Lucien Harrow.

As of this moment, Lucien was the new earl of Monthart, and one of the richest men in England. Juliette's revenge was in ashes.

Madeline awakened to find herself in a nest of pillows and blankets, curled tight against the damp chill in the room. From overhead came the sound of birds— the rain had stopped, then. She lifted her head.

Lucien sat by the fire, his boots on already, his shirt on but not yet fastened. His hair was loose around the haggard lines of his face, and in his hands he held the sheaf of papers he'd written through the night. He stared longingly at the fire, holding the papers loosely in his elegant hands. Loosely.

She sat up. "Lucien, please don't burn them."

Slowly, he looked up and met her gaze. "No." He stood and brought them to the bed, and put them in her lap. "It's yours."

From the table he took a rough blue dress, a servant's dress and many times too large for Madeline, but he gave it to her. "I want to take you home before sunrise. It will be easier for both of us. I'll wait outside."

She washed and dressed, and her fingers were clumsy with emotion. *Which* emotion, she couldn't quite say, for guilt and love and sorrow and regret were tangled as a basket of yarn. Her throat ached, and she knew it was not the weather but the force of unsaid words.

And yet, because there were no choices, Madeline combed her hair and braided it, and put on the cloak he laid on the foot of the bed. She wrapped his music in the ruined silk-and-bead dress that she was supposed to wear to her wedding.

Then she pulled up the hood and went outside to Lucien, who waited by his horse to take her home. But before he lifted her to the beast's back, he took from below his own cloak a single rose, blooming pink, the same brilliant shade as the bud he'd plucked at Whitethorn. This rose, however, was newly opened, to show the gold center. Lucien brushed his lips over it and gave it to her.

She blinked away her tears.

In the predawn quiet, they rode into London, meeting only delivery men and servants and one old staggering drunk in an alley. Sunlight had just begun to gild the horizon when Lucien stopped before Juliette's town house.

Madeline looked at the house, its shutters tight, and took a breath. Lucien tipped up her chin and kissed her very, very gently. "Be well," he said, and his voice broke. He put her down.

And quickly rode away.

Madeline gathered the too-big clothes and walked up the short steps to the house. The door flung open before she could reach it, and Juliette stood there, looking like some evil spirit in an opera, her eyes dark and hollow in her powdered face, her mouth a red slash.

"Mama—"

Juliette slapped her, a blow that left her tasting blood. Stunned, Madeline put her hand over the stinging skin and stared without speaking.

"Go to your room," Juliette said, pulling Madeline into the foyer that smelled of damp plaster. "And there you will be locked till your wedding day!" She slammed closed the heavy oak front door.

"No," Madeline said, not loudly. She stood her ground, clasping Lucien's symphony to her chest.

"What no?" Juliette's fever burned in her eye. "You'll do as I say."

"I cannot marry Charles, Mama." She shook her head. "I cannot betray him that way—he is too kind and good a man."

"Oh, do you think your precious Lord Esher will marry you? The poor and pitiful Lord Esher who has been cut off?"

"No." Again, she did not speak loudly. "I will marry no one."

"And lose your gardens? You'll toss away all my plans, all your plans, and your ancestral home for a roll in the hay with a man who's had sex with most of the women in England?"

Madeline's face burned. "Stop it."

"No, you stop it. Have a care, dear child. You'll not find a better man than Charles Devon. And he worships you."

"We will be friends always," Madeline replied, "but I will not marry him. I made him that promise."

"What promise?"

"That I would tell him if I came to the point where I believed my feelings for Lord Esher would interfere with my ability to be his wife."

"Oh, Madeline, think!"

"I am thinking. I am in love with him—and it doesn't seem to matter whether that is right or wrong. I love him. I hold no hopes of building a life with him. I have no illusions that he loves me in return—or, rather, loves me enough to remain faithful. I am willing to accept I'll not have a husband, only my gardens."

"You won't have gardens either, Madeline."

Madeline smiled. "But there's where you're wrong. I am going to open a nursery."

"Oh, dear God."

Without waiting for more argument, disaster and melodrama, Madeline left Juliette in the foyer and went to her chamber.

Where at last, holding his cloak against her mouth and nose so she could smell him, Madeline wept. And when she had wept, then fallen into deepest sleep, she awakened and set about making plans for her life.

Predictably, Charles was more understanding than Juliette had been. In fact, over the nightmarish weeks of gossip that followed, it was Charles Devon who proved to be a most steadfast friend to Madeline. It was Charles who knew when to suggest a round of cards or a walk or a bite to eat and when she needed simply to retreat and lick her wounds.

But not once in all those days did she wish she had married him. It almost seemed incestuous when she thought of it at leisure, as if he were her brother or a close cousin.

She did not burden him with such insights. Though he never reproached her, and had in fact thanked her for her honesty when she spoke to him

the horrible morning after the kidnapping, she knew
he'd been wounded.

When he left for more excavations at Pompeii,
Madeline took Juliette home to Whitethorn, armed
with a list of foods and herbal treatments. The doctors had confirmed consumption and advised them
to retire to the less foul air of the countryside,
where Juliette might maintain her health as long as
possible.

As the wet, dreary summer gave way to a sparkling
autumn, there was one more thing Madeline knew
she had to do. At the little desk in the corner of her
greenhouse where she liked to keep her notes,
Madeline sat one fine, clear autumn morning and
took up her pen.

Dear Jonathan,

*It is with urgency I write to ask you to
reconsider your very hard stand against my
mother. I know your feelings were deeply
wounded, but I know also that you loved her.
I'll wager all I have that such a love is not so
easily killed. Pride is a lonely man's bedmate.*

*You should know one more thing, too. The
doctors have said she has consumption.
Although she is much improved in health since
we left the foul city, I feel a visit from you would
cheer her more than anything I could do or say.
Please consider it.*

Yrs sincerely,
Lady Madeline Whitethorn.

She posted the letter on Wednesday afternoon, and
then was free in conscience to apply herself to the

business of preparing to open a nursery in the spring. Her vivacious correspondence took an even more energetic turn as she flung herself into the task of funding, management, and stocking.

She was going to be very good at it, and most of the time, she was able to shut down the voice in her mind that never stopped crying.

LucienLucienLucien

21

Never seek to tell thy love
Love that never told can be;
For the gentle wind does move
Silently, invisibly.
— William Blake

    Lucien rode back to Rosewood from his father's funeral in a state of grief and shock. Not grief for his father, who'd been nothing but cruel to his child, but for Madeline and all the things he could not undo. And shock because he had not been disinherited after all, and if he'd not behaved like such an animal, there might have been hope for them.

In mere days, he rode to the house at Monthart as the new earl.

Over the weeks that followed, Lucien kept largely to himself. In letters and from the stray, curious visitor he heard news. Charles Devon, the marquess of Beauchamp, had departed for Pompeii. The incomparable Juliette was dying of consumption. Word of Jonathan was scant.

No one seemed to know just what Madeline was doing. Three well-to-do suitors had been turned down and Madeline had retreated to the country. Three times Lucien sent notes to Juliette. Three times she returned them unopened. Lucien tried very hard to think of Madeline as little as possible—she deserved a man as honorable as she, though he had to admit he was glad she was not going to marry the marquess. They were not a good match.

His life quickly took on a pattern. By day he learned the layout of the grounds and gardens at Monthart. He worked well into the darkest heart of fall on it, finding he enjoyed the passion for growing things Madeline had kindled in him.

One more thing for which he had to thank her one day.

But the biggest change in his life came in the evenings, as he sat by his fire in his study. Lucien wrote music. He wrote without thought or care, wrote ballads and sonatas and symphonies and concertos. He did not throw them in a fire, either, but tossed them in a box he kept for the purpose. It perplexed him a little that the notes tumbled from him so prolifically, without nudging or drink. It was, he thought, as if they had been building up behind some dam in his soul, and he'd finally, simply, set them free.

Night after night he wrote, night after night he dreamed of Madeline. Night after night, he regained his lost self, the man he'd been going to become under his mother's tutelage, before his father crushed his heart beneath his stern boot.

He neither needed nor wished for spirits. He ate a hearty supper and sat down by the fire and wrote until he could write no more. Hundreds of images pressed in during those hours. He'd felt so odd as a child, so beyond the pale, not only for his Russianness, but for the way he always, always heard music, played music.

He heard it in the leaves and the sound of birds, and tried to imitate the sound on stools or walls or windowpanes. He made sounds with silver at the table, and with rocks upon rocks and with rhythmic slapping on the water.

He thought everyone did.

It was his mother who had seen, and taken him from the world of English lords to the harsher, kinder world of passion in which she'd grown up. He was seven. When he came home, he could play by ear any instrument they put in his hands. He played the sound of the leaves and the tumble of water and the sound of rocks banging against each other.

It made him very happy.

And now, after so long, like a bird who has forgotten to fly and remembers, he soared and swooped into the sky of his music. He hummed under his breath. And clacked rocks in tumbles upon each other. And listened to his boots thump on the earth. And tapped his spoons against the china.

And one morning, he awakened to the knowledge he must have Madeline. Not for a day or a week or an hour.

Always.

After several weeks in the country and the relief of no entertaining obligations, Juliette felt much improved. On this bright Saturday morning, she sat on the veranda overlooking the back garden. Her cough had eased, and she'd even gained back a little of the lost weight.

Now calmly making paper flowers after the fashion of Mrs. Delany, it seemed to Juliette there was more to life than love affairs and the passions of youth. When she looked back to the summer, it seemed to her that everything that had gone wrong had been only because of passion. One simply had to let one's head rule one's heart—a lesson she should have learned a long time before.

A sharp gust of wind came up and blew pieces of red paper in her face and all over the stone veranda, and stole Juliette's hat from her head. With a laugh, she stood to retrieve it—

And halted.

For standing in the frame of the French doors leading to the salon stood a ghost. Jonathan, looking aged and tired, his hair drawn back.

Juliette closed her eyes. A ghost only. She had learned to live without him, she had mended her shattered heart. To save her daughter, she would do it again.

"Juliette," the ghost said, its voice raw.

She opened her eyes. The ghost moved toward her, and she saw with a pang that his eyes were even more brilliantly green than she remembered. A wash of heat and wistful longing burst through her.

A ghost. That was all. She couldn't—

He stopped before her. "How can you always be so beautiful?" he whispered, and touched her cheek. "How is it that nothing ever touches you?"

Rigidly, she remained still, but she could not stop herself from looking up at him, drinking in his beautiful face, his wide mouth and the graceful cut of his nose. "What are you doing here?" she asked.

He opened his mouth, closed it. To her eternal astonishment, he knelt on the stones before her and took her hand in supplication. "I have come to beg forgiveness, my lady."

Juliette narrowed her eyes. "Did Madeline put you up to this?"

"She wrote to me," he admitted, and seemed unable to stay kneeling, for he leaped to his feet. "Why didn't you tell me you were so ill that day you came to my house? Why didn't you let me help you?"

Juliette pulled her hand from his. "I'd rather not suffer your pity. Please go."

"Pity." The word hung in the air like a bad smell. "Is that what this feeling is? This ache in my heart that will not let me rest? That hounds me no matter how drunk I get or how many rounds of cards I play or how many other women I find to chase you from my mind?"

Juliette closed her eyes, willing herself to keep her back turned, to keep hidden her need of him. Her knees trembled at the very sound of his voice, and a curiously thick sensation drugged her blood.

"Is it pity, Juliette?" He seized her arms and turned her around to face him, naked hunger now on his face. "Is *this*?"

He kissed her fiercely, and his hands pulled her close into his embrace. Juliette made a soft whimpering noise and let her hands come up around him. Such a dear presence—this back, these shoulders, these arms, these lips. Sweet heaven.

Jonathan gasped, lifting his head. "God, I've missed you!" He kissed her face, all over, with that peculiarly gentle way he had, and Juliette tasted tears—his or her own, she didn't know.

Then she did know, because there was no pretending with him anymore. Relief and regret and the most pervasive need burst in her and she put her face against his chest and wept. "I've missed you," she said, clutching his coat.

He made a low, agonized sound. "I'm sorry, my love, I'm sorry for all my idiocies, for my pride, for my judgments." He rocked her close. Juliette smelled the sweet notes that belonged to him alone. "I've been a fool."

"As was I." She lifted her head.

Slowly, reverently, he kissed her. "I love you, Juliette. I want to marry you. Please."

Overcome, Juliette could only nod.

Jonathan said, "There is one more thing."

"What?"

"Ask Lucien Harrow to visit your daughter. He is most desperately in love."

Juliette pulled away. "Never."

He took a breath, and unexpectedly, sighed. "He's one of the richest men in England, my love. He adores your daughter with a passion only equaled by mine for you. He's writing music and will likely be England's next great composer." He took her hands. "What more can you ask of a man than that?"

With a snap, Juliette actually heard her long grudge break. "What more indeed," she said. There was so little time—she might as well use what she could for spreading joy.

Madeline loved the autumn. It was by far her favorite season, and this year was no exception. She was, perhaps, even happier than normal with it, for her garden was finally and truly on its way to being itself again.

In the chilly fog of an October morning, she clipped dead roses and pinched out buds on sunny orange and yellow chrysanthemums, humming under her breath. It was "Lucien's Song," as she thought of it—that concerto of such beauty that he'd written and given to her. In time, she would like to learn to play it. For now it was still too painful to think of.

She wondered with a little pang what he was doing just now. Riding? Breakfasting? Had he forgotten her?

They'd heard the tale of Lucien Harrow's Great Transformation. That was how Madeline always thought of it, in capital letters, because the change was so large. He had ceased his round of parties and seductions and retired to the country where he tended his estates with an even and sensible hand.

She knew she'd had a part in that transformation. That Lucien had sought something from her, had taken nourishment from the love she bore him, and been healed. If she were another sort of woman, she supposed she'd be content with that.

Unfortunately, she was not. She grieved for him. It stunned her how he'd infected her life in a couple of months. His presence was everywhere: in her gardens and the maze and the music room; in her bedroom and the salon and on the drive. She thought of him when she rode and when she climbed the castle tower and when she wore her green dress.

Yes, she grieved. To her surprise, the things she remembered had less to do with his lovemaking—though she had to admit she thought of that too—than with his irrepressible spirits. His teasing. His buoyant energy. His sharp, witty observations. He'd become her friend during his time at Whitethorn, a fact she hadn't realized until he was gone.

With a sigh, she cut loose a pink rose and lifted it to her nose. The edges of the blossom were slightly blackened—not many frostless nights left. Soon her gardening would all be indoors.

She bent to pick up her basket, and a soft sound on

the air caught her ear. She lifted her head. There it was again—music. It sounded like music.

With a puzzled frown, she moved toward it, thinking it came from the maze. Outside, she paused, listening, certain for a moment that she'd utterly lost her mind.

No, there it was. A little clearer, now. She thought it was a violin. Her heart jumped, and she very slowly entered the maze.

And once within, the fog obscured all directional clues. She moved toward the center, hearing now that it was a violin, but not where it came from. Streamers of ground mist tangled around her ankles; she drew her shawl around her more closely.

Now she could hear the music clearly. It was the piece Lucien had composed here, then at Rosewood, the one she thought of as a tribute to Pompeii—the first part so light and free, as Pompeii must once have been. She thought of Lucien jumping the hedge the first day she saw him. So free.

She stopped, listening to the strange echoes, the muted singularity of the instrument in the fog. She smelled the faintly spicy odor of the box leaves, and damp, bruised grass. From the hidden place, Lucien played the second movement of the piece—Vesuvius stomping down, crushing the lightness, transforming and smothering everything.

And she thought of Lucien, so haggard, throwing his composition into the fire. She thought of him with his bruised face, making love to her, with such yearning and despair.

With sudden insight, she lifted her head. As he headed into the third part, the cacophonous, wild noise she'd thought represented the explosions of

Vesuvius, she thought of him storming the dress shop and carrying her away. She lifted her skirts and began to run, toward the middle of the maze.

She rounded one wall and another, listening to the crescendo build, to the crashing terrible climax—

And then there was a sharp, pregnant, expectant pause. As she rounded the last corner, into the center, where he stood in a dark blue greatcoat, his hair caught back, Lucien began to play very, very softly the refrain from the first movement. His eyes glowed turquoise against the dark of the day, against the dark of his hair and his coat and all the darkness and dankness around them.

But Lucien's face was full of light. And the shadows had gone. And he played for Madeline the sound of his fall, with a smile on his beautiful mouth. She stopped, listening to the soft sound of that golden day he'd ridden up the drive, and tears welled in her eyes.

When he finished, he lowered the violin.

"I thought it was Pompeii," Madeline said, aching with her love for him, for the beauty that had been unleashed from his soul.

He nodded. "As did I." His smile was rueful. "Instead it was my fall to love."

Madeline covered her mouth. She didn't know what to say, how to express the enormity of emotions that swelled in her just then. She couldn't speak. She felt frozen.

With uncharacteristic hesitance, Lucien put the violin on the stone bench and straightened. His cheeks were extraordinarily red from the cold morning. He touched his chin, looked at her. "Will you have me, Madeline?" he said, at last.

The simplicity of his words took her aback, and she didn't know what he meant. "*Have* you?" she echoed. She gave a little laugh.

And something in her burst. She didn't care how, she didn't care when, she didn't care about anything except that he was standing there in front of her, whole and sober and strong. So far he'd come to meet her, so carefully he'd planned it. With a cry, she launched herself over the grass and ran to him. She flung her arms around his neck and felt him catch her up with a soft groan.

"Madeline," he said into her hair.

She caught his face and kissed him. The taste of his mouth was like crisp apples, like October evenings, like all the dearest parts of morning.

"I love you," he whispered. "I could not say it before, because I said it when I didn't mean it, and then there was no way to call the words back. But there are only those words to say it—I love you."

"Yes, I know."

He clutched her close.

He opened his mouth to speak and Madeline kissed him. "Stop talking," she said. "Just stop talking and love me."

"Oh, yes," he breathed. "Yes, that I can do."

And he kissed her, deeply, sweetly, like a husband and a lover, not a rake at all. Madeline knew a wild dizzy sense of rightness, that it should be this man, with all the music in his soul, who would give her children to raise to love the maze and gardens that would be part of their legacy.

He lifted his head, and a strangely bashful expression was on his mouth. "I wonder if you might come to London this week with me."

"Why?"

Now there was undeniably a creeping color in his cheeks, not caused by the cold. "The symphony is to play my concerto. I'd like you to be there."

Madeline kissed him, long and hard. "It would be a joy." Seriously she touched his beautiful face. "I love you, Lucien Harrow."

The old devilish grin flashed on his dark face. "You can't help it."

Madeline buried her face in his shoulder. "You're right," she whispered.

Then she let him go. "Let's go tell Juliette."

Together they left the maze and wandered out into the open ground, hand in hand.

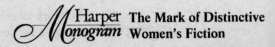

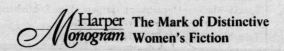